The Emperor of Carysfort Reef: Resurrection

By Jack Dunbar

Although this story follows the history and myths of Western civilization, the people and events portrayed in this work are fictional. Any resemblance to persons living or dead is purely coincidental. 4th Edition.

Dedication

This book is dedicated to my family and dear friends who have been endured repeated and annoying requests to read and comment on this story. Their help, love and support have served to water and cultivate the seeds this tale sprang, and I am grateful to them for putting up with me. I particularly am thankful to Kyle Willis who did the illustrations, and those who encouraged me as I wrote.

Jack Dunbar

Table of Contents

Introduction

Most vampire novels are always vague about the nature of the creature itself and often boorishly fixated on gushing streams of blood, sexual acrobatics, and the terror visited on victims in predictable scenarios; not to mention those fangs that magically emerge from their dental work. Although these elements all add to the appeal of this fantasy genre, I have also always felt there were so many unanswered questions regarding why vampires are all filthy rich; how they can immediately transform or to shape shift into bats, dogs or wolves; live exclusively on liquid; or move about as the animated dead and, unless killed by any variety of ways, are immortal.

This story makes an effort to make friends with physics and science as applied to the fictional vampire. Through a number of voices in the story plausible and believable explanations of their origin, power, and relative mortality of those that live in that world. "Emperor..." is also more than a vampire tale, the threads that comprise its tapestry reflect a story about loneliness, lost love and love yet to come. It is a mystery story that introduces a much broader theme of nefarious mischief afoot. It also witnesses to how sophisticated 21st century people, people minding their own business are compelled to accept the fact that vampires exist. As they go forward it details the challenges they experience in agreeing to protect the secret of the existence of vampires from becoming public knowledge, all the while tracking down and destroying the creatures wherever they turn up. Finally, as the vampire comes to us from the myths associated with Western Civilization, *Chapter I: Origins* bookmarks the triggering event at Carysfort Marina then takes you back to the colorful land of myth and legend, a land where a man first become vampire.

JD

Chapter 1

Origins

*"...When he lies, he speaks his native language, for he
is a liar and the father of lies...."*

John, 8:44

Under the glare of four spotlights Robert Hoskins
lowered the coral encrusted coffin from the boat to the
dock when without notice the primary gear of the crane
disengaged then reengaged causing the coffin to swing
wildly and bang into a dock piling. Twisting, the box
slipped free of the sling crashing end first onto the dock
with a metallic thud. The violent fall broke open the lid
spilling its contents onto the weathered boards.

"Christ, it's a man!!" shouted Alex Walsh who had
been guiding the coffin's ascent to the dock.

The creature entombed inside tumbled head over
heels onto the dock in a wave of stained sand he had been
packed. For almost 300 years he lay in the deep darkness
of confined sleep, and then in a blinding flash came

freedom. Once free of the airtight chamber fresh air rushed into his withered lungs bringing him to a semi-conscious state. Every muscle in his body either cramped or momentarily immobile, having the flexibility of dried jerky from years without nourishment. Although his body screamed in pain the creature managed to right himself and rose to his knees.

Alex Walsh stood dumbfounded, frozen in place still grasping the now limp guide line. Focused on the man, he tried to strike a balance between physics and logic, and what had just rolled out on the dock before his eyes. He was there when he and Hoskins found the coffin sticking out from under ancient ship debris on Carysfort reef, underwater, and it had been there a long time.

Hoskins impulsively rushed toward what appeared to be a crouching man. As his feet reached the sand spilled from the box, the creature turned and locked eyes with him.

***

The creature was indeed alive and certainly not of this time; a living relic and the embodiment of a long kept secret. This was a living and breathing vampire. He had just been freed from a 306 year, 54 day sleep. Why he was there, from where he came, and what he was would be the mystery that would animate the lives touched by the creature for the next several weeks, far from where he started.

He began the journey that deposited him on Carysfort Reef onboard the sailing vessel *Edith Louise* at Glasgow docks on Wednesday, July 17, 1695. Under the name of Angus Cassidy the creature and his small retinue were passengers fleeing the pressures of a vampire hunter from Cassidy's past lives. However the vampire's journey through time began long before he set foot on the *Edith Louise*. It began in a violent and distant world of conquerors, kings and emperors; the quick and the dead.

Mysia - Anatolia, 325 BC...

"You there, what are you doing?" the nasty smelling slave trader demanded as he grabbed the boy by the scruff of his neck, throwing him back onto the mud.

Putting his foot on the boy's chest he menacingly waved a short dagger at the frightened waif.

"Nothing your honor, I'm hungry and thought these scraps were thrown out by your cook." the boy responded.

"What's your name lad?

"My mother called me Demi..."

"Where is she?"

"I don't know...gone."

"Anyone else?"

"No your honor..."

"Come with me lad, we will give you some food and a new name" he said, removing his foot from the boy's chest and pulling him up.

The man led the boy past several bordello tents where loud voices from both men and women arguing, shrieking and laughing that rocked the camp day and night. Reaching the edge of the encampment where the draft animals were corralled, the man pushed him toward a group of people sitting shackled together on a large rock formation out of the animal excrement and putrefying urine. The boy turned to look at his captor when someone, pulled him back and grabbed his wrists long enough to lock them in iron shackles connected on a short chain to the others.

Wide eyed, he stared at the shackles on his wrists and suddenly felt sick and frightened. Those rotten turnips cost him more than he would know. He exhaled and sat down as he scanned the faces of the motley companions that shared his fate.

...*Where was the food he was promised?* he thought sarcastically.

***

He was fair for a Persian, muscular, with creamy skin and blue eyes. At age 17, he had just begun his new life as a commodity in a slave trader's caravan profiting from the every demand of Alexander's army as it marched east into the mountains of present day Afghanistan – past the edges of the world.

A week later he was sold to a senior Macedonian officer named Seleucus Nicator, and given the name Demetrius Keraunos. His owner was the commander of an elite infantry corps called the Hypaspistai, meaning "Shield-bearers." Keraunos learned from his first day as a slave that serving Greek military was a life filled with cruelty and depravity. Of all his "duties" he particularly detested the practice of being a sexual vessel for the men when enough females were in camp for everyone to share. He was forced to live on the cold or wet ground under edges of their tents, ate only after the lowest common soldiers were fed, carried and looked after their weapons and armor, and helped recover the dead and body parts after battles, dragging them to and piling them onto funeral pyres.

Everyone was a threat to him – his life balanced on the perceived quality of his work or compliance with demands forced on him by men who had the power of life or death over him every breathing minute. Perhaps because he was a slave and a potential threat to his masters, neither Keraunos nor any slave, for that matter, was ever permitted to bear arms, even when moving at the rear of the army as it maneuvered to contact with the enemy.

Keraunos became tough and cruel, especially to the slaves junior to him; he was a good student of the depravities and cruelty of his masters. He long planned his escape from his hated position as a slave, from the harsh treatment, sexual assaults, the cold nights, and institutional anonymity. However Keraunos did not harbor any illusions about running away and finding a fairy-tale bucolic freedom outside of the army. He plotted ways of using his wits and martial prowess to distinguish himself in front of the right people and advance within the army.

On a warm, rainy and humid day in May in the southern reaches of the Kingdom of Bactriana what would be known to history as the Battles of the Hydaspes River, Keraunos sensed his chance was near.

The carnage raged for hours as formations of mounted infantry and cavalry maneuvered from center to flank and back again near the banks of the swollen river. Searching for that opportunity to escape his lot he became distracted by the stench of the uncollected dead from previous days, then the smells of funeral pyres to the rear consuming flesh and bone in the slow flames. On this day men lay dead for as far as the eye could see across the plain. Those who were still alive moaned or screamed for their mothers or comrades, some cried and just screamed for help. Others pleaded to their comrades to kill them and relieve them of their indescribable pain.

As he stood among other slaves at the rear of the army near Nicator's command position, one of hundreds of enemy war elephants on the field was being driven directly toward them. Each elephant routinely carried an enemy bowman and javelinman, as well as the mahout, or driver but this had a second bowman. As the beast advanced through the ranks toward Nicator's position, the phalanx of soldiers was ordered to move between it and the general. Before the blocking force had consolidated it broke and the beast continued on. In the pandemonium, Keraunos broke away from the other slaves, rushing forward he picked up a javelin from a fallen soldier. It was slimy from the former owner's blood but he gripped it tightly in his right hand. He ran to the front, placing himself directly between Nicator and the lumbering juggernaut. He wasn't doing this for duty or honor, he did it for glory and promotion, to advance and gain favor. His heart raced, sweat saturated his clothing; knowing this was a chance of his lifetime – It was a calculated risk - he would be a hero or be killed. He chose to stand fast.

In full view of Nicator and the army he purposely paused to achieve the right amount of drama. He then raised his arm high and threw the javelin at the elephant advancing directly at him not more than 60 feet away. Seconds passed, all playing out in foggy slow motion as the flight-path of the javelin arched up and down toward the beast. Finally the weapon impacted, embedding itself deep in its brain, entering through the thin skull socket bone under the right eye. The beast let out a loud trumpet-like shriek, dived forward and down into the ground with a great lumbering thud, tumbling and throwing dirt and grass into the air as it expelled or crushed the enemy archers riding it!

Once the beast lay still, Nicator's personal guard pounced on the survivors and killed each one severing their heads and placing them on the tips of their spears dancing about in triumph. To his surprise one of the guards ran to Keraunos and handed him a spear with the severed head of the one who commanded the beast.

"Go forward and present it to the general, the honor is yours!"

Keraunos took the spear and ran to where Nicator was and drove the spear into the ground with the grisly trophy atop it. Keraunos gave Nicator a crossed chest fist salute, managed a slight bow then with a broad grin raised both arms high as the soldiers cheered. He was hailed a hero who had saved the life not only of Nicator, but also of his young son Antiochus, who by most accounts would not have survived if the elephant and its riders had made it to their objective.

In distinguishing himself by his bravery and martial skill, Keraunos was given his freedom and accepted an appointment as chief messenger and personal body guard for Nicator. Keraunos' life improved significantly following that day, although the legacy of Alexander discouraged the practice he was free to grow a beard as a sign of his freedom, which also reflected its owner's dignity, and wisdom - but he had still greater plans.

The campaign continued to the gates of northern India until Alexander's army came to near revolt after years of war and being away from their families and homes. After marching nearly 22,000 miles, planting towns and cities along the two million square miles of conquered territory, Alexander agreed to cease his conquest and return home. Withdrawing most of his army with him to Babylon, he unexpectedly died from an illness that came upon him just days before.

Following Alexander's death, and after taking care of some messy details associated with Alexander's wives and infant sons, his generals split up the empire. Nicator and the bulk of his army, including Keraunos, remained in

Bactriana after a large part of the Greek army withdrew. Those that stayed did so mostly because war was all they knew, they had no kin back home, many had begun families in the conquered lands, and they were very comfortable with the military comradeship developed from countless campaigns spent together. The generals that remained became guardians of the empire Alexander had built, assembling vast amounts of wealth as petty kings and warlords.

Nicator was apportioned the Kingdom of Bactriana and large border lands on its north and south in present-day regions of Afghanistan, Pakistan, and northern India. He was crowned King Seleucus I Nicator. During Nicator's consolidation of power in his own kingdom, Keraunos was given a command of his own.

Sogdian Rock, 320 BC...

Now an army commander, Keraunos had proved himself several times as a competent and ruthless adversary. He especially was known as a conqueror for ordering enemy prisoners crucified as a lesson.l to anyone who opposed him. Needing a competent resolution Keraunos was sent by Nicator with three battalions of about 1,500 *pezhetairoi*, or heavy infantry to gain compliance or kill a mysterious cult leader and warlord who refused to recognize Nicator's kingship. He was known as Angr'a Mainyu, the same name Keraunos remembered as the mythical Persian god of darkness, the eternal destroyer of good, personification and creator of evil, bringer of death and disease. God of darkness or not, Mainyu was the next rung on Keraunos' ladder to greater power and wealth.

Mainyu and his followers occupied Sogdian Rock, a fortress named for its location in the dry barrens of rock and sand in the far reaches of the Region of Sogdiana, seven days' march north. Sogdian Rock turned out to be a perfect place to defend. Its stone walls and ramparts commanded a view and advantage over any attacker on east, west and southern sides. The north side was a sheer rock wall 500 feet straight up and down. Inside was a large spring of sweet water and underground caves for food stores.

On the day of Keraunos's assault there was not a cloud in the sky; it was still cool as the summer sun rose blazing over the eastern horizon through the rocky crags of the Sogdian range onto the plain separating Keraunos's forces from Sogdian Rock. The plain was of flat terrain with scrub trees or bushes mixed in with the knee-high dry grass. As the rising sun shortened the shadows over the plain to the front of the fortress, the battlefield presented itself as largely open ground with lots of room for both sides to maneuver.

At the center Keraunos set astride his war horse flanked by his second in command and the horn signaler he used to communicate with his assault force commanders.

"Commander, by your leave....there is a rumor that has spread among the men that Mainyu ordered every fifth arrow to be tipped in solid gold" his lieutenant said as he turned his attention to the archers at the fortress ramparts.

"I know. That should be interesting. However we shall see...Move the first ranks into assault lines on the field, positioning them to advance from the east so the rising sun will be at their backs." Keraunos ordered.

With the sound of war drums and horns from each company, the assault lines moved forward toward the fortress. After advancing to within weapons range they were met with a shower of screaming arrows and spears launched from Mainyu's archers and heavy infantry from atop the fortress walls.

As the arrows screamed toward their targets, Keraunos and his troops looked skyward for the hail of gold. It was as rumored; they could see gold sparkles among the mass of arrows as they spun through the rays of the sun toward his army. The fuselage was accompanied by deafening rhapsodies of war drums and trumpets from the defenders inside the fortress.

Keraunos had expected the defenders to meet them on the plain and engage them from opposing battle lines. They did not; the gold-tipped arrows were a tactic new to him, and the result of this first long-range engagement of Keraunos' forces resulted in heavy losses to much of the first rank of his infantry.

It became apparent the assault ranks were beginning to break, not only because of the carnage caused by the arrows, but also what could be found at their tips. Here and there troops scattered in search of spent gold-tipped arrows or those sticking out of their wounded or dead comrades. His adversary was such as Keraunos had never encountered before.

Something had to be done. Keraunos galloped his horse onto the field shouting encouragement to his troops, urging them to continue the advance. A second hive of arrows rained down with one shaft piercing his armor near his neck and lodging in the flesh of his shoulder. He halted his horse, turned it about where his troops would see, grasped the arrow, broke it off where it stuck out of him and contemptuously threw it to the ground. Blood from the wound streamed under his chainmail down his chest and pooled at his waist band. In great pain he turned, spurring his horse forward. As he approached the first assault rank, the commander of the lead element was running to the rear clutching a handful of gold tipped arrows and ordering his men to follow with shouts and arm signals.

In this army, that man knew to never show fear or encourage one's troops to retreat without orders to do so. Such an offense was punishable by death. Riding to the man he swung his xiphos, or sword, in a circular motion, slicing off the top of the retreating officer's head as he passed. The officer fell lifeless to the ground before his battered brain and blood-smeared helmet hit nearby. He lay dead on the ground with the arrows still clutched in his hands. The men, who had witnessed the execution turned, forgot their hunt for golden arrows, reversed their retreat and renewed the attack.

As enemy arrows continued to rain down and take their toll, Keraunos rode up and down the ranks encouraging the troops with loud shouts, as he swung his bloody sword over his head. Moving forward between assaults of arrows and spears, the survivors finally reached the gate of the fortress, but with no means to breach it, he ordered them to give a shout of victory and withdraw before they were all killed by the defenders on the ramparts above. The field was littered with the dead, the dying, and the wounded crying and calling for their comrades as they lay or crawled back toward safety, out of the range of the deadly swarms of arrows.

After returning to his camp and having the arrow tip pushed through his shoulder and pulled out and the wound tended to, Keraunos called a meeting with his remaining field commanders to review strategy. The meeting concluded with a decision to starve the defenders out by sealing them in the fortress. Before dismissing his cadre, Keraunos awarded the commander who stood next to him at the gates of Sogdian Rock what remained of the shaft of the gold-tipped arrow that struck him during the morning's action.

***

On the 12th day of the hunger siege two riders emerged from the east gate of the fortress under a flag of truce.

The messengers carried a message from Mainyu requesting a cessation of hostilities and talks. Keraunos was invited for dinner and share the hospitality of the mysterious cult leader the next evening; and for the next several days discuss a long-term solution allying Mainyu and the new King Seleucus. According to the military custom of the day, one of the messengers was kept as a hostage and Keraunos sent his own with the second messenger.

As the sun set it cast a long shadow over Sogdian Rock. Keraunos and a personal escort of seven horsemen approached the gates of the fortress for dinner and talks. At their arrival, the great oak and iron gates slowly creaked open. Inside was a stone courtyard with a welcoming honor guard assembled to their immediate front. At the head of the troops was a commanding-looking tall young man in full battle armor and chainmail. As Keraunos and his escort approached, the tall man motioned to eight footmen who ran out to steady the horses while the men dismounted. His guard first stiffened in their saddles and placed their hands on the hilts of their swords. Keraunos waved off the defensive posture of his escort as a gesture of good will. He knew if they wanted them dead, the archers in the rampart behind them would have already loosed their arrows.

Keraunos handed the reins of his horse to the footman, dismounted and approached the young commander of the honor guard who greeted him with a right arm cross-chest salute.

"Lord Mainyu welcomes you, Commander...may I escort you to his chamber?" asked the young man in nearly fluent Greek.

Keraunos glanced at his own escort, and before he could inquire about them, the young man continued:

"Your escort will be treated well; they will be fed, bathed and provided quarters. Please follow me, Commander."

Keraunos was led down a large passageway that led to a second gate that protected the fortress keep. Oil lamps and torches lit the windowless room. His escort looked back at him and beckoned Keraunos to enter the chamber where Lord Mainyu waited.

As Keraunos stepped inside, the door closed behind him. He paused and surveyed the room from right to left with his hand gripping the hilt of his sheathed sword. A warming fire was set in the center of the room that illuminated cushions and small tables to serve as eating and drinking platforms in the Greek manner. Dark shadows dominated most of the cavernous space. The smoke from the fire smelled of sweet jasmine, circling the chimney hole before exiting. Not seeing imminent danger, he dropped his hands to his sides.

"Good evening Commander..." a voice came from the darkness on his left – this time in slightly Persian-accented Greek.

Keraunos, surprised and feeling vulnerable for being in a room with a potential enemy and not sensing his presence instinctively, pressed his left elbow against the hilt of his sword and looked toward the sound of the voice. Blinking his eyes, he could make out a tall man emerging into the light in a bright white robe tied at the waist with several strands of white cincture cord. His long greying hair and beard were braided in the Persian style of antiquity. His eyes were piercing pools of brown.

"Good evening, do I have the pleasure of addressing Lord Angr'a Mainyu?" asked Keraunos.

"Yes, Commander, I am Angr'a Mainyu...may I offer you some wine before we are served our meal?"

"Yes..." Keraunos stopped in mid-sentence, being interrupted by the appearance of a beautiful female with a flagon of wine and two cups. She locked eyes with Keraunos as soon as he noticed her enter. Serving her master first, she then approached Keraunos. The young woman had piercing emerald-green eyes, long black hair tied back to reveal her slender neck and bare muscular shoulders. Her robe was also white, cut deep revealing the cleavage between her shapely breasts that seductively moved under the fabric with each step she took. After filling their cups with wine, the woman again approached Keraunos. Sliding behind him, she reached around and began unbuckling his armor and girdle that secured his sword. He moved away, but she gently touched his arms reassuring him that he was safe.

"Please, Commander, you are my guest...please relax. It is our custom to protect our guests with our lives." Mainyu said in a reassuring tone. "Please allow her to make you more comfortable."

Keraunos smiled and raised his arms to allow the young woman to remove his battle dress. When she completed her work, she gently laid it near his couch and disappeared into the darkness of a nearby antechamber.

"Oh, I am Demetrius Keraunos...Commander Demetrius Keraunos."

"Yes, of course you are...I toast your bravery, Commander Keraunos. The young man you met when you first arrived witnessed your charge, your wounding, and the leadership you displayed on your journey to my gates. Very impressive – also impressive was how you dealt with an officer of yours who showed cowardice during the attack...Ah, what a waste..." Mainyu reflected as he took a long drink from his cup.

"And I toast your selection of a fortress and for being willing to use your obviously large stockpiles of so many expensive arrows...especially the gold ones," Keraunos said with a smile as he too drained his cup.

"Oh yes, now is a time to sit, relax and enjoy the hospitality of the evening. We can talk business tomorrow."

"Who was that beautiful woman just now? Is she your slave?"

"No, she is a daughter of sorts. Her name is Gulnar...it is my tradition to offer such a gift to my guest, so she will remain with you while you are with me," Mainyu said with a smile. With that he waved for the food to be brought in.

The train of attendants carrying trays of roast lamb, duck, rice, fruit and an endless number of wine skins was again led by the young woman who had served them the wine. Keraunos was impressed with how bountiful the feast appeared, suspecting the siege had not been as effective as he thought. As the meal progressed, Gulnar returned and supervised the servers and knelt between the two men ensuring their cups were never empty.

It had been a long, stressful campaign, and Keraunos was not used to such bountiful amounts of rich food or strong wine. He thought he was getting a bit drunk, since it had been a long time between great banquets and free-flowing wine, but in the spirit of diplomacy he pushed on. Eventually his vision began to blur, and he felt light-headed after the first cup of the new wine he had been served. It was warm and sweet, and its intoxicating effect was noticed immediately. As he lifted his cup for a second drink, he dropped it, falling into a deep sleep in mid-sentence.

With Keraunos' collapse on his cushion, all activity in the room ceased. Mainyu motioned all the attendants except for Gulnar to leave the room. Mainyu stood up and motioned the woman to position Keraunos on his back with his head and shoulders on the cushion, head turned to the right. After positioning the drugged man, she produced a small lancet and gently made an incision at the base of Keraunos's neck on his left side near the healing wound received from the arrow. As the blood began to slowly run from the wound, she looked up smiling in satisfaction and backed away. She was replaced by Mainyu, who knelt down and fed on the blood, sucking and groaning in satisfaction. After feeding for several minutes, he backed away and gazed at Keraunos, who was becoming quite pale.

Mainyu, still kneeling, sat back on his heels and arched his neck. Breathing violently in and out, Mainyu began to convulse, emitting gagging and choking sounds, and regurgitated a mixture of the blood he had just swallowed and fluids in his lungs. At the moment it began travelling up his throat, he crouched, and forcibly opened Keraunos's mouth. Placing his mouth on Keraunos's he deposited a fist size amount of a bluish-red gelatin-like substance into it. He then forced Keraunos's mouth shut, and closed off his nose to give the sleeping man no choice but to swallow it or suffocate. After Mainyu had accomplished the deed, he wiped his hands on a towel and withdrew from the room.

Gulnar returned and attended to where she cut open the feeding port, stopped the bleeding and dressed the wound. She stood by to attend Keraunos as he endured the painful transformation into what the world would call a vampire.

Although immobile, feeling in a near paralytic state, Keraunos' view of the world was through a semi-conscious drugged haze; pain radiated from his head to his toes and back again. He could hear and feel his heart pounding in his chest and the blood cascading through his veins. His skull was filled with blinding flashes of light from all directions, then in silhouette; someone, a female, was standing over him. Images of things he did not understand shot past in his dreams, images of a war being fought with bolts of lightning, vessels that flew through the air, flying through the sky and trails of light shooting back and forth and frightening noises of loud thunder claps and fire. He could smell burning flesh one moment and sweet-scented flowers the next, then his nose burned from an acrid stench. As he neared consciousness, his gut burned and his stomach churned; so much so that he erupted from both ends for what seemed like hours, then fell into a merciful sleep.

Awaking, Keraunos found himself lying in a stone tub of warm scented water. Someone was gently dabbing his forehead with a cloth. Waking more, the first thing he saw was the same young woman that had served him the wine and food. He jerked back,

"Shush..." she whispered putting her finger to her mouth as if to be quiet and all was well.

She was in the bath with him, slowly washing his body and at the same time massaging his muscles that ached from the strain and tension of the dreams he had just experienced. He felt different; her touch, her smell, the air, the warm soft water all seemed to have an added dimension of sensory impact. As she gently massaged and washed the healing arrow wound, he became fixated on her breasts, now free from the bounds of her robe, gently swaying in the water and teasing him with each move of her arms. He had not been with a woman since leaving for this campaign – much too long, he thought.

She moved closer and positioned her legs to straddle him as if he were a horse, suspended just above him on her knees. He reached out and touched her, moving his hands and tracing her body from her arms to her waist, to her bare hips and upper legs as she combed and squeezed the water from his long hair and beard. After tying his hair back with a leather strip, she pressed her body into his; her sweet smell nearly intoxicated him.

She pulled his face to her breasts, while still suspended above him she began to move her pelvis and stomach against his in a seductive rhythm until he came to full arousal. She reached under her, between his legs and grasped him, softly sliding her hand up and down his erect shaft.

Raising her hand to the edge of the bath, she produced the same lancet she had used to pierce his neck several hours before. His eyes widened, and he was about to push her away when in a single motion she pierced herself at the base of her neck, then tossed the weapon away. Arching her back she leaned into him again and offered him the pleasure of the warm sweet living nectar of her body.

Much to his amazement, he became nearly intoxicated with the sight and aroma of the blood, all adding to his sexual arousal. As he covered the small well she had opened with his mouth, he sucked and drank it slowly. She groaned, reaching down once more to him, grasped, and guided him into her as she crouched onto his lap, pushing forward, inviting him deeper. As he felt himself inside her, he stopped feeding and licked the wound before turning his attention to the rhythm of lovemaking she had begun. As a vampire at its peak, he was gifted with incredibly enhanced sensory and physical capabilities, and achieved the greatest climax he had ever experienced, one which he tried to replicate, but he never matched the experience in that bath on that night.

The next morning in the darkness of the caverns of Sogdian Rock, Mainyu shared the secrets he had successfully protected from men for over 3,000 years. At first Keraunos was angry with Mainyu, but as he processed what he had been told: a jump of his lifespan to over 5,000 years; greater physical and mental acuity; and the mysteries of alchemy – the secret of making gold and silver out of base metals, the alien science that would make him rich and powerful. There were very few downsides except for acute reactions to direct rays of the sun, and vulnerability to the prejudice of men. Both were ever-present and both could result in quick death.

Keraunos agreed to be an acolyte of Mainyu – to be his companion over the centuries and command his keepers and guardians and to take Gulnar as his mate. Keraunos and Mainyu crafted a cover story for Nicator: Mainyu would become a vassal to King Nicator with Keraunos as the governor of the region to ensure Mainyu's compliance. When Nicator was assassinated, Mainyu and Keraunos continued as their own successors under an assortment of names for several generations.

Vampire Origins...

Keraunos and Mainyu's alliance in Bactriana lasted almost 300 years; long after the Kingdom of King Seleucus and those that followed were distant memories. As they gained power and almost absolute wealth from the mysteries they commanded, eventually cover stories associated with their long lives were not considered necessary, their longevity just added to the lore and associated mysteries of the cults each lead.

The world was changing, however, in ways that made creatures of the night more vulnerable than ever before. Mainyu was not one to deal well with change or see the necessity to change. He did not see himself as part of an old order, or by any stretch of the imagination part of any order at all. He, as the last surviving member of his race on earth and father of what were known as vampires he chose to avoid temporary threats by outliving them, by not engaging them and becoming polluted by association in any way; his choice was to hide and emerge after those threats had turned to dust. As this new conquering threat came from the west, he withdrew to the ancient bastion of his kind in the underground caverns of Balkh, near the now lost city of Eucratideia in northern Afghanistan, to wait out this newest age of man.

Keraunos saw this same tide of conquest coming his way from the west, from a place called Rome, as an opportunity. The Romans appeared to be modern versions of the great Alexander with potential to surpass his glory and rule the entire world. The similarities were remarkable: Although they spoke a different language, Latin, the elite were educated in and spoke Greek. Their Gods were renamed Greek Gods, therefore vulnerable to resonating to the power and mystery of his own cult, with the knowledge given to him by Mainyu about his kind and his place in this age of man.

Keraunos saw vulnerability in their worship of nearly the same family of gods as the Greeks. Mainyu had opened his eyes to what the Greeks regarded as gods. Their gods were not gods at all, but were what the ancient Sumerian people called the Annunaki, or "...those who come down from the sky." The Annunaki had human form but were not of Earth. They were sent to Earth to watch over mankind while they mined for precious metals. Far superior to humans, they soon abused their power, mated with humans, and in their vanity accepted their worship.

Mainyu's kind was the Enki people that also plied interstellar space in search of precursors to precious metals. The Annunaki and Enki were of common ancestral origin; each shared advanced technologies and hyper-long life spans as compared to humankind. Ten thousand years before, in their home world, the Annunaki and the Enki fought a great war. The Enki lost and were exiled from their home world to one that was as hospitable and had an atmosphere that filtered out wavelengths of their sun's rays that the Earth's did not. As a result of this peculiar evolution on this world and its protective atmosphere, the Enki could live comfortably in their new home world, while the Enki on Earth and unprotected, could only emerge at night, stay in the shadows or walk about in special suits.

The Enki arrived long after the Annunaki, first appearing among the indigenous people in the Western hemisphere. Through an alliance lasting several hundred years with several tribes from what is now Mexico to Chile, they mined gold and silver and precursors for making them. As more Enki ships arrived, they expanded their exploration to the Eastern continent in the present-day countries of Greece, Turkey, and Iran. The Annunaki detected their ships after arrival and identified them as their own estranged cousins. Recalling their historical distrust, they judged the Enki as threats to their domination over mankind. They began their war anew by attacking what seemed to be undefended mining colonies.

The Annunaki's long sojourn on Earth was their undoing. Although their technology was far superior to that of man, Enki weapons were newer, having evolved beyond that of the Annunaki living on Earth. A great war ensued between the two groups with the Annunaki the original aggressors. The Enki fought back furiously with the result being total annihilation of the Annunaki, leaving what was left of the Enki as victors. The Greeks lost their living gods, and mystery cults evolved around them as stone statues of their former selves. Victory was costly, however: casualties were high, their ships were in ruin, their nutrient generators destroyed, and weapons and arsenals expended.

The survivors were marooned on the Earth, an inhospitable place to their kind with no weapons other than their own wits or what they could salvage from parts of those left after the war. Peace did not bring peace to the Enki. For more than half a millennia they failed to find nutritional substitutes for what they could no longer manufacture and most of them died from a type of anemia. Many died after being caught in the sun's rays too long. Two of the last three killed each other over a human female. Mainyu was the last surviving Enki.

He survived mainly because he did not give up on finding a nutritional substitute after their synthesizer generators stopped working for good. Quite by accident he learned the blood flowing through the veins of humans satisfied the unique nutritional requirements he needed in order to thrive. Through trial and error he learned just how to feed, as well as to "father" companions for his kind from humans to relieve his loneliness, and serve him. Mainyu became what men in their ignorance believed to be a demon or devil creature, and later called Vampire.

***

Unlike Mainyu, the creature that was once Demetrius Keraunos smelled opportunity with the Romans, but needed a venue to become one of them. Shedding his "slave" name Keraunos morphed into a character more regal sounding – someone befitting the title of "Citizen of Rome." He became Demetrius Antiochus Epiphanes, the epithet meaning "illustrious;" he felt it suited him. As Epiphanes, he was tutored by a Greek pedagogue or educator in reading and writing classical Greek and Latin as well as rhetoric, geometry, astronomy and meteorology. With these skills he could adequately pass as a man of breeding and wealth.

Epiphanes and Mainyu argued over his departure, and he was warned about venturing into the world of men, especially men like the Romans. Epiphanes would not listen to Mainyu. They argued like a wise father and a wayward son – but Mainyu relented, and gave Epiphanes half the fortune they had made and accumulated over the centuries, but would not permit Gulnar to leave with him. Mainyu reminded Epiphanes what he had told him over three hundred years before: "...she will remain with you while you are with me." To assure his wishes were followed Mainyu had Gulnar packed off to another town so she would not try to leave with Epiphanes. Angry and disappointed, he obeyed Mainyu, embraced him as if for the last time, and departed with the small army he had been given.

Epiphanes's chance came a generation later during the great Roman Civil War following the assassination of their Emperor, Julius Caesar. Epiphanes sent an embassy to Gaius Julius Octavius (Octavian), and offered to put his forces under his command in return for citizenship and designation of his forces as a new Legion of the Roman Army. Octavian hesitantly agreed.

Egypt, 30 BC...

The final land battle in the struggle for power occurred at the gates of Alexandria, the Ptolemaic capital of Egypt; Epiphanes's forces annihilated a joint force under the rebel Roman General, Marcus Antonius, and his lover, the descendant of Alexander's chief General, Ptolemy, who ruled Egypt as did Seleucus in Bactriana. That descendant was Queen Cleopatra VII Philopator, known to history as Cleopatra. After scattering the combined Egyptian forces and those loyal to Antonius, Epiphanes entered Alexandria and his forces seized Cleopatra who had been hiding in her palace on the island of Antirrhodos. The official account had it that she committed suicide by pressing an asp to her body and died from the bite. Was it poison? More likely she died from loss of blood since she was discovered dead right after Epiphanes was left alone with the prisoner after the departure of Octavian and his retinue.

The deaths of Cleopatra Philopator and Antonius closed the book for Octavian, who after consolidating his power in the Senate and Army morphed into the Emperor Augustus Caesar. Epiphanes was hailed as a hero and received his reward: citizenship and command of a new Legion given the honorific: *Legio III Gallica* (Third Gallic Legion). Assigned to Syria, Epiphanes studied Octavian's skills in politics and buying the personal loyalty of handpicked military allies who commanded legions spread across the Empire. From a slave to a general, Demetrius Antiochus Epiphanes was a quick learner and began his own quiet, yet brutal, consolidation of power and wealth. He successfully and repeatedly duped the Roman Senate and a succession of likewise cruel, perverted or distracted emperors; handing off power to himself under a variety of names and titles for the next 200 years.

Roman Syria, 168 AD...

By the time of Marcus Aurelius, the vampire had transformed himself from the Epiphanes character into Gaius Tacitus Cassius, Senate-approved Imperial Roman commander in Syria. He was no longer doing anything quietly; he had developed a reputation of cruelty and being power hungry. He was always looking for ways to take advantage of the increasing corruption and instability of the weakening Roman Empire.

He thought that this was his time, and was wasting none of it, when he received notice of the premature passing of Marcus Aurelius. Cassius, in an effort to drain support from Commodious, Marcus's equally unpleasant son among the Roman elite, declared himself to be the rightful successor and added the honorific "Caesar" to his name. He mistakenly expected the support of all the Roman Legions in the East, in Italy, North Africa, or in Gaul – now France and Germany.

The problem was that the Emperor had not in fact died; he had recovered from the illness that Cassius's spy said had killed him. Marcus and Commodious sent three reinforced Legions to arrest Cassius, execute all co-conspirators, decimate and disband his entire Legion. Decimation was a particularly harsh punishment for a Roman Legion that had committed mutiny. By lot, an officer was forced to choose one in ten men for punishment. The nine men not selected were then ordered to club the tenth man to death. As men of a Legion had often fought and protected one another during years of service and warfare, even those who lived were victimized by having to kill a friend under terms of the punishment.

Cassius had been "dying" and resurrecting himself since he became a vampire nearly 400 years before. Sensing that the time for him to "die" and resurrect himself as another was near, Cassius hatched a plan to give the Emperor the head on a platter he wanted, and the pursuit would likely end.

Cassius gathered his personal Cohort of keeper/guardians and asked them to find a soldier who resembled Cassius and bring him to his quarters. They found such a person and enticed him to Cassius's tent in order to be given a special mission. Cassius greeted him warmly, but as they embraced, Cassius drove his dagger down into the base of the man's neck deep into his chest cavity. As he was dying, Cassius gently laid him to the floor and fed on the warm blood flowing from the wound. After consuming his fill, Cassius beheaded the man and put it in a silk bag and gave it to his most trusted Centurion, Antonius Maecianus. It was then sent by courier to Commodious who then brought it to Marcus Aurelius with the story that Cassius's officers killed him in hopes of avoiding further punishment on them or the men of the Legion. The Emperor accepted the story, yet refused to view the blood-encrusted head.

In disguise, Cassius and his personal cohort of keepers/guardians fled Syria for Gaul without pursuit by way of Macedonia. Several weeks into his escape Cassius paused on a hill overlooking a plain. Looking back he saw three men on horseback in the distance. They did not appear to be soldiers but were well armed. One looked like a tracker who pointed toward him at each stop.

...Who are those men? He wondered.

Later he would learn the leader was Claudius Galenicus, a vampire of his own making. Months before the present crisis, Galenicus came to him at his Ephesus encampment as the Emperor's personal physician asking his knowledge of a plague. Cassius feared him a spy for the emperor and thought about killing him, but decided to make him a vampire and ally against the emperor. Things got out of control and Galenicus turned against him. Not deceived as were Aurelius and Commodious by Cassius' deception, Galenicus hunted Cassius and swore to destroy all he had fathered.

He eluded Galenicus for over 1100 years until in the wilds of Romania, Cassius once more feeling invincible, became notorious as a petty tyrant with a taste for blood. His behavior caught Galenicus' attention. After a losing and bloody battle between the forces of Cassius and Galenicus, Cassius fled once more; this time northwest across Europe to the far reaches of the British Isles. Galenicus pursued him there and on each of several engagements through time wrought death and destruction on Cassius' company.

By September 1659, Cassius had taken the identity of Sir Angus Cassidy on board a ship a week out of the Port of Glasgow in western Scotland. He and his remaining guardians were headed to the growing English colony on the island of Jamaica in the pirate infested Caribbean Sea. In Jamaica, Sir Angus Cassidy thought he would finally be free of his nemesis, the horrible mistake of Galenicus...12,000 leagues of ocean would see to that. He would never again be challenged, never again the weaker; never again would he have to run away.

Chapter 2 - The Wreck of the Edith Louise

"...Haggard from want and hunger, they roamed the parched land in desolate wastelands at night..."

Job 30, 2-4.

The *Edith Louise* was well fitted for privateering. She displaced over 900 tons and was built to the specifications of a 4th rate ship of the line. She had 60 guns of various calibers on 2 decks and had a draft of over 15 feet. At the gun decks from bow to stern she measured over 146 feet in length with a beam of 38 feet. Each of the crew of 250 men had English or Scottish flagged privateer or merchant seaman experience.

Enroute to Port Royal, the seat of the English colony of Jamaica the ship and crew had been consigned by the Scottish Parliament to serve as a privateer operating under a Letter of Marque for the Caribbean Sea. Its primary duty was to serve as an escort for the Scottish Darien Company ships passing through and out of pirate waters, or simply hunting pirates to collect bounties and their booty for its investors.

In addition to Cassidy masquerading as a minor peer of the Scottish aristocracy his servants and cargo, the ship carried the private cargo of the Jamaican Royal Governor. Cassidy and his entourage rarely shared the daylight with the officers on deck; regularly dined alone in their quarters or below on the Orlop deck and only seen on topside during the mid-watch.

Once the ship passed south through the Irish Sea past St. George's Channel into the North Atlantic the troubles began. Rumors spread among the crew about a curse had descended on the ship after a mysterious illness mercilessly invaded the bodies of many of the ship's company. Without a doubt the ship had been under a pall since it left the port of Glasgow. Ship's Master, Jonathan Bobb was its first casualty. The First Officer took command and made landfall at St. George's, on the English colony of Bermuda to drop off the Captain and dispatch reports back to the Darien Company regarding the change in command and status update. Although Bobb still breathed when he was carried down the gang plank – the crew watched and reckoned he was a dead man. Ship's Doctor said the Captain's plague of a high fever, diarrhea, and blisters on his throat and skin where like he had never seen before. Bobb had changed quickly, he entered the voyage a tall hardy man of 36 years, a veteran privateer, but a fortnight out of Glasgow he was too sick to leave his cabin. By the time the ship arrived at

St. George's his weight had dropped from a hefty 11 stone to no more than 8. Following report of the Captain's illness, 4 other crewmen were discovered with the same symptoms and were likewise put off with him and not replaced.

The *Edith Louise* sailed with the tide the following evening after taking on water and fresh provisions. The former First Officer Edward Coulle was now the ship's master. In hopes of arriving in Jamaica early to hire more crew and downing several drams of rum in a Port Royal tavern, Coulle hastened the passage by taking advantage of the fair winds and ordered the stunsails clewed from the topsails to the moonrakers; foremast to the mizzenmast. The winds cooperated and the ship's rigging sang and rattled while its timbers groaned as if bringing the ship to life riding its keel straight and true through the clear blue tropical waters on a south-southwest tack.

Thursday, September 16th 1695 – The First Watch

Night was approaching – Usually a time to rest and be with his mates without a thousand chores a sailor does from sunrise to sunset while at sea. Since leaving Glasgow, the crew grew more agitated after the Captain and several of the crew was taken sick, it was not helped when there also were rumors that something unnatural walked the decks at night, and to a man, everyone was racked with terrible dreams of being smothered in their sleep. Young Seaman Will Smythe now had learned to hate the night and if visited by sleep, it brought no real rest, just nightmares. About the rumors; he thought whatever it was – it also surely moved through the darkness of night – moving silently and without warning, turning healthy men into hollow eyed victims.

Now a week southwest and over 300 leagues from Bermuda, the mysterious illness had spread to all but ten of the crew. Each one of them babbled about a suffocating darkness coming over them at night as they slept; then being unable to breathe, and waking as if in a deep dream feeling weak and what looked like small wound at the base of their neck from a surgeon's lancet, like used in medicinal bloodletting practices of the day.

Thursday, September 26th – The Mid watch, the plague worsens, the whole crew is sick...

For cabin boy William Smythe this voyage was his first and wondered if it would be his last. He had just returned from bringing victuals to the watch and lay back in his hammock, thinking about his ration of beer in the morning; thinking that would make him feel better. The air was sultry and close on the first gun deck; men both close to being able bodied and those with advanced symptoms of the sickness were sleeping, snoring, or as if to be gagging for air. He crossed himself and tucked his arms to his side to keep them from dangling over the deck; for he had fear of "things" crawling up his arms while he slept. Before burying his face into a small sack filled with clothing he used as a pillow, his eyes picked up a movement in the moonlit portal of No 6 gun. He noticed a dark form moving like a ghost from the portal, making no noise descending onto the deck, pausing at each sleeping man as it passed through the chamber.

Smythe stiffened, grasping the hammock with each hand, almost holding his breath as if trying to disappear into the canvas. Moving only his eyes he watched the figure move slowly toward him until it paused over a sleeping shipmate not 10 feet from him. The figure, what appeared to be a man in a dark cloak flipped its hood back and leaned down, the brim of his hat covering its face, seemingly to study and was smelling the man's chest and throat. Suddenly the moon light gleamed off a short shank or lancet in its left hand, just before the blade pieced the sleeping man's neck just below the jaw – the man groaned but did not stir – at the same movement, the intruder covered the wound with its mouth sucking the blood flowing from it.

"Ye, there!! What are in our Lord's name are ye up to?" Smythe shouted jumping from his hammock.

The creature jerked away from his terrible feast and stared in Smythe's direction; both in frozen stances staring at each other. Smythe could not see the intruder's face, only what appeared to be it eyes gazing through it dark hair – they were haunting orbs with a fiery focus that not only reflected surprise, but also a strange sense of vulnerability. The man whose was wounded stirred and began to flail his arms; breaking the creature's embrace.

"What, what, help me! What the hell? Get off me man!!" his words were hardly audible, yet loud enough to awaken the men nearby.

Squeak O'Malley, an old salt sleeping behind the creature awoke and with a shout, lunged toward the creature. In one motion, the creature turned and grasped old Squeak by the head and snapped his neck with a crack. By the time the man's limp body fell to the deck the creature was through the gun port – no splash, just gone as if into thin air.

Smythe never had seen a man killed before, hesitated for a moment at the visual of Squeak's quick demise, and then ran forward to the gun port. He stretched forward scanning the ship above and below decks for evidence to where the creature might have taken refuge. Pausing at portal, he noticed the wind had picked up and it smelled like rain approaching. Looking down at the water, he studied the foamy waves lapping against and from the ship's hull as it slid further along in the angry looking dark sea. A moment passed when his eye caught movement below and toward the stern – it looked like someone or something reentering the ship by the lower gun portal 2 decks below. He backed inside and returned to Squeak and the sailor who had been cut.

Now the men were all awake and there was a great clamber of feet across the deck. People were tumbling and questioning and shouting at one another oaths that would make any sailor blush ...The man who was cut, common seaman Harry Coorthopp was sitting upright in his hammock holding his neck looking a bit peeked. Drops of blood dripped from the wound, but had slowed and began to coagulate.

"Whit the hell is going on here?" The Quarter Master, Tom Crisp shouted as he pushed through crowd congregated around the dead man. He stopped and knelt down to look at the body lying on its back. "Is that old Squeak? Give us a light..."

Smythe lit a passage way lamp and handed it to Crisp.

Crisp examined the deformed broken neck, closing Squeak's staring eyes, and stood up. "Did anyone see what happened 'ere?" Crisp asked to the men.

"Mr. Crisp – Ah saw everything." Smythe said. "It was a dark figure, it was a man that came in and looked like he cut a hole in Harry's throat and was sucking on the wound. Ah shouted at him and old Squeak woke up and rushed forward to get the man off Harry. Well, he turned, reached out and snapped Squeak's neck like a twig – I swear to God, like a twig - and then was gone, through that gun port..." Smythe reported, pointing to where the creature exited the deck and what he thought he saw the moment before reentering the ship on lower deck near the stern.

"Did ye recognize who it was?" asked Crisp focusing hard on the young lad.

"No your honor, never laid eyes on him before, Ah would have remember such a person."

Crisp turned and picked 2 men to carry Squeak to the Bosun and get him ready for burial at sea on the morrow.

"Seaman Coorthopp, are ye able to carry on?" Crisp asked.

"Yes Mr. Crisp, Ah am fit for duty – just a bit sore and weak, but am sure Ah will be at mah peak by the mornin' watch."

The Ship's Master next arrived and was met by Crisp who put his arm over his shoulder, turning him about and to lead him back off the gun deck to his cabin.

Turning to the First Mate and to the Master Gunner, "Mr. Poole take 5 men and search the ship with special attention where seaman Smythe noticed movement – Mr. Leeds issue cutlasses to the men and a charged pistol to Mr. Poole. Report to me at the conclusion of the search or when ye find whatever did this...and issue Seaman Coorthopp a ration of beer."

"Thank you, your honor that will do me fine!" Coorthopp shouted as the men mounted the stairs to the deck above.

Tuesday, September 24th, The Morning Watch

As Crisp and Coulle ascended to the open weather deck, dawn was breaking and noticed they were in sight of the coast of the Isla de la Florida, a foul peninsula full of unfriendly Indians, swamps and strange lizards of incredible size, and Spanish territory. They noticed the wind had picked up and a stinging rain was beginning to blow from the south east. This was in direct contrast of the evening before when Mr. Pelegran the navigator was pointing out an island off the coast the Spanish called *Cabo de Florida* inhabited by a native tribe known as the Tequesta people – not a very friendly lot.

Pausing near the port rail they took note the sea had gone from a light chop to white caps in the few hours since the mid watch. The ships rigging strained in the winds and its timbers groaned with each wave. Moving forward, holding to the bulwark, the two men entered the Captain's cabin on the stern; lit a lamp and poured themselves a whiskey.

After downing the drink Coulle asked Crisp, "What the hell is going on Mr. Crisp? We are all sick – and it looks like we all have the same mark on our necks as does Coorthopp. We now have a dead man – killed by person or thing unknown; this whole voyage has been a wonder to me. "

"Captain, there is something else – it's oor passengers. Thay are not sick and the men think thay have brought on the curse that has befallen this ship. "

"Ah, the Cassidy party. Ye know Ah don't think Ah would even recognize Sir Angus if Ah would run into him. We need...." Coulle was interrupted in mid-sentence by a feverish series of knocks on the cabin door.

"What is it?" Crisp demanded.

The door swung open, it was Mr. Poole, "Captain ye have to come with me! The men have congregated outside Sir Angus's cabin down on the Orlop deck and are threatening to beat it down unless he comes out."

"Where are your men?"

"They are between them and the hatch, but ye need to come fast sir – there is going to be trouble!"

Coulle and Crisp armed themselves with sabers, and with Poole rushed onto the weather deck. The ship was rolling violently and the rain had increased, making it dangerous to be on an open deck with no line attached – Coulle suspected they were in the middle of a tropical hurricane.

"Captain, she's blowing here, need some help keepin' 'er on a true course and to shorten sails...!" the Watch Officer shouted from the bridge deck.

Turning to Crisp, Coulle cracked "...It just gets better."

"We'll send ye a party right away" Crisp shouted back at the watch.

The lowest part of the ship, the Orlop deck was usually used to stow lines and other material – but at the request of Cassidy turned into a large berth for him and his party. Arriving on the Orlop deck, the officers came up a scene usually seen when the crew was staging a mutiny, men were packed front to back leaning to and fro as the ship was tossed by the storm, all the time demanding Cassidy show himself.

"Men, men – calm down...we've got a blow outside, and need to attend to that." Turning to Poole who stood to his right, he asked for a report.

"Well sir, we found nothing on the ship...we have not searched the passenger spaces – that is the only place left." Poole responded.

Walking through the crowd, Captain Coulle approached the cabin door and knocked on it with the hilt of his sabre. "Sir Angus, Ah need to speak to ye." Turning to the crew assembled, he ordered Crisp to secure the ship for the storm – and to do that immediately.

Crisp turned and ordered the men to leave the room and the Captain would handle the matter with Cassidy. The men slowly responded and went to their stations. The ship moved with the motion of the waves bludgeoning its hull with greater force as the storm grew in ferocity.

Turning again to the cabin door, "Sir Angus, this is the Captain."

***

Behind the cabin door was a scene of frantic activity. It concealed not only defensive preparations for the mob crashing in, but also a secret long held over the centuries about a family of men and women that served a creature of great strength and long life, but each day had to be protected and cared for as they slept, vulnerable from human fear of what they didn't understand.

Nearly twenty minutes before, Angus Cassidy, the Laird, rushed through the passage way into his quarters. He was frantic, slamming and bolting the door behind him he tossed his black cape onto the floor; pausing to listen on the other side as he wiped his mouth with the back of his hand.

"Ah let masellf be seen, and mibbe recognized…how stupid, how terribly stupid…thay will put what thay saw together and it wull naw be long before through a process of elimination to conclude who thay saw was me…!" Cassidy blurted.

"Laird Cassidy, say that again…" asked William Brodie, the head of the family group that served as Cassidy's keepers. Brodie's father and his father before him, and as long as his family history was recorded had served Cassidy as his identity evolved over the generations of the Brodie family while he lived and moved around in what was known as the Caledonian region of old Roman Britain to the present day Kingdom of Scotland.

"Mr. Brodie, expect to have a mob at the door soon…Ah was taking nourishment before laying down to sleep when one of the crew saw me, and another tried to detain me – and I didn't think - just turned and murdurred him."

"Damn it…" Brodie responded, turning to his wife "…Gillian, prepare a strong solution to help the laird sleep deeply until these men tire of looking for him…" The solution was a mixture of henbane and mandragora plant plus mandrake to induce sleep and lower the heart rate to a point where no evidence of life could be detected in the body. This mixture was handed down to Brodie through his family and often used in long transits where taking nourishment by traditional means was not practicable or dangerous due to circumstances of the journey.

Brodie's wife turned to the small ship's cupboard and mixed a triple portion of the drugs with Madeira wine enough to fill two goblets. Holding the glass cup to the flickering candle on the cupboard shelf to see that the granules were properly dissolved, she had to steady herself as the ship began to shift as the storm outside grew more violent. Turning to her husband, she gave him the concoction to give to the Laird.

Angus Cassidy, the name used by the creature for nearly three centuries had already laid himself into the brass alloy coffin moving his legs to embed himself into the sand that half-filled the interior. Lying back exhaled and closed his eyes, then sat up to receive the drug solution before being sealed into his sanctuary.

William Brodie hurried to the coffin side and gave Cassidy both goblets containing the drugs. Cassidy looked at Brodie and then the cups – for some reason each hesitated drawn to a feeling that this glance needed to be remembered. He brought the goblet to his lips and in two large sips emptied it. Cassidy handed it back to his servant. Brodie then handed Cassidy a second cup of the concoction which was uncustomary in these situations, he however drank without question. With that, Cassidy laid back and closed his eyes. Brodie gently placed a silk mask over the reclining man's face and placed his personal dagger in his right hand. In anticipation of more than normal period confined in the coffin, Brodie poured an additional drug solution over the over a folded towel over Cassidy's face, saturating it. Cassidy was now unconscious. In the last step in preparation Brodie laid Cassidy's cloak over the sand covering the body. Without a further word, Brodie shut and bolted the casket shut sealing it. To further conceal and protect Cassidy's resting place, it lay in a large wooden packing crate for transport – Brodie completed his work by securing the crate's lid.

Back on deck, the ship lurched as it was hit be a large wave. Brodie, steadying himself he made his way forward to the cabin door where he could hear a crowd of men outside demanding that Cassidy show himself. In the interval when deciding what to do, another solid knock at the door came from Captain Coulle, requesting to see the Laird.

Brodie opened the door and greeted Coulle.

"Ah am sorry Captain, we were assisting the laird at the rear of the cabin – he is very sea sick and asked to be sedated. How can we be of service sir?" Brodie said, hoping to pre-empt Coulle's likely demand to see Cassidy.

"Mr. Brodie ah presume and Mrs. Brodie..." Coulle said touching the brim of his hat with the fingers of his right hand in an informal salute.

"Ah need to see Laird Cassidy at the earliest opportunity on the morrow after the storm passes. Please ask the Laird to come and see me nearest the noon hour" Coulle said, again touching his brim before turning and ascending the stairway to the weather deck.

After closing the door, Will and Gillian Brodie looked at one another with a breath of relief before bolting it shut and securing the cabin for what they expected to be a violent storm tossed dawn.

"Mr. Crisp, we must keep oor heads if we are to save the ship..." Ship's Master Edward Coulle shouted over the howling wind to his First Officer Tom Crisp.

Screaming in their ears, the wind continued to blow from the east, and seas increased with waves crashing over the main deck. Adding to the spectacle, water spouts churned and danced in the water near the *Edith Louise* and the sky was full of lighting and loud claps of thunder drowning out orders by deck supervisors to crew members.

Moving to the bridge, Edward Coulle and Tom Crisp tied themselves to the ship's bibbs near the helmsman to avoid being washed overboard as the ship tossed to and fro. The gun crews were feverously securing the deck guns on the weather and level 2 gun deck to avoid them breaking loose and raising havoc on the decks should the storm worsen even more. The ship's galley mate in the stern below the weather deck was trying to keep the cooking fire lit in the fire hearth to make morning tea for the officers.

"Mr. Crisp, keep the bow into the wind, we are getting too close to the shore..." shouted Coulle as he strained against the salt spray riding the torrent, stinging as lead shot hitting their faces. Crisp repeated the order to the helmsman and to the sail detail below them on the main deck. Just then the ship rode high over a wave into the running sea, and came down hard with sickening sound of the hull hitting the bottom.

Crisp looked at Coulle, un-tied himself from the bulwark and struggled down the bridge ladder in the direction of the forward hatches to inspect what damage may have occurred.

Coulle thought ...*Christ we must be in less than 5 fathoms of water to have hit a reef!* "...Put the bow straight into the wind, and catch it and bring us away from the shore Mr. Murray." He shouted to the helmsman.

Although the dawn had broken, the sky was half white with swirling clouds punctuated by an ever darkening approaching front of the storm's core. It had turned deathly cold. The helmsman then saw something no sailor ever lived to describe – a giant water spout a quarter of a mile across just off the port bow closing on the *Edith Louise* that bobbed helplessly in its path.

"Captain, look!" Murray shouted over the terrible roar of the storm and pointed toward the approaching wind beast of the water spout. Coulle looked to his left front just as it hit the bow sprint and forward rigging. The sound of the torrent was like no man had heard before – grinding and snapping the timbers and sucking lines and rigging into its hungry forward wall. Crisp and four men had just reached the forecastle when it hit, blowing him, and the four men with him into the whirling water and wind. Coulle helplessly watched them disappear into the torrent and could hear their screams as it swallowed them up.

Suddenly the ship lurched to starboard; and the wind beast lifted the bow, slowly at first, then got under the keel and raised it to angle of nearly fifty degrees - every man and man-made thing on the decks, above and below not bolted down tumbled straight or end-over-end down to the stern crashing into and crushing everything caught in the middle.

Coulle, strained to untie himself from the bulwark when one of the deck guns cascaded onto the bridge taking out the wheel, crushing the helmsman who heroically was standing his post. The ships wheel was now gone, and Coulle knew he had given his last order on the *Edith Louise*. Below decks several number 2 deck guns tumbled down smashing through the stern bulkheads, and the galley; ripping down the double bulkhead of the powder magazine near it.

After passing by, the spout threw the ship back down onto the boiling sea as violently as it picked it up. The bow was breached and immediately began taking on water. When it crashed back down on the water, the lurch caused every timber on the ship to shutter from stem to stern. The heavy iron fire hearth broke free from its stone slab base and hot coals from the fire spilled onto the crumbled mass of combustibles spread about in the stern section. In seconds the fire spread into an inferno that soon spread past the shattered powder magazine bulkhead. A keg of gunpowder nearest the path of the fire had shattered and rolled forward and backward in rhythm with the tossing sea throwing gunpowder on the deck with each roll.

The inevitable finally happened, the keg rolled into the fire with the loose powder first fizzling, but when the burn reached the powder in the keg itself, it immediately detonated causing a chain reaction of explosions among the remaining powder stores. From the stern to the forecastle the ship was engulfed in an expanding ball of flame, smoke and sulfurous gases that ripped it open sending wood, rigging, men and pieces of men into the air, as well as its guns and ballast rocks to the reef below. The *Edith Louise* sunk with all hands in less than ten minutes.

Chapter 3 - The Discovery of a Lifetime

...I will give you hidden treasures, riches stored in secret places...

Isaiah 45,3

Since the unnamed hurricane sunk the Edith Louise in 1695 thousands of tropical cyclones have churned the waters and reefs of the Florida Keys. As dawn broke on Monday, August 24, 1992, the eye of third most powerful tropical cyclone to make landfall on the coast of the United States in modern times impacted south Florida just north of Key Largo, the northern most island in the Florida Keys. The sustained winds of 150 and gusts recorded to 212 miles per hour affected not only the surface, but churned and battered coral reefs to depths of 75 feet. It is estimated over 180 million fish perished, and many of the heaviest of sunken wrecks were moved or destroyed.

At Carysfort Reef, the 1821 wreck of a Spanish slave ship sunk by an anti-slavery patrol vessel was moved from its grave by the hurricane. Under the wreck were that of another; a cursed ship and a grave of a creature that would redefine ancient myth.

Near sun down on a warm Saturday evening of October 10, 1992 Robert Hopkins had just discovered the find of his life 25 feet below the surface on Carysfort Reef. While braving the low visibility in the water from the storm, he was looking for late season lobsters on a part of the reef he rarely visited. He caught a glimpse of reflected sunlight at the edge of what appeared to be a ballast pile of river rocks scattered over the coral reef. Reaching the bottom, he brushed away some loose sand around an object pushed up against a coral outcropping covered with black ballast stones. As he ran his fingers around the edge of the object, the white sand swirled in a circle around what appeared to be a gold colored bird or eagle. Instinctively he covered it with his hand and looked around to assure himself he was alone and his find was his. He also realized he was inside the John Pennekamp State Park, and the find was not his, it rightfully belonged to the State of Florida; yes only if they ever learned about it he thought. Gently pulling on the object, it broke free from the sand and coral attached to it. He gently laid it in his catch net, again looking around him for other divers.

Swimming to the surface he reached high in the water and shouted to his dive partner on the boat to retrieve it from him quickly.

"Alex, come over and take this!" Hopkins said.

Leaning over the gunnel, Alex Walsh's eyes widened he grasped the heavy metal eagle, swinging it away from the water and onto the deck. Looking back at his friend who had tossed his fins into the boat and was struggling up the dive ladder, "Wow, what the hell you have found down there?" he asked.

"I'm not sure, but mark this spot with the GPS, we are coming back tomorrow. As Walsh moved to the GPS, Hopkins took off the heavy dive equipment and laid it on the deck. Hopkins knelt down and took the eagle out of his net and held it in both his hands, scanning his gloved hand over it. At the bottom was a hollow point as if a staff or pole could be inserted. At the base carved into the metal were the Letters "*SPQR*" and below that "*Legio* ...." with the rest not legible.

"I think I know what this is, but it shouldn't be in these waters...we will definitely be back tomorrow..." Hopkins said to his partner.

Hopkins had studied the history of ship wrecks on the Florida Keys since he was a kid living in Homestead. His house was full of books about the subject – and loved to visit Mel Fisher's museum in Key West dedicated to the discoveries he and his company made on the Spanish plate ship called the Atocha. Hopkins always fantasized about finding an undiscovered sunken ship from the Spanish plate fleet loaded with gold and jewels.

The plate fleets ships assembled in old Havana each summer after taking on gold, silver, and jewels from Spanish American mines and plunder from the natives. Each year they departed Havana as fleets in convoy to avoid pirates and from just getting lost for Spain and the King's treasury. Each convoy were relatively ill-timed as they cast off in hurricane season – and the Florida Straits often was ground zero for late summer hurricanes and because they are a maze of shallow reefs even miles from shore; a bad place to be caught when one passed through.

On their ride back to Black Point Marina, Hopkins and his diving partner Alex Walsh discussed the find Hopkins had just brought into the boat. The conversation centered on what it was and their obligation to notify Pennekamp Park officials and archeologists about the find.

"Rob, you know as well as I do, anything of historical value we pull off those reefs doesn't belong to us just because we found it. The stories over the years about guys finding and keeping Spanish artifacts and gold from old wrecks and the jackpot they got in when the State or Feds got involved is pretty common knowledge." Walsh shouting now as the boat pounded over the waves of Biscayne Bay after leaving Angel Fish Creek Channel.

"Yep, yep, I know Alex, but I think we can keep looking around for more, and then make a decision about letting Pennekamp know what we found and where we found it."

That discussion was the last they had about telling anyone about their discoveries on Carysfort Reef. Upon their many return visits to the site, they found gold coins from both wrecks as well as jewelry – just enough to keep them coming back, but not enough, they thought to constitute a need to share with Pennekamp officials. Their cover story whenever approached by a marine patrol officer on the water was either fishing or lobstering.

When in the water the diver always carried a catch net and tickle stick; a 40 or so inch fiberglass rod with a hole drilled in one end for a key ring that held a lobster carapace measuring tool. Each diver also pulled a "diver down" flag float and had a fishing and lobstering license – everything as not to attract attention or instill a need for further investigation if questioned.

Coins were the most remarkable discoveries they made in their visits to the mysterious wreck. The coins were also not what were normally found in Florida waters either. In addition to a dozen or so Scottish hammered gold coins dated 1601, minted during the reign of James VI of Scotland, the greatest numbers of them were clumped together copper or silver coins of lesser value. A few of these coins turned out to be Scottish farthings, pennies and half pennies after Hopkins he pulled them for an electrolysis bath in his Kendall garage. What kept both men going back was the first find – the gold Eagle. Gold was on both men's mind – although after the nearly 10 year search yielded very little, and both were getting discouraged.

On Friday afternoon, November 8, 2002, Hopkins and Walsh were anchored about 100 yards west of the first pile of ballast rocks Hopkins had found the Eagle. Alex Walsh was on the last 1000 lbs. of air in his scuba tank, swimming the edge of a sea grass field and sandy bottom leading east to the reef. Instinctively he scanned under the hollow cave-like area carved into edge of the sea grass for lobsters that may be hiding there. Swimming over a rise in the grass he noticed in a gap in the grass and murky sand what looked like a few black ballast rocks.

Walsh bled a few squirts of air from his buoyancy compensator (BC) vest and settled on the bottom putting down his lobstering gear. As he settled on the bottom, he kicked up some of the murky silt that would make it more difficult to see if he was not careful. He ran is hands over the rocks, and pulled a small one up confirming what it was. Looking around for similar rises, he saw none. Apparently as the bottom of the ship moved in the violence of its demise, it shifted away from where most of its ballast had pulled the hull to the bottom and deposited some here at the rise...not too unusual since when a ship goes to the bottom, there is no formula for where everything winds up. Ballast rocks are a promise to treasure divers, but sometimes a hollow one.

To the east of the rise of grass and sand covered ballast rocks ran the edge that cuts toward the ballast rocks. Walsh shifted and glided to the edge and peered down into the hollow. Although obscured by shadow and murky visibility, he could see to the back of the cave-like hollow under the grass. He stuck his fiber glass tickle stick into the sand; first into soft sand, soft sand, then struck something solid. He poked the same spot again, landing on what seemed to be a flat hard surface. After assuring himself there was nothing that would grab his hand by sweeping the area with his stick, Walsh reached to the back surface and clawed at the sand where he felt something solid. Although he could not see inside the hollow because of murky water, he felt a flat surface. He made a fist and tapped on the object which sounded like it was metal. Running his hand left to right, up and down he tried to determine its size. It was big, and was unable to determine where it began or ended. Pulling out, he headed to the surface.

Surfacing, he swam to the boat, leaving his diver's down float, line anchored to the bottom as a marker. As he came up to the diver ladder he was met by Hopkins. " Rob, I need to put on another tank; and maybe you should come and help me to find out what I found in a sand cave at the edge of the sea grass bed near the reef" Walsh said as he handed Hopkins his fins as he ascended the dive ladder.

Hopkins tossed the fins on the deck and pulling a full tank from rack he asked, "Ok, what did you find?"

Climbing the ladder and stepping on to the deck Walsh recounted his discovery and the mystery of what it was. "Do you have anything on board that we can dig with?" he asked.

"I have an old Army entrenching tool in the cuddy cabin for getting off mucky flats I run up on when missing the channel, will that work?

"Yep, I think so – if whatever it is, is covered by ballast rocks, it has got to be associated with the early wreck we found the Eagle and English and Scottish coins; it's got to be." Walsh said. After changing his air tank and dawning his BC, Walsh helped Hopkins put on his equipment, and both were over the side. After achieving correct buoyancy, both ascended to the spot where Walsh found the unknown object under the sand and rocks. Walsh circled around Hopkins who had stopped to survey the rise of ballast rocks under the sea grass. Walsh slowly descended to the sand cave and peered inside where the water that had cleared in the 20 minutes he had been gone. He switched on the flashlight he brought with him from the boat when he changed tanks. As not to stir up the bottom muck, he steadied himself with his fins in the sand and one hand on the bottom. He slowly swept the light inside the sand cave. The light came to rest on patch of metal showing past a thin film of sand that had settled on its surface after it had settled. Slowly he reached in and gently brushed away the sand revealing a green encrusted metal object. He moved more sand away scanning the object with his hand in search of an edge or corner. Sand swirled as he moved his hand. He paused not to obscure his search with more sand into solution.

Hopkins slowly glided over Walsh, hovering about five feet above him to a point where he was in Walsh's air bubbles. He then moved to his left and tapped the valve to release a bit of air from his BC and ascended to a position beside Walsh. As not to stir up any sand to obscure Walsh's search he backed off into the sand, all the time straining to catch a glimpse of the object Walsh had found.

Walsh concluded it was time to explore a bit more aggressively with the entrenching tool. Glancing to his left he motioned Hopkins to back away. He then opened the blade and configured it like a spade. He began by slowly chopping away at the sea grass and sand outcropping of the cave's edge. Sand, bits of grass and bottom muck began swirling in water nearly obscuring both men's view of their work. From time to time all work had to be suspended until the water cleared from the muck and sand that was being stirred into solution. Walsh eventually moved through the rock and sand to the object – his tool striking with a solid metallic thud. After locating it, he found its upper edge and began to clear the debris from its top on the left and right. He motioned to Hopkins to scoop away the material obscuring the object to his left. After lifting rocks and scraping coral they uncovered a corner of what appeared to a brass or maybe gold colored box. On the exposed corner was a large corroded nut likely one of four used to seal the box, they both knelt on the sand staring at the partially exposed box, then at each other.

Walsh remembered they had been working a long time and checked his pressure gauge. It registered about 350 lbs/in^2 of pressure and about to run out of air. He motioned to Hopkins, pointing at his watch, and then made a sweeping motion on his throat to signify it was time to go. Both then covered the object with the grass and sand and as much as possible to obscure any sign of a disturbance on the bottom. After restoring the location they then marked the moment with a high five, and pushed off toward the surface.

Back on the boat after stowing their dive gear, they each opened a beer and stared at the water.

"Okay Rob, now what – what do you think that is?" Walsh asked taking a large gulp from his beer.

"Christ, Alex, I'm not sure; it could be anything. My sense it could be full of gold and jewelry, or....not."

"Rob, according to what you have read on this, neither of these wrecks we have been diving on are treasure fleet ships – nothing we have recovered except for the Eagle, and now this box points to anything to get excited about. However, didn't you say the Eagle we found was an Imperial standard carried by a Roman Legion?"

"You're right about there being nothing to points to a treasure, and God knows in 10 years we have not found anything that's going to make us rich – or even anything we can sell without getting into a jackpot for not reporting it, and losing it, and not making jack."

"...And the Eagle..?" Walsh reminded him.

"The Eagle, the eagle; right, well each considered to carry the soul of the military unit – it represented something like the colors or unit flag of a modern military organization. When a unit is organized the Roman Emperor gave it its Eagle to protect and take care of, and if they lose it in battle, the Legion is disbanded and the name of the Legion is forever dishonored; like the IXth Legion that lost theirs in Scotland I mentioned to you earlier."

"So, this was not a Roman wreck, how do you suppose it got on board on a ship sailing in these waters sometime in the late 16 hundreds"

"I just don't know, just don't know Alex" said Hopkins, draining his beer and tossed it into one of the deck buckets. He continued, "Unless you have a better idea, I suggest we get 2 Carter 2000 pound lift bags – rig them on each corner of the box after we dig it out without being caught; then fill them with air from a couple of dive tanks without being caught, lift it to the surface and then without being caught, pull it slowly to the marina and lift it to the dock while no one is there and open it. Did I mention, we need to do this without being caught?"

"Let's get in and see if we can borrow the lift bags, those size of bags are over $ 500 apiece." Hopkins observed as he started the outboards and Walsh pulled the anchor for their return to the marina.

Their plan worked well, and didn't get caught. They didn't reckon on what they would find inside the box.

Chapter 4 - Saying Goodbye

*"...And all this could be such a dream so it seems
I was never much good at Goodbye..."*

Night Ranger, *Goodbye*, 1985

It was less than two months since Coleen and her family lost her brother from the automobile accident near northern Scotland's Loc Awe on the A86 after leaving the ruins of Kilchurn Castle. Although he was driving the utility vehicle for Dr. Galen, Galen was not hurt, bruised or showed any signs of surviving a fatal accident. She thought this was very curious, but had not pursued the anomaly.

The day of his funeral was a sunny August day, not one that would otherwise mark a solemn occasion. After the minister had concluded the service Coleen stood transfixed on the scene in Glasgow's ancient Govan Old Parish church yard, the coffin and the thinning crowd. Although the parish church is no longer active and burials are limited in this small park like campus, her family had been members since before it's founding in the 6th century. Her father approached her, and put his arm around her shoulders and gave her a hug. As she turned to him she wiped a tear streaming down her face.

"Coleen, there is someone you need to meet, he is just down the way waiting in his car," said her father Robert Jones.

Robert had retired the past year from his association with Galen. She was soon to learn the Jones family had been keeper/guardians of Galen since his arrival in Roman Britain around the date AD 304. Their association had always been limited to direct descendants of the living patriarch of the Jones family following his retirement. That was about to change.

Coleen looked at her father with a puzzled expression, but without questioning him, she turned and walked across the neatly cut grass, past rows of ancient tombstones to a parked black Mercedes Benz in the church car park off McKechnie Street. As they approached the car, the dark tinted passenger side window rolled down with an electric hum. Inside was a 50ish man with a salt and pepper beard dressed in a black business suit. He wore dark sun glasses, a black fedora and what appeared to be grey lambskin gloves.

Both bent down to the seated man's level.

"Coleen, this is Dr. Mark Galen; Dr. Galen, this is my daughter Coleen," Robert said.

"I am very happy to meet you Dr. Jones, your father has been singing your praises for years. Please accept my condolences regarding the loss of Andrew. He was a remarkable and courageous young man. May we have a word about a very important matter?" asked Galen.

Glancing to her father who was planning to meet with family members immediately following at a local pub, he returned her glance with a nod. "We will be there for a while and you can join us after..." Her father said as he turned and walked away.

Turning back to Galen, "Yes, of course" she said, opening the door and stepping inside the limousine.

She sat opposite the man who seemed a bit fidgety, trying to find the right way to begin.

"Dr. Jones, this is very difficult for me; as you know, your brother Andrew was serving me as did your father, and his father before him." He paused, "I am a bit of a special case, and need a personal assistant with your qualities immediately as a direct result of Andrew's death. I need you to come and work with me in a very important series of projects...and I need you now...there I said it." Galen said as he took off his sun glasses and looking her directly in the eyes.

Coleen felt a jolt; she had not expected this - this is not what she wanted. This was not the future she had planned for herself. Andrew was always with his father when he worked with Dr. Galen; it was Andrew that was primed to succeed his father, not her.

"Dr. Galen, this is such a surprise, and such as shock. The first of my first inclinations is say thank you very much and take my leave. As you can see, I am not a male, and certainly not my brother Andrew. No, I can't do this sir."

"Ms. Jones, there must be something I can do for us to reach an accord. As a scholar, you will also need time to do your own work when not engaged in a project with me, and I understand that."

"Your offer sounds intriguing, but I know nothing about what you expect me to do except to drive your car and manage your itinerary. I am trained as a classical scholar, not as a personal assistant. Your offer for me to forget all that I have worked for and sit behind a computer or steering wheel looking for the best hotel deals!" Coleen said with a bit more passion in her voice.

"Dr. Jones I am not speaking about being a personal assistant as you describe. At the time of your brother's death we had just learned of the existence of a sealed jar in the ruins of a 1st century AD Christian monastery in Turkey. That jar is said to contain parchment scrolls that are partially completed of the Hebrew text in Greek. The calligraphy is written over what we believed to be palimpsests of a work of the Roman historian Gaius Sallustius Crispus; part of his *Histories*, of which only fragments are now known to exist."

"Are you saying you know where there is possibly a full text of *Histories* existing as palimpsests, and written by the same Gaius Sallustius Crispus, known to classical scholars as Sullst?

"Yes Dr. Jones – we, or I have some reliable sources that have confirmed this information. Andrew and I were there not a month ago."

They were there? Coleen thought – she was not paying close attention to where Andrew was all the time, but was unaware of a trip out of the country.

"So you are suggesting my job will also include research and data collection directly from primary sources and time to pursue personal work as well?"

"Yes Dr. Jones that is exactly what I am saying. I need your help to decipher these particular palimpsests which I believe to contain some very important information. Alone this discovery is amazing, but what Gaius Sallustius describes is of great interest to my own research, research I have been working on for a long time."

Coleen thought this was an intriguing opportunity to go into the field and actually collect artifacts that would contribute to her discipline as well as an opportunity to study them and ultimately write and deliver an award winning paper on her findings. Avoiding distracting Galen with visions of her future scholarly acclaim, she thought to establish her terms, to include salary.

"Dr. Galen, the prospect of collecting and studying the Sullst palimpsests changes a lot for me. I however am still focused on continuing my work independent of yours. I will accept your offer only if I am permitted to continue to research and publish on projects of my own when it does not interfere with yours. I also need a salary of at least £ 45,000 per year." Coleen said feeling a bit uneasy about the high salary she had just demanded.

"Excellent, I accept your terms Dr. Jones." Galen said replacing his sunglasses and opening the car door. "Will a fortnight be long enough to conclude your present obligations?

"A fortnight will be splendid Dr. Galen."

"Excellent, I will call ahead and send a car for you and show you around your new office and my lab...." Galen said with an uncharacteristic smile.

Coleen smiled back, collected her purse and stepped out of the car, shutting the door.

Galen opened the window again, and as she presented her hand to shake his, he added "...oh yes, I reject your request for salary, I paid Andrew £ 125,000 per annum; you will be paid the same. Use this card to order computers and other equipment you need and have them sent to the address on my business card." He said smiling pressing the credit and business cards into her hand as they shook goodbye. He motioned to the driver and was gone.

Stunned, Coleen stood motionless staring at the limousine as it disappeared onto McKechnie Street. She looked at the credit card and the address on Galen's business card, then remembering the salary she just landed.

"...£ 125,000! Wow!" She whispered out loud.

Turning, continuing to smile, Coleen walked briskly to her car at the corner of the church car park. As she passed through the shadow cast by the old parish church, she glanced into the cemetery toward her brother's grave. Her mood slipped into a more somber one, remembering what had just happened, and how much she would miss her dear "Andy."

The Three Judges Pub was just across the river on Dumbarton Road, but by car required taking the Yoker-Renfrew Bridge. Coleen used the time to begin to mourn the loss of her brother, meeting Galen, the proposition she was given regarding the Sallst palimpsests, and the incredible salary offered. It was all kept cycling in her mind, to include her boyfriend, the love of her life, at least her lover until recently.

***

She met Michael when in post graduate school. He was sitting in front of her in a document imaging class. She paid more attention to the back of his neck and his hair than she had to the professor. His hair seemed to always need to be brushed although his beard was regularly trimmed. He wore a daily uniform of corduroy pants, plaid shirt and Campbell tartan tie to class. He was the outdoorsy type, very sexy she thought in a 1960's way. She was aroused with the way he sat, showing off his long athletic looking legs. She stared at those two lovely appendages throughout the lecture. She found the class to be a joy to attend.

He confessed later he had noticed her looking at him, and decided to approach her after the lecture was over. It was difficult to chat as people were milling around mixing their voices with theirs. He asked her for coffee.

In the days that followed Coleen soon felt she was slipping out of control. She tried to get herself back on track and figure out how to manage the relationship. She needed to stop spinning out of control every time she saw him. After all, she had plans of her own for her career, and didn't need distractions associated with a man in her life, a man that would make demands, have expectations and try to change the course that she had already set for her future. On the second date they shared a bed. To say they shared a bed sounds a bit more than it was and not as descriptive as actually occurred. But it was wonderful.

Michael and Coleen had dinner together in one of the better moderately priced Lebanese restaurants in Glasgow – a place she could have lamb, one of her weaknesses – and she indulged them all when she was being treated. For her first meat course she gorged on *kibbeh*, generously-seasoned lamb meatballs all washed down with a sound Scottish ale. This was followed by a main course of *meshwi* - rare, tender, with herb seasoned charcoal seared **lamb with** crispy edges. Too full for dessert, they closed the meal with cups of mint tea. After, they shared a taxi to her flat near the University.

The evening was cool with small pools of water on the street following an early evening rain shower. The air was heavy in an almost musky dampness. After arriving at Coleen's flat – both anticipated the usual impending awkward moments associated with a first kiss. As the taxi idled in the street, they silently gazed into one another's eyes, each squeezing the other's hand waiting for the other to make a first move. The driver having witnessed these moments countless times, glanced at the couple in his rear view mirror and wondered, when!

When they finally leaned into the kiss, before their lips touched, the taxi driver's radio crackled with the almost metallic voice of the central dispatcher calling for a driver to pick up a fare. Both jerked back, releasing each other's hands.

"Will you come up for a coffee?" Coleen asked.

Embarrassed from his failure to capitalize on the first kiss, and fumbling the chance to taste her lips, Michael said "Thanks Coleen, perhaps it would be best to say good night."

Coleen thought this a bit offish..."Does he not find me attractive? Did I eat too much? What's wrong?" she thought to herself.

"Fine, thank you for a wonderful dinner; will I see you tomorrow afternoon at the lecture?" Coleen asked, thinking she may have given up too soon.

"Right, at the lecture" Michael responded fidgeting a bit.

Coleen turned and stepped out of the taxi, subtly trying to draw him to her. She slowly shut the door, releasing the handle as the latch clicked into place. She paused and looked back at Michael sitting in the dark back seat. After a moment she finally spoke.

"Good night Michael."

"Good night Coleen." Michael said with a nervous smile.

Coleen walked to her door, unlocked it and went inside closing it behind her.

Both the driver and Michael watched the young woman walk away and disappear inside.

"What are you thinking? The driver asked Michael.

"Excuse me?

"If there is any woman I have seen that really was inviting you in, this was one – I'll tell you mate, I am an expert on seeing these things develop. You are messing up – you are bloody crazy if you don't go after her."

"I think I need to go." Michael said.

"Not in this taxi....so, off you go..." The driver said.

Surprised, Michael turned to the driver, "What, you are not taking me?"

"No mate, I will not be a party to you disappointing that young woman, so off you go..." the driver said, reaching back and opening the door.

Perplexed, Michael dislodged himself from the back seat and handed the driver a £5 note, who drove off without another word. Michael stood in the street, first surveying the empty street and then at where he had last seen Coleen. He felt cold drops of rain dancing on his face, then looked at an increasing crescendo of droplets in the puddles on the street: No good night kiss, kicked out of the taxi and then being rained on – Michael's evening was getting even better.

Inside, once Coleen had shut the door to her flat, she leaned back against it, closing her eyes clutching her purse close as if in an embrace. For the longest time she stood there without moving, contemplating what had just happened and how much she wanted Michael, how much she wished to relish his touch, feel him inside her, and to hold him close in the quiet darkness.

Breaking her near contemplative trance, she walked to her kitchen to fix a cup of tea after tossing her purse on the couch. As she filled the pot with water she thought she heard a knock at her door. She turned off the water and stood still – a second double knock. "Who could that be this time of night?" she thought. It could not be Michael; he seemed too embarrassed to follow through

– kind of cute; a bit wimpy and very disappointing. She went to the door and looked through the fish eye security portal to the outside. It was Michael! He looked so vulnerable, like a little boy running an errand for his big brother; one he was not sure if he would live to tell the tale. She smiled finding this very sexy.

Coleen opened the door so quickly, a surprised Michael moved back wide eyed just in time to accept the woman's embrace. In her rush, her front teeth banged into his; both smiled in amusement, as if they both had done that before. In a second attempt, both located and found each other's open lips. Michael tasted Coleen's sweet mouth and tongue as both exchanged wild kisses. As they embraced she wrapped her left leg around both of his, then, stepping back she grabbed him and pulled him inside – all the time smothering him with kisses and not letting him say anything to stop her, not to put off what she longed for this evening.

Michael's shock at Coleen's aggressiveness soon gave in to enjoying not having to work through the awkward moments of kissing, to petting, to making love. For each first time for him, he was never sure if he was reading her correctly and reacting appropriately. She had successfully skipped all that and removed all doubt as to what was on her agenda. As they moved together to her bed, she was shedding clothes and using her hands to bring Michael to full arousal.

They fell into the bed as one. She laughed, rolled over and leaning over Michael, Coleen used her fingers from both hands to gently trace down the outside of his hips, then moving them together until that met at a very erect "Michael." She grasped him in her hands, slowly moving her fingers up and down from the base to the soft pear shaped tip. She then put him in her mouth, sucking and using her wet tongue to bring him close to climax. As his passion heightened, he gently pushed her away, sat up and lifting her to her feet and kissing her on the neck, to her breasts – pausing at and giving special attention to each pink nipple – to her navel and then running his tongue over and between the sweet lips of her secret place nestled below her soft curly hair. Finding her aroused most sensitive of spots that beckoned for attention, he teased it with his tongue. Coleen stiffened then groaned in approval; opening her legs as she sat back on the bed pulling him onto her.

Once down, finding themselves horizontal, they rolled to face one another and for new opportunities to explore each other's bodies. Coleen ran her right hand over and down Michael's hairy chest, across his stomach and gripped him hard - moving her hand back and forth on the hard shaft. Michael passionately groaned as he kissed her ear, smelling the sweet smell of her hair while tenderly caressing her breasts and tracing around each base and tips of her erect nipples. Whispering something

Michael could not male out, Coleen looked up, their lips clashed together and passionately sucked and kissed as if to consume one another; their tongues dueling in anticipation of what was to come. Michael could taste her passion – the breath of passion fire from deep within her, peaking in near ecstasy.

Rolling to her back Coleen grabbed Michael by the shoulders and pulled him over her. Opening herself to him and pulling her legs back, she reached for Michael and guided him into her. Michael slowly moved forward, as Coleen gave a soft gasp, she arched back, permitting Michael to slide deep into her. Their eyes met as their bodies joined. They gently kissed, caressing one another...as each moved their hips into the other ever so gently at first; but as their passion increased, they soon became lost in a mutual cascading rhythm of love making and passion.

After that night they became constant companions in days of magical passion and emotional intimacy. Aside from his brains, he was an outdoorsman. She shared a love of the water and swimming with Michael. He added a dimension to her life by introducing her to scuba diving. As a scuba instructor he took her on as his prize student. In no time she was joining him in underwater archaeological research surveys of sunken ships in the western Mediterranean when on holiday trips to Barcelona and closer to home in the cold Irish Sea.

Although happier than she had ever been, she had a moment of clarity: Coleen realized her life was being defined by Michael's. That was not what she wanted. It came to a head a month earlier after Michael told her he had received a major grant. He asked her to leave the University and accompany him on a protracted study in the Red Sea surveying ancient wrecks. The clarity came when she had to decide between her own career and Michael's. Bottom line, the sex was wonderful and he was beautiful, but she had no interest being his cabin mate while Michael pursued his professional dreams; and hers sidelined. She told him no, and that's when it became emotional; she stuck to her plan, and he was gone and out of her life. This was when she decided to give up men, at least for a while. She took comfort in thinking the streets were full of good looking smart men and that the sun and all the stars were not in orbit around the density of their own testosterone.

***

Before she was ready, the large front windows of the pub came into view; she parked and walked through the front door following the "private party" posted on a stand just inside.

Pausing as she approached the wake, she turned to the end of the bar.

"Hello Coleen, sorry about Andrew, he was a great guy – can I get you anything? Asked the barman Harry Devine.

"Thanks Harry, how about a short Grouse and a pint of Buck Fast ale. It looks like they have a head start on me..." Coleen said looking toward the party.

"We're out of Buck Fast, sorry..." Devine responded.

"Okay, make it an Easy Rider...how come I never get here in time for Buck Fast?" Coleen said with a smile.

"Dunno darlin', that's about the 10th time today I have had to say that" He said putting down two bar napkins followed by the whisky and ale.

Coleen looked at the two drinks for a second, picked up the scotch and lifted it toward the people at her brother's wake, and made a toast - "Here's to Andrew Jones..."

She downed the whiskey in one long gulp, and then followed it with sip of ale. She wiped her lips with her bar napkin and reached for her purse to pay for the drinks.

"Those are on the house; for Andy, go inside and the rest is on your Dad," Devine said before moving to another customer at the bar.

Coleen picked up the pint of ale and walked into the room where everyone was enjoying emotional stories about Andrew; laughing at times and shedding tears in another. The Three Judges was Andrew's favorite watering hole, and many who were present were his friends and school chums that also considered this pub their second home. The Jones family was small, as their calling to be keeper/guardians of Galen and manage his business affairs were so consuming - there was no room for many friends beyond their work. With the whiskey making its presence known in her system, Coleen began to doubt her decision to take her brother's place – she wanted a life, and a family of her own, not an end where her only family were people she met in a pub.

"Coleen, come and sit with me for a while," her father shouted over the laughter and conversations.

Robert's voice interrupted Coleen's mood as she looked up to see her father Robert standing near a small corner booth motioning her over. She smiled and wound her way across the room and slid into the seat opposite him.

"Can I get you something to eat or a whiskey" her father asked. Coleen smiled and waved her hand over her glass which was about half full.

"No thanks Dad, just had one at the bar – giving that time to settle before moving on...I'll stick to my ale for now" Coleen said glancing to her drink and the several empty whiskey glasses around the table in front of her father.

"Did Dr. Galen ask you to come and work for him?

"Yes Daddy he did..."

"Well, don't keep me in suspense Coleen darlin'...what did you say?"

"I told him I would...with some provisions, most importantly for me is that I can pursue my own research and publish as long as it was not a distraction to my duties in his employ"

Jones smiled and leaned back against the back of the booth.

Leaning forward as not to be overheard Coleen asked in a low tone "Daddy, who the hell is this guy, and there is something he said about you and grandfather serving him...this guy doesn't look that old. Grandfather would have had to be his baby sitter if he served him as Dr. Galen said."

Leaning to meet his daughter, Robert looked around at the crowd to assure that no one was listening and replied, "It is a long story Coleen – Dr. Galen is a lot older than he looks. All I can tell you now is that a long time ago he was infected with a virus of the blood that altered his genetic characteristics. It rendered him rather unique, he is not like you and I."

"Altered his genetic characteristics...That is incredible...I'm not a geneticist, but I don't think that's possible!!" Coleen said, raising her voice above his.

"Dr. Galen is a geneticist and will explain it better than I can, obviously" Robert said leaning back and sipping from his whiskey.

"I'm sorry for raising my voice at you Daddy, this is a pretty emotional time for both of us, and I personally am still trying to process what I can grasp, to add an element I do not understand is a bit overwhelming." Coleen said as she picked up her ale, taking a long drink of it as well. Putting the empty glass on the table, she glanced to the room full of people and decided now was time not to think of the on-going mystery of Dr. Galen, it was rather a time for some distraction.

Chapter 5 - Vampires are People Too

"...Travel with me if you choose, into a land of notions
Through the ruins of yesteryear..."

Gordon Lightfoot, *Whisper My Name*, 1980

At 7:30 pm, two weeks to the day that Coleen had agreed to work for Dr. Galen, her cell phone rang. Not familiar with the phone number on the caller ID, Coleen was hesitant, but answered the call.

"Dr. Jones, this is Mark Galen, do you remember me?"

"Oh, yes – good evening Dr. Galen, how are you? Coleen responded.

"I am fine. Are you ready to come by and see your new office and a tour of my lab?

"Yes, of course – I was getting a bit concerned. I have been waiting all day, thinking you wouldn't call."

"Forgive me, I do most of my work in the evening; I should have told you that when we last met."

"No worries. The answer is yes, I will be waiting; do you need my address?"

"No need, my man is waiting for you on the street outside your apartment building, I look forward to seeing you then, goodbye." Galen said and hung up.

Coleen paused as she glanced down on the screen of her cell phone and pressed "end" and tucked it into her purse. She walked to the window pulled the drape aside and looked down to the street. The same black limo she saw Galen in the day of the funeral was parked at the curb. She grabbed her jacket, tablet, purse, and a couple of pens and rushed out the door.

From her apartment on Park Circus Place near the University of Glasgow the limo headed south onto Clifton Street, then wound its way to an open field and a helicopter with its engine running! The driver pulled the limo to the aircraft.

"This is yours Dr. Jones. The helicopter will take you to Dr. Galen's home a lot faster than I can. Please hurry, the neighbors always become cross about the noise." The driver said as he motioned to the pilot.

As Coleen approached the aircraft she was met by one of the pilots who had exited the aircraft. He motioned her to approach from the side and lower her head until she got safely into the helicopter. Once she was seat belted into her seat the man sitting next to the pilot handed her a headset with a microphone. She put it on and adjusted it on her head and positioned the microphone.

Through the headset intercom the pilot introduced himself.

"Welcome aboard Dr. Jones, my name is Philip Jameson. We will be in the air for just over a fifteen minutes, and have you to your meeting before you know it. If there is anything you need before we get started?

Coleen shook her head no.

"Oh, in order for me to hear you, press the little button here on the push-to-talk switch..." the pilot said as he twisted in his seat and pointed to the place on the cable he was referring.

"Thank you Mr. Jameson; I'm fine, just didn't expect to fly today." Coleen said, pressing the button as instructed. The intercom buzzed on...

"Also, release the button when not speaking...okay?" Jameson added. Coleen nodded back a bit sheepishly.

With that the pilot lifted the helicopter off, turned its nose left and ascended into the vesper light of the evening. The aircraft headed southwest from the city and eventually over what looked like the Firth of Clyde, a small bay to the west of Glasgow. From her window she could see the lights of Glasgow disappear behind her and approach what appeared to be an island in the bay. On the north end of the island lights defined some craggy high ground shaped like a big smile. The pilot approached and circled a large compound of buildings nestled inside. No sooner did the lights of a helipad come into view did the pilot descend and land the aircraft.

The co-pilot exited the aircraft, stepping back and opened the passenger compartment door for Coleen. Coleen removed her headset and laid it on the seat. No longer buffered by the headset, she noticed the loud whine of the aircraft's engine and air agitated by the rotating blades blowing tiny pieces of sand and leaves into eddies through the helipad's spotlights.

"Dr. Jones, Dr. Galen is waiting for you inside – oh, and here is your escort. " the co-pilot shouted over top of the aircraft's engine; steadying her by the arm as she stepped out of her seat and onto the helipad. Putting her briefcase strap over her shoulder, she looked up at Galen's residence. It appeared to be a restored stone manor house – very impressive she thought. Her escort offered his arm and walked her to and through the gate to the building.

Inside she was met by a middle aged woman identifying herself as Mrs. Campbell, Dr. Galen's housekeeper/guardian.

"Forgive me for being forward, Dr. Jones, but I was so sorry to learn of Andrew's death, he was such a nice young man. Please accept my condolences...Dr. Galen will be with you in a few minutes. Please come with me to your new office and he will join you there." Mrs. Campbell said.

Down the portrait lined hallway Mrs. Campbell led Coleen to the last door on the right. Grasping the knob, the woman hesitated as if to listen for something on the other side before entering. With a twist, the door unlatched and Mrs. Campbell opened it. Following her inside Coleen entered a room about twice the size of her apartment while in undergraduate school. Inside was a large wooden desk with an executive style chair, several overstuffed chairs circled around a small conference table, a fireplace, planters filled with live plants, and on the exterior wall axis large windows overlooking the bay. The floor was covered in a plush oriental rug, and stacked on the conference table were various components of the computer equipment she had purchased and sent to the house. Through a second smaller door was her private bathroom to include a shower, large closet; all fully equipped with towels and linen.

Mrs. Campbell remained silent while Coleen scanned the room. As Coleen approached boxes of computer equipment, Mrs. Campbell continued. "I had all the deliveries of equipment purchased for your work brought here. The computer equipment has been stored here in your office, and the other boxes in your laboratory through that door..." she said pointing to the set of double door doors across from where they stood.

"I hope you will find everything you need Dr. Jones..." she said, leaving the room.

As she left, Galen came into the room, pausing to collect himself before addressing the young woman. Coleen had her back to him looking over the boxes on the desk.

"Good evening Dr. Jones – welcome to my home."

Turning, Coleen stood face to face with Dr. Galen. He was not as tall as she thought he was – then one's height is often deceptive when sitting. He was dressed in grey trousers, white shirt, blue tie and white lab coat. With his grey beard and close cropped hair he looked to be in his late 50's.

"eeeer, good evening Dr. Galen" she said as she took his outstretched hand and grasped it tightly

"Good handshake, I like that in a person; shows character and focus." Galen said motioning her to sit down at the small conference table.

She sat, opened her briefcase and pulled out her tablet to make notes if necessary. Galen sat down opposite her, pausing as if to select his words carefully.

"May I get you some refreshment, tea or coffee; have you had dinner?"

"Thank you, no Doctor I am fine. I ate earlier and try not to take anything after 7 pm."

"Well then, we can get started. I will first tell you a bit about the job, my expectations; then I will tell you about me and my life until now and the focus of my research and the importance I place in your help. After, I will give you a tour of my and your labs – fair enough?" Galen said.

"Fair enough" Coleen responded with a smile.

"As you have seen my staff consists of several men and women, but you will be the keystone of them all – you will be not only my personal assistant, there is nothing you will not know about my work, or about me. You also will manage my entire enterprise." Galen said, pausing and handing Coleen a computer thumb drive.

"This device contains the numbered accounts I have in various banking institutions as well as the passwords Andrew set up for them. You are welcome to change them and inform me of course of any changes." Galen said smiling.

"Now, my expectations are rather straight forward – you are a professional, at the top of your field and highly disciplined. I am looking for you to be yourself, a professional and highly disciplined. I also am hopeful you will be open minded and retain your sense of humor. Your father has told me you are very funny and are quite out of the box, as they say."

"Thank you for your confidence in me Doctor...Daddy always laughs at my jokes, but recently there has not been much to laugh about." Coleen said looking toward the floor.

"...And there is something you must know about me..." Galen said hesitantly.

Coleen looked up, and looked directly at Galen with a puzzled look. "Yes, what is it Doctor?"

"Coleen how old do you think I am?"

"I'm not too good in guessing age, especially when it comes to men...I would say in your mid 50's." Coleen replied.

"Coleen, I am approximately 1,897 years old..." Galen said with a slightly pained expression.

Coleen sat back in the chair as if she had been pushed. She then leaned back toward Galen who sat silent awaiting her response.

"What did you say? Did you say 1,897 years old? You have got to be joking Dr. Galen!" Coleen said with half a smile, but her eyes were narrowed in disbelief.

"Coleen, I am what you might call a vampire." Galen said as he stood and walked to the nearby window and stood with his back to her.

"Vampire...vampire! Daddy told me you were different, but now I can't decide who is loony here – you or that I am for taking this job!" Coleen said, standing up, beginning to collect her tablet and returning it to her briefcase.

Galen turned back to her, approaching her at the conference table. "Coleen give me a chance to explain" he said quietly, hoping to calm the surprise she just experienced.

"Your father was right, I am different. For him, he did not have to overcome learning of my affliction as you just did. Once your grandfather came close to retirement he trained Robert in his future duties; he also gently – more gently than I just did – told him about my...my condition, shall we say. The same with Andrew; Robert brought him up as my keeper/guardian as was his father. I am sorry to have to give you this news without warning and without the delicacy required." Galen said placing his hand on hers resting on the table.

"You are serious, aren't you?"

"Yes I am Coleen."

"The same vampire as we read about, the same blood suckers on the television and the movies?"

"Well the mythology surrounding vampires is somewhat more myth than truth. I don't have fangs; I do not turn into a bat when alarmed; I don't burst into flames when sunlight hits me – although I am very sensitive to it; and I am not the walking dead or immortal...Most of these myths came from primitive and superstitious people having brushes with my maker or those like me over the centuries. Story tellers took these myths to a level where my kind became the "vampire" – and today the mythology portrayed in motion pictures about vampires reflects unearthly powers and titillating, blood sucking sexual acrobats. Nothing is really farther from the truth...well mostly...I was made what I am by another through a process of chemical genetic mutation. My own research indicates my genes have suffered what is called a missense mutation - This type of mutation involves a change in one DNA base pair that results in the substitution of one amino acid for another in the protein made by a gene. In this case, vampire mutation involves a radically mutated proto-protein that has resulted in a reliance on human blood as a staple in the diet; long life span, and increased sensory capacities...Coleen, that's what makes a vampire, at a risk of being boorish - not like what you read, and watch in horror movies about some undead creatures...creatures with mystical evil and manipulating personalities. Evil and cruelty live in the creature before transformation into a vampire – it does not result after..." Galen said returning to his seat as he sensed Coleen relaxing and listening more than reacting.

"Okay, but I am still shocked, and I think rightfully so...just how all this happened to you?" Coleen asked sitting down.

"Can I have a whiskey...a large whiskey?"

"Of course..." Galen said, standing and walking to the corner cupboard, opening it and producing a bottle and two glasses. Returning to the table, he poured each glass half full. He handed her the drink and tapped it with his and took a long sip.

"See; and you thought vampires couldn't drink alcohol...no way!" Galen said with a smile. "May I tell you my story?"

"Yes, I am a bit more receptive now – good whiskey" Coleen said leaning back into the chair with both hands holding the glass to her chest.

"...I began life as a Greek named Claudius Galenicus. I held Roman citizenship much like the Christian evangelist known to the world as Saul, then became Paul I think...never could understand the Hebrew and Christian take on creation out of nothing. But I digress. I was born in the city of Pergamos; a province in Anatolia in what I think was about your AD 131. I am known to history simply as a physician and scientist. I received my first medical training in modern day Smyrna and Alexandria. I became famous first as a surgeon who tended to wounded gladiators from the arena of my home town – I received a lifetime of knowledge about trauma wounds there. Since I was successful in patching up and returning valuable gladiators back into the blood sport for their owners, Roman authorities noticed and eventually I was summoned to Rome during the 5th year of the reign of the Roman Emperor Marcus Aurelius.

With a bit of drama caused by the retinue of physicians already serving him, I was appointed his personal physician. My story that has led me to you began when I was 35 years old. My work as the Emperor's physician brought me to the fortress city of Aquileia in Northern Italy. A plague had broken out among the troops that had recently arrived from the command of General Gaius Tacitus Cassius in the city of Ephesos, a place better known to you as Ephesus, the capital of Roman Anatolia, in the present country of Turkey. This caught my interest as I had family there. Cassius was widely known as being particularly cruel and politically ambitious. Word also had it; this plague had its root in the nearby province of Lydia. My work among the sick resulted in a list of symptoms of high fever, diarrhea, and inflammation of the throat situated immediately behind the mouth and nasal cavity, as well as skin eruptions appearing on the eighth or ninth day of the illness. I couldn't clearly define the nature of the disease, but scholars today believe it was smallpox. I was soon to learn personally, it was not all smallpox.

I wrote to Rome describing the plague and need for more research. A return message from the Emperor's secretary dispatched me to Anatolia and to find the source of the plague. Three years after I had first set foot in Aquileia, I left Rome and proceeded to the great city of Ephesos or better known as Ephesus. Upon my arrival by imperial galleon, I was met by a Centurion from the palace guard of Co-Emperor Lucius Aurelius Verus, who was at his eastern palace in the city, gravely ill. The Centurion described the same symptoms of the great plague.　I asked, but the Centurion denied me the opportunity to first visit my relatives, but his orders were to have me go directly to the Co-Emperor's chambers. I was ushered into the private chambers of the Co-Emperor who was surrounded by his personal physicians and his wife.　As I approached his resting place, he motioned for everyone except for me to leave the chamber. Following their departure, he asked me "...*How is Marcus, I pray to the Gods his health is better than mine...*"

"*Yes Emperor, Marcus was well when I last saw him. How can I serve you? I asked standing a respectful distance from him.*

"*Come closer and give me the letter you were given for me to read, and also that cup of wine on the table.*" Lucius said in almost a near whisper.

Producing the letter I gave it to Lucius.　He unrolled it and held it toward the nearby torch for more light. After seemingly passing through it twice, he rolled it up and laid it on the bed near his side. Silent for a time, he again addressed me after a sip of the wine...

"*Marcus and I wish for you to visit the commander of The Third Gallic Legion, General Gaius Tacitus Cassius, who is headquartered in a palace near here.　We both believe he needs to be questioned about the plagues in Aquileia; the widespread maladies that I am told you have direct experience. A plague carrying similar consequences has taken root here. The larger concern is that the preparedness of the army here has been threatened by the plague, and measures must be taken to stop and reverse it, or we will become vulnerable from some very present threats to our east – and as you can see, it has affected me as well."* Lucius said as he presented his frailty with a wave of his left hand from his head to chest.

I stepped forward and recognized some of the topical symptoms of the plague I had studied at Aquileia. Looking closer, I noticed a small wound that was healing near the base of his neck where it met the shoulder. I asked him about the wound. He responded that he had no memory of how it was inflicted, or when.

"Your excellency, although you cannot precisely remember when you received the wound, can you recall any coincidence of noticing the wound and becoming ill? I asked

"No...yes! I first noticed the wound when it was scabbing over, and a few days later I fell ill, do you think there is a connection? Lucius asked

"If something bit you, venom or other poison could cause the reaction you are experiencing." I responded.

Just as he finished, several servant girls entered and circled the bed. They were dressed in short white bathing robes and carried towels.

"Time for my bath Doctor...Go see Cassius and report back to me what you find out as soon as you can." Lucius said as the young women helped him out of his bed and toward the adjoining caldarium - the room containing a hot immersive bathing pool.

Lucius was known for skipping the cold and lukewarm baths that most Romans traditionally bathed in before the hot bath. He was after all, the Co-Emperor of the known world, and liked what he liked...The next day I was taken by wagon to a meeting with General Gaius Tacitus Cassius. On the way to his palace evidence of his harshness and cruelty was displayed on both sides of the stone roadway for nearly a ¼ mile. Staggered were wooden crosses with bodies tied with ropes or nailed to them in various stages of decomposition – there were men, women, and one or two children. This practice of crucifixion was a time honored means of torture, death, humiliation, and deterrence used since ancient times, but perfected by the Romans. If my Plutarch serves me correctly, this spectacle paled to the mass crucifixions that resulted after the final battle of the Gladiator revolt lead by a slave named Spartacus. The Romans took approximately 6,000 of his surviving followers and crucified them along the main road between Capua and

Rome. Like Spartacus' rebels, each had committed an allegedly capital offense: Stealing food, theft of any sort, cowardice, insubordination, or mutiny – not too much was not a capital offense to Cassius. Each had their offenses written on a board in charcoal tacked above their head. As I was a guest for dinner, these sites and smells distracted me from enticing thoughts of the impending feast.

By the time I arrived the sun was sinking in the west over the city from the sea. Cassius' palace would have otherwise been in the dark shadows on the eastern slope. It was however bathed all around and inside by light from torches and cooking fires. Upon my arrival, I was whisked into Cassius' private apartment with the large door slowly closed behind me.

"Good evening Doctor Galenicus – please tell me the Co-Emperor is doing better." Cassius said as he entered the room.

He was dressed in a purple toga embroidered with lots of gold thread. This caused me to pause as what he was wearing; a *toga picta* customarily was reserved for wear by a Roman general during special occasions such as at a triumphal parade – not dinner with a visiting physician as me, even if I weren't also an emissary of both co-Emperors. It became clearer to me how much he was impressed with himself, on impressing others and advancing his place in the Roman hierarchy.

I responded that he was ill, but still had a good taste for life – and was hopeful he would recover. During our dinner we traded small talk about the politics in Rome and Cassius' current campaign in the East. In his belt was a small lancet – or blade the size of a large paring knife, strange I thought, but he was a soldier after all. I also thought it odd that none of his command staff had joined us, or any attendant present after we had been served food other than a single slave girl who sat between us keeping our cups full of wine...Bottom line, that was the night that Cassius drugged my wine, fed on me and like a collector – added me to his collection of bastard children as one dependent upon him and human blood.

When I awoke several days later I was spent and hungry; soon discovering that food and wine no longer fully satisfied me. He educated me of my new status, explained the nightmarish sleep and pain I had experienced, and the mysteries he had learned from his maker. I felt all powerful and drunk with the increased sensory capabilities and added strength that came with my transformation to vampire.

I returned to Lucius indicating nothing was amiss with Cassius – with a bit of the creature flowing through my veins, how easily I lied to the Co-Emperor, and in my boldness, I too fed on him after drugging his wine during a private audience. Lucius died a few days later. Although I felt nothing about taking his life, I did not consider men or women to be nothing more than blood sacks as did Cassius.

In moments of reflection while visiting my family in the villa near the city – I was reintroduced to their kindnesses, humility and their pride in my new found position as personal physician to the Emperor. The kindness and humility that resided in the genes of my family had survived my transformation and it became clear to me that I had become an abomination and had to seek ways to reverse my need for human blood for being a parasite. After all, I was a scientist and knew a great deal about herbs and cures, but first needed to identify why human blood had properties that sustained me, Cassius, and others of our kind.

After much meditation I also concluded that it was my duty to either cure or kill any of my kind I came across – beginning with Cassius. As you might have guessed, Cassius would not hear of my plea to help me find a cure for both of us. When I returned to him he offered me riches and a life of comfort where we could dominate lesser men for centuries. Not distracted from his offers I demanded he submit to my research. Well, he had me expelled from his palace and escorted back to the city to think over his offer for an alliance and untold wealth and power, or I would simply disappear – probably on one of the crosses no doubt...I returned to find his palace deserted. A rumor was that he had been killed by his officers before he could be arrested by troops sent from Rome by the Emperor and his son Commodious. That story turned out to be a deception. Cassius and a personal Cohort of guardians had left for Gaul via Macedonia just hours before I arrived. Instead of returning to Rome, I set out for Gaul in pursuit. That's the short of it – I nearly had him several times; once in Dacia in the present country of Romania; once in northern Scotland; and once about 300 years ago near Glasgow. He disappeared but reappeared as Angus Cassidy on a ship bound for Jamaica, the ship never made it there. The trail turned cold..." Galen finished, sipping the last from his whiskey glass.

"I'll stay..." Coleen said, still nursing her whiskey, yet now staring past Galen, her thoughts being well beyond the room and this conversation.

Chapter 6 - Carysfort Reef Marina

*"...The sea gave up the dead that were in it, and
death and Hades gave up the dead that were in them,
and each person was judged according to what he had
done..."*

Revelation 20:13

The man who tumbled out of the coral encrusted box; the same who had just locked eyes with Hoskins was not of their time, not really a man at all.

Now freed the creature rolled over and stiffly came to a defensive crouch. Squinting to avoid the painful light, he made out two figures, and could smell the sweet blood in both, and an irresistible need to feed.

Convulsing images from his past flashed through his mind – his life as slave in Alexander's conquering army and a siege where he was made a vampire. The tumble onto the dock and dizzying light brought dreamlike images of the ancient vampire who made him, then the face and piercing emerald-green eyes of a servant girl, the sex with her, then cascading recollections of his many identities, and finally the face of the one of his own making who pursued him throughout time.

Shouts from the two men ripped through the fabric of his hallucinations...

Reaching into the sand, the creature's right hand found the dagger his keeper always placed in the chamber with him. He moved toward Alex Walsh still transfixed, just standing there when the creature backhanded him on the head with the hilt of the weapon. The blow sent Walsh flying backward unconscious into the dark undergrowth near the dock. Returning to a crouch, his head clearing, and eyes adjusting to the bright light; he sensed the second figure rushing toward him.

The creature turned and in one quick moment thrust the dagger into the man. He ran the blade up his body, from the navel then ripping into the heart, and withdrawing it at the base of the neck. Hoskins emitted a choked scream, arms flaying toward the dagger, then the wound, and finally landed gently onto the creature's shoulders, then fell back motionless onto the dock. The creature hesitated over the body, the smell of the blood was nearly intoxicating; he then put his mouth deep into the wound and shivering heart, moving it up and down and side to side; convulsing as he consumed the warm foamy sweet liquid covering his face in blood.

After sucking and licking every drop he could from the man, the creature's head began to clear from its 300 year sleep.

***

He watched the rain drops sparkle as they danced through the lights from traffic on his windshield. What a night he thought...to be dicking around doing bullshit follow-up reports when he would much rather be watching the New York Jets play Miami at the Tavernier Sports Bar wall to wall televisions near his apartment. It was also Veteran's Day weekend and he was not motivated to get involved in anything that took effort. It was a slow evening, and his mind turned to dinner. He hadn't eaten since breakfast. Detective Rusty Nash's police radio crackled now and then with security checks of boat yards and calls by uniformed deputies to meet with each other or the shift commander to bitch about something, just anything.

Nash had just passed Pennekamp State Park north bound on the Overseas Highway in Key Largo when he remembered on Sundays Jimmy was in the kitchen at the "Cracked Conch" restaurant just ahead. He made the best creamed alligator soup he had ever had outside of Durgin-Park's version of New England clam chowder in Boston's North End. Nash caught sight of the red neon "open" sign of the restaurant ahead on the right just off the road in a small grove of banyan trees. In a flash, he was in the parking lot, and into the restaurant, slipping into his favorite booth. Without a word, the waitress shouted into the kitchen to Jimmy that Nash was there. In no time a steaming bowl of the creamy concoction was served up with a side of fried conch fritters for the detective. The first spoon-full had just touched his lips when his department cell phone rang. Nash thought about sending it to voice mail, but last time he did that it turned out to be an error in judgment. Pulling it off his belt, he answered...

"Nash" he spoke into the speaker, continuing to scoop soup and conch fritters into his mouth.

"Nash, this is Captain Evans, are you near Carysfort Reef Marina?"

"Yeah Phil, I'm about 2 miles south grabbing some supper." Nash said, scooping more soup into his mouth at a faster pace, knowing there was something at Carysfort Reef he would be seeing shortly.

"A couple of tourists looking for a rental tied up at the marina found a body on the dock, at least what was left of a body. I'm calling you on your cell to keep the call off the radio so the newspaper doesn't pick up on this yet – same for the first responding officer already there and she called for you."

"Keep it off the air – what the hell is this, and what do you mean, what's left of a body?" Nash shot back, trying not to be overheard by those near his booth.

Evans shot back - "That's what I said and that is what I meant Nash, they told the 911 dispatcher blood was everywhere, with much of the guy's head and torso looked like they were shredded....The responding officer confirmed this and has the marina manager there, and he thinks he knows who the guy was...anyway, the Sheriff wants this kept quiet until we figure out what is going on...and you are the "Stuckee" to find that out Detective...one more thing, you are to call and brief him as soon as you can make a preliminary assessment of the situation, right after you enlighten me – I'll be in my office at the Roth Building in three fourths of an hour."

"Okay Phil, I'm on my way." Nash said as he put the bowel to his face, gulping down the last of the sweet alligator chunks swimming in creamy sauce. Wiping his face with a paper napkin, Nash rose and went to the register to pay, hoping they still would "comp" the soup and fritters. As he stuck his left hand into his pocket for cash, Lilly, Jimmy's girlfriend waved him on with a smile.

"Thanks Lilly, tell Jimmy everything was great – sorry I didn't have more time to savor Jimmy's specialty, but duty calls." Nash said over his shoulder on the way to his vehicle.

***

Nash watched for the entrance to the Marina, like most mom and pop marinas up and down the Keys, the road was a narrow coral gravel road to the docks, with no real sign. As he approached, and turned down the lane, he recalled the place used to be a great diving marina with almost immediate access to several old and new shipwrecks in relatively shallow water. Its channel dumped into Pennekamp Park waters, so it was "look but not touch" for things found swimming or on the bottom. Now, with no money or paying customers to upgrade the ramps or with a hotel or restaurant/bar on site, the chicks and land sharks following them migrated to the trendier combo Tiki bar marinas down the Keys.

As Nash turned down the lane he drove up to the marked vehicle near the dock; in his headlights he could make out a young man and woman, and what appeared to be the marina manager. The rain shower had passed and the air lay heavy with saltwater smell and humidity. Pulling next to the marked unit he turned on his own interior blue lights. As Nash exited the air conditioned car into the soupy evening he noticed the body was near the parking lot on the bleached out wooden dock. He paused without speaking, and stared at the human-sized lump under a tarp in the rotating lights of the police car.

Nash came to South Florida from Boston after he separated from the Navy. He planned to bask in the sun, chase babes, and dive. He didn't plan on getting a red headed Russian fireball Marathon Key bartender named Viktoriya pregnant after a wild weekend in Key West. She claimed to have been brought to the U.S. by a Russian family in North Miami, but they expected her to do tricks as a payback for the trip and green card. Things just got better after that. He decided to do the right thing; to settle down in the Keys and marry Viktoriya. He later answered a public safety recruitment advertisement and landed a job as a road deputy with the Monroe County Sheriff's Department. Four months later his wife had a miscarriage; no baby just a wife with other plans. That was seven years ago. He often said it just gets better. His wife apparently fell out of lust with Nash – and 2 months ago Viktoriya took her beagle and the bank account to Virginia along with a cop from up there somewhere who, interestingly enough was in Florida to bask in the sun, chase babes, and dive.

Nash had always prided himself in not taking things too seriously; especially women. However his close encounter with permanency had an effect on him he was not prepared to admit. The good news was he loved being a cop, and really didn't miss his wife, but Nash did miss something, something he couldn't put his finger on. He knew however he did miss the dog.

"Hey Rusty, how you doin'?" asked Deputy Sheila Brown turning away from the couple, still writing on her field note pad.

Her words brought him back to the business at hand, "Not, bad Sheila – did dispatch call the ME yet, and are Bob's crime scene guys on the way?"

"Yep and yep" answered Brown. She had been hired a few years after Nash. Brown's family was from Jamaica. Her father was a senior officer in the Jamaican Constabulary Force, and after he retired decided to settle in the Keys and start a business. Her slight Jamaican accent was exotic to Nash and loved to hear her speak. Typical of a small law enforcement agency, Nash and Brown had met socially and Brown tried to make friends with Nash's wife. After Viktoriya left, Shelia said she too missed the dog.

Nash identified himself to the marina manager and the young couple that had found the body about 30 minutes before. He went forward to the tarp.

Before he moved the tarp away from the body, he looked over his shoulder and asked them to step back away from the sight he was about to reveal.

***

Standing over the body, Nash turned on his Kellite, and more detail of the carnage came into view. As his hand moved to the tarp, his eye caught marks on the weather beaten wooden dock. He leaned closer to the deck; he could see deep gouges that looked like heavy drag marks trailing from the body to the coral gravel parking lot heading north in the direction of the mangrove swamp. That wasn't the only creepy thing. Nearby, partially dangling from a dock hoist was a heavy looking coffin-like metal box. It was partially covered in barnacles, coral and bottom growth. It looked like it may have slipped from the hoist and crashed onto the dock, breaking open. After hitting the dock, the top hinges looked as if they gave way and snapped, sending the domed metal top back off the dock into the nearby mangrove. The box came to rest on its left side, and spilled its contents of sand that had been stained brown by something inside. Shreds of what appeared to be rotten fabric and sand littered the dock from the box to where the body lay.

Looking inside the box, near its middle, just inside the bottom on opposite sides were things that looked like handles.

"...what the hell...?" Nash murmured, leaning forward flooding the area with his flash light.

Moving the light along the edge he also made out what looked like latches...he ran his hand over them and then one of the handles. Pulling on the small handle, he met resistance, then it gave way, and the latch moved.

...Christ, why would this have handles on the inside? Nash pondered.

Nash's eyes shifted back to what was under the tarp. No matter how many times Nash had seen dead bodies: dead Iraqis and GI's in the Gulf War, floaters, crispy critters, or just plain victims of crime or old age, he had a revulsion to all of them – and each of them stayed with him long after. He prepared himself for a new horror. With that he took a deep breath and exhaled slowly. He pulled the tarp from the body, he gasped quietly as he gazed upon what was hardly recognizable as a human being, more a tangled mess of broken bone and torn flesh. Nash's stomach churned, and for a moment his thoughts returned to his alligator soup, hoping to keep it down.

Blood was smeared everywhere; the victim's wet suit top was unzipped, and so too it seemed was the body's torso. It was ripped open from top to bottom revealing a great gash from his throat to below the chest cavity. The head still only attached by a shred of flesh, lay atop its former owner's left shoulder. It was covered in dried blood, wide-eyed, tongue protruding from the mouth. The T shirt the man had been wearing showed signs of being slashed with a sharp object. Looking closer,

Nash could make out trailing slashes in what appeared to be in groups of three or four, like fingers.

Nash stood back up, feeling a bit dizzy, he steadied himself; and looked away to the light dancing off the water and breathed in the soft salty night air. He wondered *...what or who the hell could have done this to this guy, and what the hell was the motive?*

After gaining his composure Nash turned and looked into the darkness of the north end of the parking lot – in the direction the drag marks led. He always felt when staring into the dark that there were about a dozen mother-fuckers out there looking back at him. He backed away and walked back to where the dock ended and the gravel lot began. The drag marks at this point had stains of what looked like blood mixed in. The gravel was a combination of crushed light colored coral rock over compacted coral over the living or dead rock, the stuff that made up the Keys themselves. He looked in the direction of the drag marks and moved forward, tracing the direction with his Kel-lite and possibly a clue as to where who was dragging what.

Nash expected to find the end of the drag marks where logically a vehicle was parked and loaded with whatever that came out of that box. But, there was no obvious end to the marks – they disappeared then reappeared; but did not end in the lot but to the north end and continued as disturbed leaves and vegetation into the mangrove swamp. Nash stopped, staring into the mangrove – he was drawn to follow, and stepped inside the tree line, surveyed the ground and saw a patch of flattened grass and leaves – as if someone stopped and laid down a load for a time before moving on. It looked as if what or whoever it was did move on, but no longer dragging whatever it was, but carrying it.

"What the hell happened here? Why did they go into the mangrove instead of just getting away?" Nash murmured out loud, staring first into the mangrove, then toward the parking lot.

Walking back to his car Nash dialed Evans…"Phil, we are going to need a tracking dog team up here at the marina." Nash sighed as he kept looking around and over his shoulder, trying to shake off the creepy feeling the place gave him.

"Right, I thought about that and called FDLE – they will help us, but it will be awhile, they are detailed to the park service looking for some lost hikers somewhere north of Flamingo in the Everglades. It could be awhile…" Evans said.

"Great, can Dade County send down theirs?"

"Nope, they are tied up too, that's why we are in helping in Flamingo – Any news from Brown?" Evans asked.

"Not yet. I need the dog team ASAP – it looks like the perp or perps never left the lot by vehicle, but looks like they went into the mangrove on the north end of the lot." Nash said.

"What the hell could be up there that they would go to in order to slip out without being noticed coming from the marina?" Evans asked.

"There is a house just north and west of here, but there is nothing but mangrove practically to Ocean Reef...there also is the old Nike Hercules base about 2 - 3 miles north. It has been abandoned for nearly 40 years – it's overgrown and leads nowhere. If anyone was hoping to find an escape route or intentionally moving into the mangrove – they don't know what they are doing...Phil this doesn't make sense. Bad guys always want to get away; the trail doesn't make sense when access to a fast escape is clearly the road by way of a vehicle – not humping something through a swamp after gutting a guy to get it." Nash said.

"Yep, this is why we are trying to get a handle on the why's and who's before the newspapers arrive and pull the Sheriff over the coals. I'll try to get a dog down there tomorrow." Evans said.

Returning to the scene, Deputy Brown was interviewing the tourists; Nash motioned for Nick Ciccone, the marina manager to follow him to his car, out of ear shot from the others. Ciccone was a little drunk, a common condition for the Keys, but wasn't about to discount the information he was about to get. Nash, thinking about it, would have had to discount about half the information provided by witnesses or victims - it seems alcohol plays a big part in both comedy and crime in the Keys.

"What can you tell me about who this guy is or was, and what do you think he was doing with that box on the dock?" Nash asked.

"Well, I think the guy's name is Robert Hopkins, or that is the guy who has been paying me for the slip for that boat. He works, or worked at the UM, the University in Coral Gables, not sure what he does there. As far as I know he was a sport diver, diving for lobsters and did a lot of spear fishing...I'll be damned if I know anything about that box..." Ciccone answered.

"We'll need to make a copy of the rental agreement – address, phone number and any other contact information on it. Do you ask for an emergency contact? Nash asked.

"Yep, it's over here in the office if you want to get it now"

"Sure do." Nash replied, turning to Brown, "Deputy, I'm getting the next of kin and contact information on the victim; anything you need, let me know, I'll be right back." Nash said following Ciccone as he tried not to zigzag away from the scene. As he walked, Nash had a creepy feeling about those drag marks – looking back into the darkness he knew if the case was going to be solved it would involve finding out what was being dragged, and what or who was doing the dragging.

In the office Nash noticed through the window a couple of small well used houseboats in the channel opposite the dock where the body was found.

"Mr. Ciccone, I also need the names of everyone who has a boat or business in the marina, with special attention who is living on those houseboats" Nash said looking out the window in the direction of the houseboats.

"Oh, sure can...by the way only one of the houseboats is occupied right now. The red one is for sale. The other one at the end of the dock is rented to a guy named Holmes...here is his information; his first name is Seth...he works at Captain Billy's Tiki Bar down by the Holiday Inn; he's a real weird fuck if I don't say so" Ciccone said, as he fed the rental contract into his photocopier.

After getting the rental contracts and next of kin information from Ciccone, Nash returned to the scene. It had been transformed into what may have been described as a flood light lit Hollywood set. The forensics team was working the area – photographing the body, the open metal box, the dock area and the blood smudges into the coral rock parking lot. An additional 2 marked patrol units had arrived to seal off the scene to keep anyone from contaminating any trace evidence that was available to be collected. A third was circling the north end of the parking lot shining its flood light into the mangroves – no vehicles, nobody was running from the scene. A Florida Department of Law Enforcement/FDLE helicopter circled overhead, flooding the nearby road and mangroves with light from its high powered spotlight.

Nash, pulled his cell phone off his belt and called the Zone 7 Commander, Phil Evans reporting what he thought would certainly focus interest to the scene.

When Evans answered Nash asked "Phil, who the hell called FDLE?"

"FDLE, what are you talking about? Remember I called them about the dog team but did not ask them for anything else!" Evans shot back.

"There's a goddamn FDLE helicopter circling us and if the Sheriff wants to keep this low key, this is certainly not the way to get that done. You know as well as I do the Miami Herald, any of the Keys papers or better yet Miami television crews and reporters will be crawling up our collective asses if we don't put a cap on this right now." Nash shouted over the overhead noise.

"Got it Nash, we'll make a call." Evans responded and hung up. In a number of minutes the helicopter banked north and disappeared into the dark night toward Miami.

Trace evidence is something left behind by the perpetrators of any crime. It is well known that when someone enters a room or sits down, they leave something behind. The trick is to find that thing, link it to a particular person, and its meaning to the case. In this case the forensic team was looking for anything left in the body by the perpetrator that might identify who or what killed the man. The body would be moved as soon as possible to reduce the probability that any chemically based trace evidence might evaporate or deteriorate before it can be collected and analyzed.

"Hey Nash, did you touch anything around or the body itself?" asked Lieutenant Robert Hernandez, chief of the forensic team standing just inside the yellow police tape.

"Nah, just stood by it and pulled the tarp off to have a look; wished I hadn't" Nash said.

"Okay, just trying to figure out how many dip-shits tramped all around in my crime scene." Hernandez said eyeing Nash in jovial manner; keeping up his reputation of the most anal officer on the Special Investigations Unit.

"Let me know when the Medical Examiner is planning to do the autopsy, this one will be a real treat." Nash said as he looked out into the darkness of the mangroves at the north end of the parking lot. A feeling returned to him that someone or something was returning the favor of looking back at him.

"Bob, how long do you think the guy's been dead?" Nash asked as he looked back at Hernandez.

"I can't say for sure, it's pretty warm, like all stiffs down here, he's room temperature – judging from the rigor it looks like he's been dead no more than three hours – just after dark. I'd say time of death about 8 pm. What's interesting is we should see some evidence of lividity; you know, the dark purple discoloration of the skin from blood pooling in the body. Funny thing, Nash – there is none. I don't think there was enough blood left in this guy to pool, period." Hernandez said.

"I've got to go to the boss's office and give a preliminary report to him and the Sheriff, then I'm going home; send me anything you can tomorrow, ASAP, okay!!" Nash said, turning and walking back to his car.

Chapter 7 - Dynamite Docks

"... Surely the darkness will hide me and the light become night around me..."

Psalm 139.11

About 10 feet into the mangroves at the north edge end of the marina parking lot the creature crouched down to the form, its nose nearly touching the rising and lowering chest of the unconscious man lying next to him in the shallow dark rotten smelling swamp water. Breathing in deeply, it filled its dry lungs with the sweet smell of the life pulsating under the skin.

Slowly its head turned toward a distant bubble of pulsating white and blue light from where it had just awakened. The lights were the brightest it had ever seen; there were no lamps that shown so brightly with long beams of light... even at this distance it could clearly see people moving back and forth; with one standing, looking in his direction. Pointing its nose toward the lights, it opened and flared its nostrils, to smell and taste the air for clues – the air was filled with a mix of the sweet smell of food as well as something like pungent burning oil.

It turned and while moving, the creature glanced back one more time toward the light, before dragging the dead man's partner deeper into the dark mangrove thicket.

To the north of the marina through about a quarter mile of mangrove swamp lies an ever decreasing number of overgrown, dilapidated cement block buildings that used to be Battery "B" of the U.S. Army's HM-40 Nike Hercules missile coastal defense garrison. It closed nearly twenty years earlier in June 1979, and occupied what is now both the Crocodile Lake National Wildlife Refuge and Key Largo Hammock Botanical State Park on north Key Largo. The base used to house both missile launch as well as a supporting radar installation on the small base. It had all but forgotten and hadn't seen a human in years. On the southern end of the base is an overgrown road cut-through in the dense hammocks built by the Atlas Power Company to transport explosives during construction of the base from the ocean-side location called "dynamite docks." The old base is just north of the dynamite docks road.

Still dazed and in a confused state, the creature moved slowly north away from the flurry of activity and a unworldly noisy light in the sky – what manner of creatures inhabit this place? Its memory and decision making skills were blurred from years in silent darkness and lack of liquid and nourishment. The drug laced wine he last remembered drinking worked well – but was not meant to last for whatever the time he spent sealed in his transport chamber. He recalled last handing his faithful keeper the cup, and a second after drinking the potion its next memory a shocking and jarring return to the light in a strange place.

He suspected something had gone terribly wrong after coming under the drug's influence. Things were not as they should be – he should be in Jamaica with Brodie and his wife heading for their new enterprise in the English Caribbean – he would set up his plantation out of the reach of his nemesis that had been pursuing him through Germania, Gaul, Britain and Caledonia. However, when he awoke, he was starved and acted out as days of old, in pure survival and instinct, in a way that surely would bring attention – something he had learned to avoid over the years. He suspected the activity and lights near the dock where he was returned to the light resulted from his ill-advised feeding frenzy.

He recalled, after being revived unceremoniously head first onto the dock in a sea of sand he had been laying, the fresh air rushed into is withering lungs – the oxygen brought him to a semi-conscious state. Two men were there. The first he knocked out and was now his captive. He killed and fed on the second.

As he sat panting next to the dead man, he noticed on the ground nearby what looked to be water gushing from a tube the first man was holding. Taking it, the creature tasted the sweet water; he drank and drank then washed the blood from his face, hands, clothing and his loyal dagger. At that moment, he recalled the last known vestige of his former life. The sensation of nourishment and liquid filling his organs and brain was a balance of both ecstasy and pain.

The creature sat on the dock surveying his whereabouts and situation. Nearly every boat tied to the docks had no sail with the exception of 2 or 3 tied nearby. The rigging was also strange with a single mast just forward of amidships. The strange construction of the boats and brightly painted metal and glass things sitting on 4 small fat black wheels in the gravel yard were also baffling; where they conveyances of some sort? There also were no horses nearby or customary village built around this tiny port.

He struggled to come to full consciousness recalling the name he claimed at the time he last could remember was Angus Cassidy – he had established himself as he evaded capture in Scotland as a wealthy Scottish Laird heading for Jamaica. That was September 1695. However, this was not likely to be Jamaica and it did not appear to be anywhere close to the year 1695.

Cassidy's attention was now on the man lying next to him in the dark wilderness. Unknown to him, the man was Alex Walsh, his partner was Robert Hoskins – the man whose life he had just taken. Hoskins and Walsh had been diving the wreck that Hoskins had found Cassidy's Eagle years before. It was Walsh that discovered the encrusted gold-like stasis chamber, the coffin they raised and were off-loading when the sling slipped and the coffin crashed down and broke open, freeing Cassidy.

His captive appeared to still be breathing but unconscious. He was clothed in a manner Cassidy found intriguing. His pants covered only the tops of his legs – stopping at his knees. The top garment was made of material much like that of stockings, but was loose with the words "Pirate's Cove" written above the design of a skull and cross bones – were these pirates? Realizing he had to seek a refuge and safety to sort out his new circumstances and time to decide whether to feed on this creature or to attempt to question him about his whereabouts and circumstance of his awakening, and the whereabouts of the Brodie's. As he continued to survey the new world he had been reborn to, two points of light accompanied by a growling noise appeared and moved across the far end of the gravel yard. Cassidy froze, and then decided those strange lights portrayed danger, stood and plucked the man from his resting place and quickly dragged him into the gravel yard away from the lights. Sensing dragging was too slow by the time he reached the edge of the forest, still clutching the dagger in his right hand, he threw the man over his shoulder and moved into the hammock. He paused about 6 feet into the bush to watch and get his bearings. He breathed heavily from the strain involved with transporting his heavy load, and closed his eyes to rest. In an unknown amount of time he was jarred from his unconsciousness by what sounded like a series of screams sounding like a female shrill in the direction of where he had come. A short time after, a second 4 wheeled thing with bright lights on its front and bluish rotating lights on its top rolled into the open gravel yard and stopped near the first, and a figure emerged from inside.

He turned and moved deeper into the hammock of coastal undergrowth away from the bright lights, again paused to get his bearings - he could see the sky to what he thought was the east beginning to glow into a new day – was actually the glow from the lights of Miami to the north. Stopping to kneel into the brackish water he rinsed more of the blood and shredded flesh from his face and arms. He knew shelter would have to be found soon to rest and gain more strength.

After about an hour, he had come to an overgrown track running from his left to right. Laying the man down, he stood erect to his full height of 5 feet 9 inches, a tall man from the age he had come. His clothes were wet and encrusted with sand and appeared rotted and needed to be replaced in the style of the era he now had found himself. He stared to the west along the track and made out what appeared to be several ruined buildings. He stooped and throwing his unconscious prisoner over his shoulder once more, and hurried to what was hoped to be his sanctuary. As he approached the first ruin there was a sign with a message written in a form of English, "*US Gov't Property, No trespassing...United States Army Nike Hercules Installation Key Largo.*" It was curious, what is the "United States Army...United States of what...? And the last parts are words he had not seen in centuries, names of the goddess of victory and the son of Zeus – perhaps beliefs that have survived through the centuries, and opportunities for manipulating those who still worshipped them.

Looking inside the stone like walls, he could not see anything that would provide shelter and security while he regained his strength and oriented himself to this new and curious world he had been resurrected. As he was about to move off Cassidy caught sight of what looked like a stair descending to a lower level. He stepped through the broken roofing material and overgrowth and pulled away an overturned piece of metal furniture that revealed a stairway to an underground chamber. Leaving his prisoner, he slowly descended the stairs. Ground water dripped into the large chamber; the floor was wet and had a strong musky smell of the mangrove and decaying plants. It was dark, damp, where no sun had reached in years. It was perfect he thought!

Returning to his prisoner, Cassidy retrieved him and located the driest spot in the underground chamber where rest could come in relative safety; but first there was a need to find a way to bind the prisoner so when he regained consciousness could not get away before he could be questioned or fed upon. In the upper room Cassidy found a line of high strength but had a strange box shaped contraption made of a light smooth metal like material, but not metal, attached to it and broke it off. He tied the man's hands together behind his back, and then looped it around his own right wrist. He withdrew to a far corner of the chamber taking account of his new environment and closed his eyes once more. His body and organs slowly began to hydrate from the life giving blood and water by way of his shriveled stomach. He felt full and yet close to becoming sick, but could not afford to lose the red nectar he took from the gift package he encountered on the dock...he still needed solid food to complete his physical restoration, but for now needed rest more.

Cassidy closed his eyes and gripped the line attached to his prisoner lying close to his feet. Soon a familiar cloak of darkness came over him – his thoughts drifted from the present confounding place he found himself back to the last memory of feeding on a crewman on the ill-fated vessel; the last exchange of glances with William Brodie, and the look he gave him that now he understood; the look was he knew it would be for the last time.

As the sun rose Cassidy slipped into an almost drug induced sleep. He stirred hours later; noticing it was dark, but felt powerless to move, with just enough energy to heal and rejuvenate. The man he had made a prisoner was to him no more than a sack of fresh blood and source of information about the time in which he had been awoken. He was conflicted about what to do with him, ultimately, what to do with anyone he encountered here or anywhere. He did need to feed again if he were to gain enough strength to move about in this new world.

***

Cassidy focused on the man...if he were careful he could drink slowly and take care not to injure him. Keepers were not considered blood sacks to be fed upon, they were more important to his kind – they conducted his business in the world of light and did not carry the smell and aura of a vampire. This was important for his survival – the keeper then is able to move back and forth between the world of light and darkness and not serve as a trail back to him. The Brodie family had served him for nearly 400 years – before that had been a string of keepers whose ancestry was unbroken for 1,000 years, at least until Josephus Galenicus; a vampire of his making who turned against his kind and began a pursuit of Cassidy and his band from Italy across Gaul, to Britain to northern Scottish sea known then as *Mare Duecalidonium* to the island of *Hurtha*. In a savage battle Galenicus' band of warrior keepers killed them all except for Cassidy who barely escaped with his life. Retreating south, he recovered, and recruited Seanus Brodie, the first keeper of the Brodie family into his service. All was well for several hundred years. Cassidy had become almost respectable – successfully becoming and evolving as a series of Scottish patriarchs with help from cover stories and deceptions concocted by the Brodie's – at least until he became prominent as a leader of Scottish Royalists during the Scottish War of the Three Kingdoms. During the Third Civil War, he evolved into Rupert MacCahan, Marquess of Logie and found himself on the losing side and, in retreat reverted to his ancient ways – committing atrocities and leaving a trail of victims drained of their blood. This caught the attention of Galen McLeod, who officially commanded a ramshackle band of volunteers that pursued rouge remnants of Royalist forces. As it turned out McLeod was the ancient nemesis of the then Rupert MacCahan: Josephus Galenicus. By the summer of 1659 his band had been reduced to a handful when near the shores of Firth of Forth, accompanied by three score armed warrior-keepers, McLeod attacked him once again. A fierce battle raged with heavy casualties inflicted on MacCahan's forces. On the second day during a lull in the fighting, the Brodie's located a small sailing craft, and after loading MacCahan, and as much of his treasure on board, escaped. Landing near Glasgow, and with a price on his head, MacCahan became Angus Cassidy, the 5th Laird of Logie. In September he and his keepers set sail for a new life in the new world of Jamaica – putting thousands of leagues of ocean between politics, Galenicus and himself, forever.

***

Cassidy noticed the man had things stuffed in his pockets. Patting a side pocket he heard a crackling noise – he reached in and pulled out a clear bottle like vessel with a colored label. Inside appeared to be a clear liquid that likely was water. He tried to pull off the top, which didn't work, but when he gave it a twist, the top gave way. Bringing it to his nose he smelled it – nothing, no smell, strange for water. He brought it to his lips and sipped it – it was wonderful. Looking in the pocket opposite he found a package. It was wrapped in a paper like material but was also transparent. Inside were several identically sized square biscuits. He ripped it open and smelled them...had a salty and wheat smell; he bit into one, it was very salty but an appealing flavor. Cassidy quickly consumed each of the small biscuits and drained the water from the bottle. He would not feed on the man, just now.

After the second day in the dark chamber, the line tied to his wrist tugged as the man, now awake tried to make his way up the stairs. Jerking back violently, Cassidy pulled him backward onto the debris strewn floor, and he landed with a grunt. Light from the sun bathed the top several stairs making it easier to see the features and the manner of dress his prisoner exhibited, especially his strange rubber soled shoes.

"Who the fuck are you? What the fuck are you?" Walsh shouted as he lay on his back, squirming and turning his head from side to side as if to catch a glimpse of his captor who was behind him as he lay on the cement floor.

To Cassidy, this language was a dialect that sounded like that used by the English, but a strange accent he had never heard before. It had no relationship to the Scottish brogue he was accustomed to hearing for the past several hundred years before his voyage here.

Still struggling, Cassidy stood and crouched over the man and placed his cold wet right hand over the man's face and forehead applying pressure to still him.

"The question, m' lad, is who you are and where is this place?" Cassidy calmly responded.

There was a long pause from both. Walsh moved his eyes to focus on the fingers and the hand on his face. His head throbbed and back stung as if he had been dragged around all the rocky coral of Key Largo. He struggled, but more pressure resulted.

"What did you do to my friend?" Walsh asked, rolling off his arms to his side attempting to get a glance of his captor.

"Your mate is no more m'lad...he is dead.

"Dead, you have got to be shitting me! What did you do to him?" Walsh demanded.

"Dun'na worry about him lad, I have questions for you." Cassidy said. "First, what is this place and what year is it?"

"This has got to be a fucking dream. You can't be real – you fell out of the metal box that had been under ballast rocks and encrusted with coral at Carysfort Reef, a box that has been there for over three hundred years – and are now talking to me in this shit hole and asking me so nicely about where you are and what day it is." Walsh replied in an exasperated tone.

"300 years?

"Yep, big guy, Rob estimated the wreck he had discovered was that of a ship lost around 1695, and probably covered up by another wreck 150 years later. We found you as the little jack in the box because about 10 years ago Hurricane Andrew swept the upper Keys to Miami and moved the earlier wreck off where we found you."

Thinking of the impact of this information Cassidy asked "Then this is some time in the 1990's?"

"Since I am talking to a fucking phantom, I'll play along, today's date; if I wasn't out longer than I thought is Monday or Tuesday November 11th or 12th , 2002." Walsh shot back.

"...And where are we?" Cassidy followed up.

"Florida, you ass hole; Key Largo in the Florida Keys." Walsh added sarcastically.

Cassidy sat back again into the corner and stroked his unkempt beard and mustache. He remembered Florida as a colony of the Kingdom of Spain – the place where they sought the fountain of youth – whose waters bestowed the immortality of youth on any of those that drank from it. That myth was over 400 years old. Now for him the struggle to come to grips with the prospect that he had been in the chamber for nearly 300 years and these 2 men had just retrieved it from the bottom, freeing him before he would have eventually died.

"...and this is the United States?" Cassidy recalling the sign he had seen coming to this building.

"Yes, the United States."

"The United States...of what?"

"Of America – Have you been in a fucking box? You smell like you have...you need a shower and a haircut man." Walsh added sarcastically to mock him.

Cassidy concluded the Brodie's were likely lost when the ship went down – and after 300 years gone anyway. This meant he was alone without means, without help, and no knowledge of life in this foreign place and time, and how he was to recover what he had lost. This man did not seem the type he could depend upon soon enough for help. Perhaps he should find out as much as he could and feed on him as he did his mate. He did however need a keeper to replace Brodie – and to teach him the mysteries of his existence, formulae for the concoctions he needed from time to time, the alchemy necessary for his wealth, and to do his bidding in the painful light. Perhaps he would try to convince the man to change his tone by offering him the ancient mysteries of his creator to make him wealthy beyond his dreams. It was worth a try, especially since he would have to start over again with another.

"My name is Angus Cassidy, Cassidy of Logie, and what would your name be?

"Cassidy of Logie, wow, this is really fucked up....my name is Walsh."

"Splendid, tell me Master Walsh, was there anything else found with my chamber, I mean any other items?" Cassidy asked Walsh.

Lying on his back, Walsh felt as if he were experiencing an out of body experience. He remembers recovering a large heavy metal coffin like box, making sure the marine patrol did not discover the two men taking items from the reef inside Pennekamp Park. He remembers helping to float it to the surface and towing it into Carysfort Reef Marina; and when lifting it the wench line snapped and out popped this guy. Next thing he remembered was waking with his hands and arms tied up with telephone cord somewhere in a ruined building with a throbbing headache and double vision.

"Rob found an Eagle, what he thought was a Roman military standard; he was researching it...it was out of place; was that something to do with you?"

Cassidy did not answer. It was getting clearer; something terrible must have happened after Brodie sealed him in the chamber. His beloved Eagle, his Imperial standard; the one he had made during another life as commander of the Roman Legions in Syria during the reign of Marcus Aurelius 2,000 years before. Cassidy was tired – closing his eyes to pass the hours until sun down and for an opportunity to begin collecting the necessities for his new life in Florida.

"One more thing for now Master Walsh, what were those four wheeled metal and glass conveyances that people now ride around in...?

"...four wheeled metal and glass conveyances that people now ride around in..." Walsh repeated.

"You mean cars, they are cars; boy I am really fucked – you are who you say you are, aren't you?"

"How do these cars move around?" asked Cassidy who was intrigued with this new technology.

"Engines, engines that burn gasoline..." Walsh responded closing his eyes.

"Ummm..." Cassidy responded, stroking his beard as he thought of how he could use them in his new life in Florida and the 21st century.

***

Walsh could hear Cassidy's labored breathing, and sounds of sleep. He looked about his surroundings and tried to figure out where he was. This definitely was not the marina or anyplace that was close to people...Judging from his recollection; this must be the old Army missile defense base north of the marina. He had never been there, and would not know which way to run if and when he got away.

For the umpteenth time he ran his fingers over the telephone cable binding his wrists together and tethered to the creature Cassidy; he slowly fed the cord into his hand until this time he felt something in the line. He was sure because he could not see what it was, but believed it was an old style telephone line extension jack. If he could find and activate the line disconnect he could free himself and slip away to safety. He calmed and listened for Cassidy's breathing.

From what Walsh could guess it was around noon. He was hungry and very thirsty = actually the first time he noticed it since he woke up from what he suspected was a mild concussion. He patted his pockets but had apparently lost his water bottle and peanut butter crackers. Walsh was weighing the methods of successful escape, but escape to where? Since coming to, Walsh was constantly disoriented; things were blurred together, and had no clue how far away he was from help. He knew one thing; this guy was not your normal run of the mill dude that just fell out of a box. This guy was not a human that lived and died according to the same schedule the rest of normal people did. This guy was different - just smelled old – and pretty nasty as well. His clothes looked like he stepped out of a Three Musketeer's movie, his hair and beard looked like they had been growing for years, and those gnarly broken finger nails. Walsh had a very hard time visualizing this guy was in that box alive, sealed in, underwater for 300 years until Hopkins and he found him – until the box he was in crashed onto the dock, broke open and freed him. Walsh thought if this guy or whatever he was killed his friend Rob, it was likely only a matter of time before his number came up – he had to make a run for it, first choice secretly without a confrontation, one in which he probably would lose.

Lying on his side on the cement floor of the basement of an abandoned building he lay is head slowly down onto the cluttered surface. The floor smelled like a mixture of ground-in vegetation mixed with cold wet sandy concrete. Listening for Cassidy's breathing – by the sounds he made, he was sleeping soundly. Watching to see movement on the part of his captor, Walsh did a finger over finger pull of the telephone cord connecting him to Cassidy's grip. As it moved through his fingers, the line disconnect slid into his hand. He could not make out how much slack was in the line between him and Cassidy so assumed there was none.

Trying to remember where the release was on the old extension jack – he ran his finger over it softly feeling for any button or slight protrusion that was the release...until he found it. The trigger like mechanism was on the side – he squeezed it slowly until he heard a feint click, but it did not disconnect.

"Shit," he thought, "...probably corroded and a pull would release it."

Lying there he knew he now had to detach himself from Cassidy; if not the next time he awoke and pulled on the line it would likely disconnect and he would be retied to something he could not get out of as easily. Walsh slowly rolled over top of the line where his weight would stabilize Cassidy's end while he pulled against the corroded release.

As he rolled, Cassidy stirred – he froze still. He got away with it, Cassidy's head turned and he returned to a deep sleep. He pulled on his end and felt the line release give way. Walsh then paused and again listened for any movement by Cassidy. He continued to sleep deeply and Walsh decided it was a time to leave.

The hard part was rolling back quietly and getting into a position where he could get on his knees with his hands tied behind him. It was not easy, and he almost fell onto the sleeping Cassidy. Once on his feet Walsh walked almost on his tip toes up the stairs and out of the decaying building into the daylight. It wasn't until after his escape that he noticed his clothes were soaking wet with sweat, with long streams of the salty liquid covering his face and stinging his eyes. He thought to find a way to wipe it off, but realized he had better move out and find help while he was able.

He ran as fast he could across partially overgrown bits of asphalt parking lot toward the tree line on the opposite side. Once several hundred yards south of his captor Walsh stopped and began to peel away the overlapped loops of telephone cabling. Once he untied he tried to get his bearings. Remembering his Boy Scout days, Walsh stood to put the sun on one side of his body; supposedly if it were on his left side late in the day, he was facing north, to the rear south, and to his right was east. Unfortunately the sun was overhead. He guessed which way were the directions and headed west, toward a north-south road in hopes of finding help and completely escape this strange creature calling himself Angus Cassidy.

Heading in what he thought was west, Walsh began to realize he had guessed wrong, he was in fact heading due east! The sun had moved, but now was to his rear, not his front if he were heading west in the late afternoon. Just as this revelation came to him he could see patches of blue through the underbrush. Continuing further he came to the ocean side edge of the Key. The little seagull droppings encrusted island just off shore gave it away, it was what he and his partner called "Bird Shit Island" – he was standing on old Dynamite Docks, and had to go back, past where he left Cassidy in order to find the north-south road and help! That was not his first option.

Sitting down, he thought there might be a passing boat that might pick him up...he and Rob had passed by here hundreds of times while lobster diving – someone would pick him up for sure. He was also concerned about the approaching night, if this guy slept during the day and roamed around at night; night was a bad time for Alex Walsh. Thinking quickly, he decided to swim to the Bird Shit Island, try to wave down someone and hide from Cassidy as well. It sounded like a plan.

After wading to the island, Walsh positioned himself on the eastern most part the mound, obscuring clear view of him from the shoreline. He felt weak, and began to get dizzy – the blow to his head and lack of water for the last 48 hours had taken a toll on him. He lay down with his feet nearly in the lapping water and hid in the lengthening shadow of the rocks. As he looked at the bobbing trash that had washed ashore from passing vessels he noticed several water bottles snagged in the flotsam. He got up, after first looking to the shore and picked one out of the water. It was empty; however the second was nearly full. He untwisted the top, forgetting his fear of unknown lips on it before him and drank the fresh sweet water to nearly the bottom; stopping to save some if he needed to rely on it further.

Walsh looked out to sea – the darkening horizon was clear – no boats of any description were visible. He knew he would probably not be able to wave down anyone – and began to plan his walk past Cassidy in the sunlight of the next day. If Cassidy's lair was due west from where he was, he could probably go south along the shoreline back toward the marina; as he recalled there was a path or road just north of the marina, and he could follow that to the road and certain help. That sounded good...for now, he thought best to rest and sleep; and maybe try to snag something swimming by in the shallows for breakfast. He lay his head down and sleep overtook him.

Cassidy awoke, with his eyes still closed; he pulled the line to assure himself he still had someone at the other end. It pulled free, his prisoner was gone!!

Chapter 8 - Station House Blues

"...Workin' on mysteries without any clues...
tryin' to make some front page drive-in news..."

Bob Seger, *Night Moves*, 1976

Before leaving Carysfort Reef Marina, Nash checked in with Rob Hernandez about anything new since the medical examiner had arrived.

"This is really one for the record books," Hernandez observed, sorting through his evidence collection locker.

"Look Nash," Hernandez holding up a clear baggie containing a bloody yellow piece of something that looked plastic. "You know what this is and where we found it?"

"Rob, I haven't got a fucking clue, surprise me." Nash said, becoming impatient.

"Well detective, this is a fingernail – the artifact is approximately 135 millimeters in length, that's about 5 inches to you. That would mean it has been growing for almost 4 years under normal circumstances; anyway I found it inside the wound, in the victim's chest. I found several other fragments inside and in the sand on the dock. This is a new one for me; well, I guess it's your job to figure this out Mr. Nash." Hernandez said nonchalantly as he placed the evidence baggie back into his field locker.

"Oh yeah, the autopsy is tomorrow at 1000 hours at Mariner's Hospital in Tavernier." Hernandez said over his shoulder as he walked to his van.

Nash noticed that Deputy Brown had been replaced from the shift relief Zone 7 Deputy. He was a bit disappointed, as he was looking for an opportunity to share a beer or five with her before heading home. As he opened the door to his car, he again felt either of being watched or something was near; the same unexplainable sense he had felt often while in Iraq – he used to think he could smell people, and it served him well. Glancing out to the north end of the lot one time he turned the ignition key and the engine came to life.

The Plantation Key Substation is home for the Sheriff's Upper Keys Criminal Investigative units covering patrol Zones 6 and 7 – it was about 20 minutes south of Key Largo just off U.S. Route 1 Overseas Highway. Nash thought about this case – definitely one he had not had experience with in the Keys. Maybe there were similar nasty murders in Miami but never a murder like this in his experience. With light traffic, Nash made it to the his office in no time, but not in enough time to process the scene in his mind or emotionally, at least not enough to report it thoroughly to the Sheriff himself – but first had to deal with Evans who Nash considered a pain in the ass most of the time.

After exiting his car in the parking lot, he had the same sense of being watched – or a presence as he had experienced at the Marina. This was new for him. Never had this feeling followed him away from crime scenes, but seemed stronger as the evening progressed.

He collected the field notes he had made and was buzzed into the squad bay by the desk officer. He stopped at her desk and pulled out the next of kin information Ciccone had given him at the Marina.

"Good evening Mizz...Garcia-Ramirez; how are you this fine Florida evening?" asked Nash sarcastically.

"Just peachy Nash, what's this? She asked of the note card he was handing her.

"It's the next of kin information for the victim at Carysfort Reef Marina – call the Metro police in Dade County and ask them to go by and make the notification.

The victim is **Robert Hopkins, here is his address in West Kendall, and his wife's name is Elizabeth.** I also need a time when it would be good to go up and interview her tomorrow" Nash replied.

"Okay Nash, they will probably want you there for the initial contact on a murder, but I will try." Ramirez replied. ""Oh by the way, Captain Evans has been pacing by your cube for the past 20 minutes and has finished off nearly every candy jar in the squad bay – please go back and talk to him before he broadens his grazing to my lunch in the refrigerator."

With that, Nash smiled and headed to the detective squad bay on the second floor.

"Nash! It's about time – fill me in so we can call the boss and get started on this" Evans said from Nash's cubicle chair.

"Good to see you too Phil..." Nash said pulling up a chair from the adjoining cubicle.

"Bottom line this is it: The body was discovered about 6 hours ago by a couple of tourists looking for a boat they had rented...they were in the wrong marina, and paid for being lost with a sight they will not soon forget. The victim is a white male by the name of **Robert Hopkins,** approximately 42 years of age, and lived in West Kendall. He was found lying on his back with a massive wound running from his belly button to his throat, in what looks like made by a knife or other large sharp instrument..."

"Christ! Just one long wound?" Evans interrupted.

"Yes – blood was smeared everywhere, but inside the wound not much pooling of blood – pretty clean in a gory sort of way. The circumstances – this is where it gets creepy: He, and from what we can determine, someone else was off-loading a large coffin shaped metal tube thingy when it slipped the strap and crashed onto the dock. It was partially filled with a sand-like material that spilled out when the top broke open after hitting the dock."

Evans interrupted again – "Was he caught up under the box, was there anything in the box except sand? How was the wound inflicted? and why is this a murder?"

"In all good time Phil, This is where it gets weird and creepy – to answer your question it appears that something was inside the box; contents unknown. Hell, it is even possible that the something inside could have killed Hopkins."

"Wait a minute; you are not a rookie detective on his first case. That doesn't make logical sense Nash. It seems more probable that he the perpetrator was someone on the dock, someone interested in maybe what was in the box. You said that someone was helping him?"

"Yeah, too many moving parts for a single set of hands to handle, someone had to be helping..." Nash interjected.

"Yeah, okay, person or persons unknown - wouldn't that be a more logical immediate theory?"

"Yes, except for what Bob Hernandez found inside the wound at the crime scene."

"And what was that?"

"What appeared to be a human finger nail..."

"A fingernail – so what?" Evan interrupted.

"A fingernail five inches long...with fragments of others spread about the wound." Nash finished.

"What the fuck? You are telling me whatever or whoever killed Hopkins had fingernails that hadn't been cut in..."

"Four or more years..." Nash said, finishing the sentence.

"Christ, how are we going to tell the Sheriff this and not sound like we are nuts or drunk, or both?

"Well tomorrow we will have pictures Bob and his people took tonight, or last night at the crime scene, and the autopsy is scheduled for 10:00 am; in about 7 hours at Mariner's in Tavernier. I will meet with Hopkins' wife sometime in the afternoon. The picture should be clearer by then. How about we just tell him the facts; and the circumstances are unclear surrounding the murder – leaving out the part about the murderer might have popped out of the box. We will go with those unknowns as persons of interest; how about that? Oh yes, let's ask him to avoid a full media circus as long as possible. That also means securing the crime scene as is until I can get out there and look at the box in more detail in the daylight – like later today. I think Bob took samples of the sand, the fingernails, and other shit he found and sent it to the lab – let's also see what that tells us."

"Nash, it looks like you are scheduling yourself for working 24 hours a day – you need some help with this...wasn't Deputy Brown the responding officer on this case?"

Nash paused; pleasantly conjuring images of Deputy Brown in something other than her uniform or maybe even without something altogether. "Well she knows a lot about the case already, and we have worked well together before...yes, I do need help..."

"We will contact her and her shift supervisor; I'll take care of the assignment and have her meet you at the hospital for the autopsy later this morning. She will be detailed to you for the duration of the case. Maybe she can do the leg work while you concentrate on the details."

"Okay, now let's call the boss – I'll put him on speaker so we both can report. I'll do the talking up front and you support my story, got me detective?"

Nash nodded, already lost in lust about his new partner.

***

Arriving back at his condo, Nash stepped in and closed the door with his foot, gripping his field notes, bag of burgers, and his jacket. He tossed them on the coffee table in front of his television. It was now 3 am and he was spent. In the kitchen was what used to be a half-gallon bottle of Bacardi rum, but now only a trace of the amber liquid remaining, enough for one strong drink. He went directly to the bottle and mixed the liquor with ice and some sweet tea – his favorite but strange concoction he had come across while serving with an Army Special Forces team during his stint in the military. The mix was born the night more rum was left at the end of the coke, and the large supply of sweet tea on hand was the only logical solution.

He plopped down on the sofa and took a long draw on his drink. He often used this time after coming home from a busy evening to decompress – only this night he was alone – and this night he was consumed not with bull shitting with his colleagues or trying to get into his date's shorts – this night he stared into the blank TV screen thinking about the events of the evening and the bizarre case he was now trying to figure out.

The rum began to lay warm in his stomach with the alcohol entering his system distracting him slightly – but did not relieve him of the vision burned in his memory of the body and the horrendous wound that lead to its demise, and the circumstances – circumstances that did not make sense and had to be discounted for the moment because logic and the laws of physics were not on his side of his theory. Nash could not get the dead man out of his head, so too was the nagging "presence" he sensed at the crime scene – both something he had not experienced before on the job. Everything had always been business – nothing that he had carried home or kept him awake as this one.

He also thought of how he subconsciously reacted when Evens assigned Deputy Brown to him – not as an opportunity to spread out the work and cover the bases more quickly, but his license to get between her legs. He was lonely, and believed he had come to regard women as objects, something he had to fight against if he was ever going to have a healthy long term relationship again. In reality he knew this and that Brown would not be his partner in solving the case by day and his bed companion by night. She was a sweet girl, one that looked up to Nash, someone who had shared some social time together over a few beers and commiseration about lost love, not someone that was looking for a sex partner from work.

As much as he denied it, Nash carried a hole in his soul after Viktoriya left him. Despite what he often said, Nash probably still loved her, or maybe just felt betrayed in the way it ended – he really didn't know. He recalled the day he found her gone; he felt a deep emptiness come upon him, and walked around the Key for hours before going back to the condo they had shared. To compensate, he tried to fill his emptiness with a series of no-name relationships with women he met after; tourists, a nurse, even a woman who owned a couple of lobster boats he called "Tugboat Annie." The depth of each encounter became less and less as he tried more to find meaning it them. He was a mess and he knew it; so enough of the fantasy about screwing Brown was not going to happen.

Chapter 9 - All the Gory Details

*"...I really do appreciate the fact you're sittin'
here...Your voice sounds so wonderful But yer face don't look
too clear..."*

Jimmy Buffet, *Why Don't we Get Drunk*, 1973

After waking on the couch at 9:20 am, Nash hastily showered and shaved and found a clean outfit in his closet – he was usually pretty good about keeping on top of laundry and general condo appearances, but this day he was behind on both counts.

Sipping black coffee from his travel mug Nash pulled into the Tavernier Hospital parking lot. Brown's unmarked patrol car with blind tags was already there, probably for hours. In the police world blind tags were ones that are issued to a law enforcement agency that lead nowhere. When these tags are checked on a vehicle data base by legitimate or other authorities, they will come back as "...not on file." This could mean they are new and not in the system, or the system is down, or they are on a law enforcement or undercover vehicle. The last guess is the ones most cops make when coming across them.

Exiting the car he took the last gulp of the coffee and put it on the passenger seat.

"Hey, Rusty...good morning"

Nash turned and his fantasy about her raised its ugly head once more; it was Deputy Sheila Brown walking toward him in civilian clothes. She was dressed in dark pants, and white cotton blouse. Both were very complimentary of her small waist and generous bust. Over her right shoulder was the issued hand gun bag designed to look like a typical woman's shoulder bag. Judging from the way she clutched it, inside was her full sized Glock semi-automatic pistol with probably enough ammunition to qualify on the range. Her straight black hair was tied back tightly on her head with a tropical colored hair bow. She looked stunning he thought, and then fought to disconnect from his long running fantasy and concentrate on the business at hand.

"Good morning Sheila, err...Deputy Brown" Nash stumbled.

Brown paused, thinking Nash was trying to be a bit overly formal, but ignored it. "It's about 10, shall we go in? Dr. Bhatnagar is already in there – he is the Prosector." She said as she met Nash, and tucking her arm into his right arm as they walked arm in arm through the front automatic doors.

Autopsies generally are conducted through the partnership of two people. The Prosector is the person directly performing dissection of the cadaver. In this case Bhatnagar is a Board-certified pathologist medical Doctor. The Prosector is typically assisted by a person called a Diener. The Diener is responsible for moving the body from the cooler and placing it on the autopsy table and assisting the Prosector as he or she slices and dices the cadaver. Although the Diener is not formally trained, most come from the funeral home industry and are competent in handling bodies and assisting in the grisly business.

Opening the door to the autopsy room when one is being performed often includes an image and smells that will last a lifetime. As they entered Nash glanced at Brown who hesitated as she entered. This was typical he thought but not something anyone might witness regularly – and happy he did not. Nash motioned to Brown to put on surgical gloves, a frontal gown, shoe covers, and plastic face shield.

"This often gets a bit messy and things can squirt..." Nash whispered to Brown with a smirk. Brown looked as if she was reconsidering this assignment but finished putting on the protective gear and followed Nash to the table.

Simon Drake, the Diener, had just placed a body block under the body's back to expose the trunk. The next step was to make a Y shaped incision from each shoulder meeting at the breast bone, then down to the pubic bone. In this case the murderer had already performed this at the crime scene.

Generally, before the pathologist begins his scripted and recorded examination, he will answer any immediate questions from police or officials present, since typically they do not have an interest in the whole procedure. This morning was no different.

"Good morning Detectives, as you can see, our subject provides us with some challenges..." Bhatnagar noted as he motioned to the large wound cavity.

"Good morning Doctor" Nash responded. "Correct me if I am wrong, but this wound is the cause of death, not blunt trauma or other cause which this might have occurred subsequently, correct?"

"Correct, there is no evidence of trauma anywhere else. As you can clearly see the head and face are intact and without any sign of blunt force anywhere." Bhatnagar responded.

"What do you suspect was used to make this wound Doctor?"

"It appears to have been a knife or other similar sharp object, probably about 30 centimeters in length entering the body approximately 10 centimeters up from the pubic bone and running approximately 47 centimeters to and through the xiphoid process of the sternum." Bhatnagar observed, pointing to the beginning and tracing to the end of the wound; surmising the upward movement of the thrust used by the murderer.

Leaning forward, and turning the overhead lamp closer onto the wound cavity, he continued, "Also involved were the entire intestinal tract, liver, and heart. The implement penetrated and ripped as it went....There is also evidence of foreign material inside the wound, what looks like sand, bits of the victim's clothing, pooling of a gelatin like substance here near the top of the heart; the *aorta ascendens*, as well as bits of a fibrous keratin material; likely to be fragments of fingernails. Remarkable."

Nash recalled the long fingernail Hernandez had pulled from the wound at the crime scene, confirming Bhatnagar's initial observation. To Nash, the smell of gelatin like material near the victim's lacerated upper heart seemed to overpower. The lacerated intestines filled his nostrils...it smelled old. The presence he felt the evening before seemed to radiate from the glob. He shook it off.

"Thanks Doctor, I think we have got what we came for, at least for now. I know you are busy, but please try to expedite your report soonest – this is a very unusual case and will no doubt attract a lot of attention and we want know anything you discover to help us put the pieces together." Nash said.

"I understand detective, I will try to have a preliminary report and lab results to you as soon as I can, but you know the lab is often the slower of the two, and will not submit mine without that." Bhatnagar said peering over his glasses as he collected samples from the cavity.

As they deposited their gear in the toxic waste container on the way out, they heard the whine of a Stryker saw used to cut through the cranium and remove the brain for examination. Nash did not miss not seeing that, and unknown to Brown was very happy to have left when he did; he hated dead bodies.

As they walked into the morning sunshine from the hospital Nash asked "What did you think of your first autopsy Sheila?'

"Oh, this was not the first; we went to one while at the academy, but we didn't stand at the table, more like in a gallery over the process." She responded.

"Right, let's get some breakfast, I am starving!" Nash said smiling.

***

Not far from Mariner's hospital they pulled into a breakfast and lunch place and together were ushered to a table on the outside deck to the rear of the restaurant. Nash and Brown ordered coffee. Brown opened her menu and noticed Nash was looking toward the water as he sipped from the mug in what could be described as a "...ten thousand yard stare." He was thinking.

"I thought you were starving..." Brown noticed.

"I know what I want – although I like to cook, but don't do that very often for any one either than me. Therefore...I am a regular at nearly every decent restaurant or watering hole in the Upper Keys."..."that will give you half price or comp your meals.." Brown completed his sentence with a smile. Nash smiled back, knowing he opened himself to the joke.

"Well, what is good?"

"If you like a hearty breakfast - eggs, bacon, biscuits, grits and gravy with a side of fried crispy yellow tail snapper are my favorites." Nash said rubbing his hands together in anticipation of his meal.

"Christ, I won't eat for a week; okay, make that two..."

After ordering Nash got down to business. Looking to their nearest neighbor on the deck, he began at a level he would not be overheard, leaning toward her.

"Tell me what you think about this case – you were the first officer on the scene, made first contact with the complainants, and first to see both the crime scene and extended area around it."

Brown reached into her shoulder bag and took out her field notes pad. Leafing to the case she began:

"I arrived at 1925 after a call from central dispatch on my department cell phone. I thought it was pretty strange to be dispatched over the phone instead of the police radio, but found out I was being dispatched to a pretty strange call. Upon arrival I met the complainants who discovered the body. They were tourists named Osborne from North Carolina looking for a rental boat they hired online. They were lost and at the wrong place. They reported to have arrived, and at first saw nothing unusual. With the meager lighting in the marina they were drawn to a couple of spot lights shining onto the dock from a boat tied up to Dock #1 along the main channel. That's when they found him and called us." Brown said, reading from her field notes.

"What did you see as you entered?"

"Well, I saw the same thing, nothing unusual either – only two cars in the lot. You know the marina is not a busy place, only a few boat slips and a couple of houseboats, with only one occupied. That guy works nights and is not unusual to be gone at that time."

"Did you run the plates of the two vehicles you observed?

"Yes I did – the Ford Explorer came back to the victim, Robert Hoskins. The second, a Toyota Tundra pickup to a guy named Alex Walsh."

"Did you make any connection between Walsh and the case?"

"Nope, not yet."

"Walsh may be the guy who was helping Hopkins when the murder occurred. Now, here is the elephant in the room, what or who do you think killed Hopkins, and the motive."

"Those are the big questions. From my perspective there are at least two theories. The first is that a person or persons unknown knew Hopkins and that whatever was in the box was valuable enough to kill him for it – the motive was theft. The second is a non-affiliated person or persons killed Hopkins as a thrill killing and stole whatever spilled out of the box." Brown said as she paused long enough for the breakfast plates to be placed in front of her and Nash.

"Another big question; what the hell was in the box and where did it come from...it looked like it came off the boat, and if it came off the boat, it came from the water, and since it doesn't look like it would float on its own – it came from the bottom. The diving gear on the boat and floatation bags point to it having been raised from the bottom, most likely illegally from the Park." Brown continued.

"Do you think Hopkins could have done this by himself?"

"Hell no, too many moving parts and too heavy for one person to handle. You are a diver Nash, could you have positioned the boat, secured the box to it, inflate the bags and keep them inflated as the boat towed its half-submerged cargo miles in the open ocean?"

"Do you think anything could have been alive in the box and when it broke open could have attacked and killed Hopkins?"

Brown was caught in mid chew of her breakfast, and nearly choked, "Are you shitting me Nash? You are the expert at this table – what facts, at least those not based in the SyFy Channel are you suggesting that supports this third approach?"

"I'm not sure there are facts yet to support that, but there doesn't seem to be anything inside the box of any weight. If it were, there would be marks on the dock where it came out – logically this makes me believe if the thing or things inside were not of sufficient mass to mark the deck or whatever it was, was not rigid – maybe like cash or dope....if it would be cash, we would likely have found a bill or two missed by the perp, even if it was wrapped. If this were dope, it would fit to include the vicious nature of the killing – a message to anyone stealing their product," Nash observed as he nibbled on his bacon.

"There is one more thing, the drag marks in the gravel at the end of the dock I saw and photographed last night. They could be drag marks from the sack of drugs. Then they should stop somewhere where it was loaded into a vehicle, right?"

Brown nodded as she finished her breakfast. Placing her knife and fork on her plate and wiping her mouth with her napkin she asked "What is the plan Rusty, what do you want me to do?"

"Okay, I'd like you to drive up and interview Hopkins' next of kin and go to the address registered to the Tundra and find out what's going on there. I want to know who Alex Walsh is, and why his truck is parked at the crime scene. I'll go back to the marina and look at it in daylight, try to find out where the drag marks end, and interview the manager some more as well as the guy in the houseboat, I think his name is Holmes."

"Okeydokey" Brown said, reaching to pay for her meal.

"It's on me; this is a special occasion – your first post autopsy meal, a passage each cop eventually experiences. Call me on my cell when you get back. I am very interested in learning what you find out.

It was then 11:30am. After Brown left for West Kendall, Nash approached the cashier and went began his traditional kabuki dance at trying to pay; he put his hand into his pocket, was waved off, and ended his performance with wave of the hand and a shy boyish "...thank you." After a short walk to his car he was enroute to Carysfort Reef Marina, a very full and happy camper.

Chapter 10 - The Story

"...Alibis, angles and tales from the tropics...Come to my mind, so easy and quick...that's my story and I'm stickin' to it..."

Jimmy Buffet, *That's My Story And I'm Stickin' To It, 1989*

It was nearly 12:30 in the afternoon when Nash arrived back at the crime scene. As he approached the turn off from northbound Monroe/905 to Marina Lane, he could see officers assigned to protecting the crime scene speaking with a two young women. Behind them was a Miami television news remote broadcasting van – Channel 71 no less. The technician was in the process of erecting the satellite communications tower for live broadcasting – apparently they had just arrived.

Nash pulled to the right along the road near the tree line about a quarter mile south. Still looking to the emerging drama at the yellow plastic tape used to mark the edge of the restricted area, he dialed Captain Evans from his cell phone.

After one ring Evans answered – skipping his customary sarcasm; Nash began - "Phil, I'm at Carysfort Reef Marina – well, Channel 71 is here too, remote broadcasting van and everything. We are busted – can you get the PR guys here to meet with the reporters? I don't want to get wrapped around the axle with these people."

"Yeah, the *Keys Herald* reporter called just now and the officer at the crime scene just called in about Channel 71...Doug Harris is on his way. The official line he will report is it appears now to be a murder – not releasing the name of the victim just yet. Metro has not got back with us to confirm they made contact with next of kin – but likely did...whatever. We confirm it appears the murder was connected with the contents of the metal box, avoiding the reference to "...it looks like a big coffin", and finally, believe it could be drug smuggling; end of story right now... Harris' message will also be about a news conference update at the Sheriff's Headquarters Building tomorrow at 7:45 am. You have until then to fill in some of the gaps that we need to release making this sound like a "bim-bam, thank you mam" drug related murder, nothing more...Did Brown make contact with Hopkins' wife yet?" Evans asked.

"She left right after breakfast, and following the autopsy to conduct the interview. I haven't heard from her yet – she's probably still enroute. You did say right now we have not released Hopkins' name yet, right?"

"That's right – Now sit tight until Harris gets there; makes a statement and announces the press conference before you try to get past the media there...maybe they will go away so we can do our work."

"Understand; I would rather have all my teeth pulled out than talk to them...I do know a back road into the Marina – it's a bit south by way of a house building site closed down because an endangered lizard lived under the slime in the coral rock, or some shit...I'll turn around and go in that way."

"I forgot you were such a touchy-feely guy Nash...be careful not to disturb them critters on your way in..." Evans said sarcastically.

***

After maneuvering his vehicle past the coral rubble of the housing site, Nash made it to the southern end of the marina gravel parking lot. He slowed the vehicle to reassure himself no camera carriers or reporters were loose near the crime scene. Driving to the dock area he noticed a public auctioned Dade County Police vehicle, still sporting the green and white color scheme. The star and badge logo and "police' decals had been scraped off. It was parked in a space near the houseboat where the only occupant of the marina lived. Good luck he thought, he could interview him – but was puzzled how he got in, probably the same way Nash snuck past the barricaded access point. He drove to the dock and parked near where he had the evening before. He was met with the interior security officer, Deputy Tom Noland.

Exiting the car, Nash asked Noland, "Hey Tom, did any of them get past the entry-way before they were stopped?"

"No they didn't see anything beyond the entry-way and likely not the crime scene itself." Noland responded.

"Not the dock or box?"

"Nope, we stopped them first."

Nash nodded and walked to the blood stained dock, taking care to walk around the red smudged wood planks as he approached the box, half suspended by nylon straps, attached to a hoist contraption built onto the deck of the boat and tied to the dock. The coffin-like box had apparently slipped from the strap opposite from the one still holding it up as the hoist was being manipulated over the dock for a soft landing. When it slipped, a soft landing turned into a crash causing the retaining bolts securing the lid to break, spilling most of the contents onto the dock. And what were those contents? Nash asked himself as he looked inside the box.

As he stretched closer to the box's interior, still avoiding stepping on the blood stained dock, Nash sensed the same presence he felt the evening before, and the smell was the same as the glob of gelatin like material inside Hopkins' chest cavity at the autopsy. Nash repelled from the smell and presence, feeling a slight dizziness. He backed, stood straight and collected himself, and wiped with both hands over his face, wondering why the hell he was reacting to these things like he did.

The dogs had yet to arrive and probably would not until tomorrow since at night the handlers refuse to run their dogs through mangroves and swamp – too many toothy critters, especially crocks and dangerous down falls.

***

The houseboat was tied at both bow and stern to the docking area reserved for larger vessels – where at one time at least one lobster fleet called Carysfort Reef Marina home. Those days were gone. The channel had pretty much silted up and at low tide it was tricky getting out into open water. The houseboats were owned by the Nick Ciccone's boss as rental income. Houseboats are pretty much the same as regular boats – holes in the water that owners throw money into. Both had seen their better days especially the one rented to a character named Seth Holmes.

Nash did a registration check on the beat up surplus police cruiser parked next to the dock to which the houseboat was tethered. It came back to Seth Edward Holmes of this location. A quick FDLE check on Holmes revealed he had been arrested and did a few months in Dade County jail for petty theft and drug possession, nothing remarkable since nearly everyone Nash had business with these days had a record of some sort. Jail records showed Holmes had a psych discharge from the Navy where he had been trained as a barber. Evidently Holmes began talking to himself to people who were not there while in the lock up, got evaluated by the jail shrink but with inconclusive results.

After calling in and advising central dispatch his location and his visit to the houseboat, Nash exited his vehicle and stepped onto the houseboat deck. There was no sound coming from the main cabin. Nash knocked on the door and waited for a response. There was none and knocked again with a mop handle he found propped on the bulkhead next to the door.

"Holmes, Seth Holmes, I am a detective from the Monroe County Sheriff's Office. I need to speak with you about a crime that occurred in the marina last night..." Nash shouted into the door.

Nash heard some rustling in the cabin and locks being turned behind the door. It opened slowly about two inches and on the other side were a pair of blood shot eyes attached to a short balding white male in a dirty T shirt and baggy khaki shorts. His dark rimmed glasses and bushy mustache reminded Nash of those Halloween mustache and glasses gag masks.

"Mr. Holmes?" asked Nash displaying his badge and credential case to the man. "I'm Detective Russell Nash assigned to investigate a murder that occurred around 8 pm last evening on the dock just down from your houseboat on Dock 1."

"Mur-der! Christ! The man said.

"Are you Seth Holmes?" Nash asked again.

Yeah, that's me – what murder are you talking about...?" Holmes responded.

"A boat owner...can I come in?

Opening the door, Nash was not disappointed in what he saw – a mess: Clothes and empty food containers littering the furniture and floor. A television sat across from a couch with animated images of an online game playing out, and all mixed with a smell that the trash had not been taken out in a while.

"...Err, sure, sorry, I work at night and didn't get back here until 3:30 this morning – I saw the road block and came in by the construction site...an officer met me when I got into the lot, and explained to her I lived here – so he let me come in."

Nash wondered why the officer didn't report the contact with Holmes and note that on his log. These types of lack of attention to details screw up more cases, and often are the reason why cases are lost in court...a big annoyance to Nash.

"You can see, I live alone and am basically a slob; Hey can I go over to see where it happened; maybe I can help – I live here you know..." Holmes said as he retreated into the main cabin and sat down in a chair opposite the door.

"No. Mr. Holmes you said you were working last night...what were the hours and where were you?

"I work at Captain Billy's Tiki bar by the Holiday Island Inn at mile marker 100. I wash dishes and bus tables   and do a good job. I watch people too, a lot; maybe I can be your helper..."

"Mr. Holmes...last night." Nash said trying to keep the man on track.

"...Err, anyway I went to work around 7pm and got home, like I said, around 3:30 this morning."

"Did you see any activity on Dock 1 as you were leaving for work Mr. Holmes?"

"Is that the one over there?" he asked, pointing toward the crime scene. Nash nodded in response.

"Oh, yeah...the boat that had been tied up there for the past couple of months came in just before dark. The two guys I had seen on it docked around quarter to six. They were dragging something in the water: I could see yellow bags sticking out of the water beside their boat, had no idea what it was. They fucked around and were pulling something under the bags out when I left; that's all I saw... I was late...does that help? Did I say something good?"

"Yes, that was very good; was there anything else Mr. Holmes?"

"Nope, I try to keep out of other people's business – but I do watch...The guys on the dock had been back and forth since they were here. Are they dead or did they kill someone?"

"One of them wound up dead last night – killed there on the dock..."

"....Ummm, did the other guy kill him...you have got him, right?"

Nash's cell phone vibrated just in time before he would have to dance around what he did not know. Pulling the cell phone from his shirt pocket, caller ID showed it was Sheila Brown. He got up, excusing himself from Holmes and stepped outside and shut the door.

"Hey Sheila, how'd things go?"

"...Rusty, about three-quarters of an hour ago I left Alex Walsh's house and before that had a long visit with Liz Hopkins, our victim's wife. I got some interesting information and saw some equally interesting stuff he and his partner, Alex Walsh have been taking from a wreck in the Park since after Andrew came through in 1992...where can I meet you?" Brown asked excitedly.

"How about the parking lot at the Shell Man gift shop in Key Largo?" Nash responded.

"Perfect, I'll be there in about half an hour" Brown said and hung up.

Reentering the cabin, Nash found Holmes back in front of his television, fixated on the game.

"Mr. Holmes, something has come up, can get I back to you tomorrow?" Nash asked.

"G-g-g-r-eat!" Holmes pushed to Nash a piece of notebook paper with his free hand, "...here is my cell phone number and phone number at Captain Billy's..." Call me anytime – I can be your helper! I'm off for the next two days so will be here tonight through Thursday. I leave for work around six thirty."

"I'll call you to set up a time..." Nash said just before Holmes shut the door and returned to his game.

While Nash walked to his car, Nick Ciccone's words echoed in his head about Holmes being a "weird fuck." Nash thought Holmes wasn't just a weird fuck; he was the president of the Weird Fuck Society.

***

Nash drove south to the rendezvous point and got there before Brown. He pulled out his field notebook and recorded his conversation with Holmes. The information about pulling something in on Sunday afternoon just about dusk, and the yellow bags confirmed that the lift bags found in the boat were used to get the coffin off the bottom, and if in the Park; probably illegally. He made a note to call the park administrator to determine if these guys ever pulled a permit to excavate where they were diving. He also made a note to review the report of the search of Hopkins' vessel. He was hoping to find any obvious drug smuggling or other evidence pointing to illegal excavation of a sunken vessel, as well as the on board GPS receiver. Made a note to have the lab give him a list of all latitude/longitude waypoints stored on the device to help him determine where the two men had been visiting and where they likely would have picked up the box. He needed to do that ASAP.

Okay he thought, Brown found out these guys have been diving on a wreck for over ten years; they apparently found something, and enough of it to keep going back; they just recently found the box or coffin, or whatever it is, lifted it off the bottom; and brought it ashore early Sunday evening and were off-loading it when it slipped and crashed onto the deck. By about 8 pm that evening Robert Hopkins lay dead on the dock and Alex Walsh went missing.

Evans suggested it was a drug or counterfeit money smuggling deal gone bad – the box contained either some high-end cocaine or heroin, or a bale or more of fresh one hundred dollar bills. By extension of that theory, Hopkins and Walsh were meeting a buyer of the contents, they arrived and the discussion may have turned bad for some reason - when whatever it was fell out of the box and the bad guy or guys killed Hopkins and grabbed Walsh or killed him as well, and threw him into the channel and the tide took him out to open sea – overlooked after dark when it floated beyond the dock lights. But, why would they grab Walsh instead of just killing him as well...maybe to find out if they had recovered more than what was in the box and it was at either of their residences? If that was true, Brown should have learned of any strange visitors to either place...but she didn't mention anything about it earlier.

It was now about 5 pm, and he was getting hungry. His late breakfast with Brown had long since gone. Thinking of a solution, Nash also remembered the Cracked Conch was closed on Mondays...so he would have to settle for a burger somewhere – too far north of the Lorelei, his favorite watering hole and place to eat south of Key Largo. It was about 20 miles south, and there was much to be done before kicking back for the sunset ceremony at Lorelei, a 1-5-1 floater, stone crab soup and conch fritters. He only usually had one of those giant rum runner slushy thingy's crowned with a shot of 151 proof rum floating on top, but this case might cause him to reconsider that limit.

His visions about relaxing over a strong drink and food was broken when Brown pulled in opposite him where each vehicle driver could chat with each other – something learned while on patrol when officers gathered to gossip and still remained behind the wheel.

"Okay Sheila, you were pretty excited when you called – what do you have?" Nash asked.

"A shit load Nash...I took some pictures of the loot Walsh and Hopkins had been taking off the wreck in

Pennekamp Park and had a long talk with Elizabeth Hopkins. Although she freely showed me the stuff, do you think we should get a search warrant to confiscate the stuff they picked off the wreck....?" Brown chattered on.

"Hold on Sheila, slow down – I think the important part is what Elizabeth Hopkins had to say, and any others that might be involved in this case..."

"Oh yeah..." Brown tried to continue.

"Wait, let's pick up some burgers and fries and continue this at my office in the Plantation Key Substation

...we can spread everything out, print pictures and think this through a bit" Nash interrupted.

"Okay Rusty, I'm too juiced up to eat, but could use a coffee." Brown said.

"Sounds, like a plan. It's 5:20 right now; I'll meet you in an hour at my cube, second floor, at the Substation. Oh yes, I know this will be a hassle and make it a really long day - if you can find a judge, get search warrants, contact Metro Dade PD to assist us. You and I will serve them both at the Walsh and Hopkins residences after our meeting. We really need to take possession of anything that was illegally taken in the Park and will help us in this case....One more thing - Evans is likely to still be there so be prepared for that."

Brown nodded and pulled south on U.S. 1.

Nash sat down at the conference table in the center of the detective squad bay. He had a couple of Keys special double cheese burgers with fried onions and fresh avocados, and about a half pound of French fries from a little joint that caters largely to cops and members of the local fishing industry – guides, boat crews and pirates. The grill probably hadn't been cleaned in years, and flavored the burgers in a way the chain fast food places couldn't touch. After unwrapping his first burger, he was in half bite when Captain Evans and Community Relations Director, Anne Harris came out of Evan's office and sat down opposite him. Nash took his time chewing, silently staring back at the two men.

"This stuff is great! Sheila found out some interesting stuff in her trip north today, as well as me during my daylight visit to the marina and interview with likely the last person to see Hopkins and Walsh alive." Nash said after swallowing.

"Good, we need some facts; at least enough to sound competent at the press conference tomorrow at 9...here is the list of GPS waypoints you requested from the on-board unit. Note that one is listed as "Eagle," and best we can figure was visited last, but not sure exactly when." Evans said.

"Wow, great, thanks..." Nash said licking his fingers and wiping them with a paper napkin before taking the print out.

"Rusty, I need you and Brown to write and submit your preliminary follow-up reports now so we can use them for a press release soonest and of course for the conference tomorrow. The Sheriff will be the spokesperson and we need to give him as much information on this as possible...I will be meeting with him after I leave here." Harris said.

"Will do Anne. Err, Director – getting my notes in order and when Deputy Brown arrives will look at what she has and make a consolidated report and submit this evening."

Downstairs the desk officer buzzed in Sheila Brown; she hurried up the stairs where the men had gathered around the table.

"Good evening Captain Evans, Director Harris – Rusty..." she said, placing her shoulder bag, brief case, large coffee and a half eaten oatmeal raisin cookie on the table and sat down with a sigh.

She took a sip from her coffee, sat it down, and pulled out her digital camera and field notes from her shoulder bag. Looking over to Nash she asked "Are you ready for this?"

"Start from the beginning, we will try not to interrupt you..." Nash said, glancing to Evans and Harris.

"Oh-kay..." Brown started.

"I arrived at the Hopkins residence and met with Elizabeth Hopkins, wife of the deceased. She is still in pretty much shock about this whole thing; I guess anyone would be...anyway..." She stopped as Nash interrupted.

"Did Metro Dade show up when you were there?" Nash asked.

"Yeah, so did an agent from FDLE; he was helpful..." Brown said.

"Helpful..." Nash parroted.

"Yes Rusty, I know that's hard to believe. Anyway, I asked her about her husband's reason to be at the marina, Walsh, and anyone else that she knew to be associated with why he was there. She told me that Robert and his friend Alex Walsh were longtime friends – hunted, fished, lobstered, and dove together for years. Although the boat belonged to Hopkins, Walsh helped to outfit it with a state of the art GPS, hoist, and other related dive gear such as the large industrial strength yellow lift bags. According to Mrs. Hopkins, they discovered a wreck in 1992 right after Hurricane Andrew came through. It was under another wreck – apparently

Andrew moved enough of the newer wreck, if you can call a wreck sunk there around 1827 newer. Anyway, Hopkins theorized the wreck that lay on top was a Spanish slave smuggling/pirate vessel named the *El Pepe*. Hopkins told his wife he believed the older wreck had sunk there likely in a violent fashion in mid or late 1600's because of the stuff they brought up, and where they found them; many of which had been mixed in the *Pepe's* debris field. This is where it gets interesting: The first thing they found in 1992 was very valuable; it also really screwed with their minds – it was gold alright, but it was not typical treasure find, it was a gold figure of an Eagle and inscribed banner at its top. Hopkins researched it and discovered it was called an "Aquila," a standard that was carried on a long staff ahead of a Roman Legion as they marched, and into battle. In ancient times the eagle was a symbol of strength, courage, and immortality – very powerful "ju-ju" to The Romans. Normally these things were made of silver, or maybe bronze – not gold; very unusual. I asked Mrs. Hopkins to release the Eagle to me. She did and I gave her a written receipt for it, and this is it..."

Brown, to increase the drama left the Eagle at the doorway. She turned to Nash...".

"Rusty can you help me with it?" She said walking toward the object wrapped in layers of newspaper secured by duct tape.

Gently laying the Eagle on the squad room table, she cut open the wrapping and exposed the artifact.

"...As you can see it is in almost perfect condition except for the part of the banner at the top – you can see clearly an inscription of "SPQR", this according to what the deceased told his wife, stands for *Senatus Populus Romanus*; an honorarium used by the ancient Romans much like we use USA. I remember seeing it on public buildings when visiting Rome a few years ago, was always curious of its meaning. The rest of the inscription, according to Mrs. Hopkins likely named the Roman Legion or military organization it represented. Aside from the Eagle, everything else except for the box was pretty standard stuff coming off a wreck of a particular period. In the rest of the cases there were pieces of pottery, encrusted globs of cannon balls, silver and gold coins; stuff like that. Hopkins had everything cataloged and on display in a special room he had built for his loot, to include the Eagle, which as you can imagine took a prominent place in his little museum."

After getting over the initial shock of seeing an artifact of solid gold, they sat door around the table.

"As far as I can tell, neither Hopkins nor Walsh ever sold or tried to sell anything that came off this wreck. Money apparently was not their goal, unlocking mysteries, and just finding interesting shit was their hobby. There seems to be no one else Hopkins involved in this deal; his wife said she only ever remembers hearing Robert speak of Alex Walsh." Brown reported.

"How about Walsh...any sign that he was into anything else other than working with Hopkins and the self-satisfaction of finding stuff from old wrecks?"

"No, none, I spoke with his roommate who is a cop at the UM in Coral Gables, and said Walsh was always over at Hopkins house or out on the boat with him. He is divorced and lives pretty spartanly I might add; no girlfriend right now as far as the roommate knew, no guys in long overcoats coming around either. The roommate has not heard from Walsh for about 72 hours."

"The roommate does have a name, and you got the contact information, right Brown?" asked Evans.

"Yes Captain, he does, and I did, and it will go in my report." Brown said rolling her eyes.

"You've been around Nash to long already..." Evans said with a smile.

"Tell us about the box. Did Hopkins mention any of that to his wife?" Nash asked.

"Well, he did – they found it last Friday, on the 8th and wasn't until this Sunday were they able to get it out of the coral and barnacle growth around it and float it. It apparently weighed a lot and they were working to avoid being caught by the Marine Patrol or Park authorities." Brown answered.

"That pretty much answers the question about whether they pulled a permit to excavate the wreck, but I still will confirm that." Nash said.

"Anything else Deputy Brown? Evans asked.

"No, except for my personal sense that, although these guys were illegally pulling stuff off a wreck, they were not making any money doing it, and considering the apparent length of time the box was on the bottom, which I might add was at least 350 years – the same box that is key to the theory it contained dope or hundred dollar bills – were not smuggling drugs or counterfeit money, just being at the wrong place at the right time...and what the right time was, and who killed Hopkins remains a mystery that cannot yet be explained in a context we understand." Brown responded.

"Considering the new information on the box, and what we have just learned about activities of a 10 year period, the original motive theory for the killer or killers pretty much is out the window. It appears the box had been on the bottom for a lot longer than we originally thought, and likely did not contain dope or dollars. So is the box still central to our murder? And if it is, what was in it that was so important that it was worth a man's life?" Evan observed as he looked around the table.

The phone in Evan's office rang, and he got up from the conference table to answer. While Nash was thinking about the new information, he picked for remnants of french fries at the bottom of the burger bag. Harris suggested..."Well, we may be talking about a treasure related murder then..."

"I agree with Phil, the dope or dollar theory doesn't make sense anymore...I think the box held something, something that cost Robert Hoskins his life, but what? If Alex Walsh is not dead, I would really like to talk to him – if he did not kill his old friend and partner, he knows who did and why. I think Walsh is key to our investigation at this point...I asked the Marine Patrol to keep a watch for a floater between the marina and reef in case my key witness is also dead" Nash said as Evans returned from his phone call and stood by the table after having picked a sucker out of a candy jar on Nash's desk.

"Rusty, you are going to love this. The pathologist who did the autopsy this morning got a call from what has been called a "distinguished colleague" from Scotland named Dr. Mark Galen, who offers to consult *pro bono* on this case. Galen and his assistant, Dr. Coleen Jones are flying in from Turkey on a private jet just to help work this case. The Sheriff has approved it and you will be getting more help as of Friday morning. They arrive at MIA tonight and will be staying at the Bayside Resort in Key Largo. You are to meet his assistant Dr. Coleen Jones at the hotel restaurant on Friday at 9 am sharp" Evans said smiling sarcastically.

"That's fucking wonderful" Nash said under his breath as he took the last gulp of his soda.

Nash didn't like working with civilians, especially those called "distinguished colleagues." This all sounded like code words for dorks; dorks that would get in the way, dorks that he would have to explain things to...

Chapter 11 - The Acolyte

"...Thrilling to think, poor child of sin! It was the dead who groaned within..."

Edgar Allen Poe, *the Sleeper*, 1831

Running up the stairs from the basement sanctuary, hoping to catch a glimpse of his escaped prisoner, Cassidy became painfully aware that the sun's rays were not a friend to his kind. As he reached the top and turned toward the outside doorway, the Florida sun bathed his face in its glow with the delicacy of molten lead. Recoiling from the pain, Cassidy retreated back into the shadows. His kind endured a genetic transformation as a price paid to join the community of vampires. A vampire's skin exhibits high sensitivity to all three ultraviolet radiation wavelengths from the earth's sun – reacting with immediate formation of free radicals and triggering germicidal-like attacks on his living cells as if they were foreign bodies. This condition obligated him and his kind to live a life in the shadows, totally covered, or as a creature of the night.

This was a time of decision. His fresh food source was now gone; he knew very little about the land he now was forced to inhabit, and no keeper or guardian to look after him. He was also very much in need to feed again soon, as well as more solid protein food, and water, lots of sweet water. He could only reconstitute properly if he had these and now, awake and exposed to the open air; otherwise he would wither and die. Cassidy concluded he needed to return to the only other place he knew, the place where he was awakened and seek out answers and nourishment there. First, he realized he needed to attend to his appearance. A glance at himself in broken piece of glass revealed a person that would, if discovered by the other inhabitants of this "...Florida" would certainly command some interest; the kind he now needed to avoid. Using the sharp edge of his dagger, Cassidy trimmed his hair, finger and toe nails – the latter were especially tender having been confined inside his shoes and grew in a curious circular fashion. Lastly he successfully shaved his full beard into a goatee and mustache of the fashion he was accustomed to while in Scotland. Finding some pooled rain water from a recent shower, he washed his face and hands of any remnants of the ghoulish enterprise he engaged in at the dock.

At sundown, Cassidy abandoned his hiding place at the old base and began the walk back to Carysfort Reef Marina. He found the trail he had made through the mangrove, carefully avoiding a highway he could hear to his right as he walked. He also sensed the salty expanse of the sea to his left. He kept each smell to his flanks and walked between the two to the marina.

In about an hour Cassidy approached the edge of the gravel expanse he had dragged his prisoner. He surveyed the area for the people he remembered seeing that night. There were no pulsating blue and red lights, but there were the same black and white horseless vehicles Walsh described as cars parked near where he was so abruptly dropped onto the dock. To the right was another of them with a single person sitting in it – blocking entry from the outside.

He chose as his destination the buildings on the other side of the open area. He decided to conceal himself in the trees leading up to the car with the single person inside. As he approached through the darkness he heard strange gravelly voices coming from the car and the person seemed to be ignoring them. First one would speak and then another – but they were nowhere to be found in the car or outside of it; the person inside just sat silent as he read from a book by way of a directed beam of light with no flame. How these people have mastered light and energy sources he knew nothing about – or at least not yet. The car was also emitting a foul smelling smoke from two pipes at one end. This was the same burning oil smell he experienced the night he was forced to flee this place after he was awakened.

Passing behind the car in a crouch, Cassidy walked past the distracted deputy in the patrol car. As Cassidy crept, the Deputy heard or sensed something and looked up. He looked in his rear view mirrors above the windshield and on both sides of his vehicle. Cassidy stood motionless in the brushes just to the left of the car. The Deputy, seeing nothing in his mirrors went back to his reading and coffee.

Proceeding toward a cluster of small buildings away from the activity, he smelled an aroma of food being prepared. It was heavy and sweet smelling, a sensory stimulation he had not experienced for a long time – even before the voyage, before he was forced to flee from the likes of Galenicus. He could see light coming from a house floating on pontoons in the water at the far end of the dock. It too had one of those cars parked near it. He concluded cars were the way these people get around in this time – they were the new beasts of burden. As he approached he noticed the door to the cabin was ajar and could see inside.

Seth Holmes had just put several pieces of fried conch, broiled yellow fin tuna, and french fries on an oversized paper plate into the microwave for his supper. The assortment of seafood was from what he had collected from plates while bussing off tables at Billy's Tiki bar, where Holmes had been working for the past three months. He worked for minimum wage, and considered "hardly touched" seafood, steaks, burgers, and fries he collected in "to go" boxes each night as his fringe benefits. On good nights what he brought home was enough food to feed him for several days at a time.

The sun had set, but the warm tropical air hung heavy after a late afternoon rain shower. Holmes didn't have central air conditioning on the old houseboat so it was his custom to open his cabin door and several windows to get a cross breeze to cool off his living spaces. The buzzer rang as the warming cycle expired on his microwave. He got up from his television where he had been playing a game all afternoon and walked into his kitchenette to retrieve his dinner when a voice from the doorway diverted his attention.

"Good evening mate, I smelled your food cooking and couldn't resist not coming by and complimenting you on it..." Cassidy said as he smiled and bent slightly at the waist with a flourish of his right hand.

Holmes turned wide eyed just in time to see Cassidy's flourish. Although still startled, his surprise subsided and collected himself enough to respond.

"Wow!! I nearly shit my pants – didn't think anyone else was in the marina, err, allowed inside the marina since the murder...and the police are all over the place..." Holmes said nervously as he squinted past Cassidy in the open door, toward the police cars at the dock area and then at the entrance.

Cassidy also turned to understand what the curious little man was describing. Quickly, Cassidy assessed the situation on the floating house. It was remote, out of the way, but accessible to the outside world, and most importantly he now learned - a source of nourishment in all forms, and likely water to complete his recovery from the centuries in the suffocating dark.

Holmes' glance returned to the stranger at his door. He thought the man was dressed in clothing much like a celebration of "dress like a pirate" day at Captain Billy's – but that is in September...a bit odd, but the Keys was a harbor for odd things and people... Holmes also considered how this guy had got past the police who were all over the place – and what exactly he really wanted? Beside the pirate garb, he noticed the man's hair was scraggily cut and he could certainly use a bath. His Scottish accent reminded him of Sean Connery in the

Highlander movie, also a title of one of his favorite video games. Holmes was convinced the guy was homeless, a condition he had shared and knew well for most of his life after being discharged from the Navy at Key West.

"Please come in, are you hungry?" Holmes asked as he put down his gaming device on the counter by the microwave.

"I am delighted to join you – truth be known, I haven't really eaten a real meal for eons." Cassidy said in a tongue and cheek fashion.

As Cassidy entered his eyes locked onto the television set – one side of the square box blazed with moving images, color and sounds that further added to the mystery of the time he found himself.

Holmes laughed nervously and turned to dish up the fish and french fries onto two paper plates. He reached into the plastic bag he used to bring the food home from the restaurant and produced two plastic forks. He gave a plate and fork to Cassidy.

"Can I get you something to drink?" Holmes said, remembering to be a good host.

"Aye, anything will do, ale, beer, wine, or water." Cassidy replied.

"I do have some beer, would that be okay?"

"Aye." Cassidy said as he began eating with his hands, disregarding the peculiar instrument his host had handed him.

Holmes opened a can of beer and handed it to Cassidy, who focused on the can as he took it. How curious he thought as a vessel for beer. He particularly noticed its cold temperature, and the circular hole at the top. He looked at the refrigerator, not understanding how the can stored inside that box was so cold. He brought it to his nose to smell the bubbling liquid; then smiled and took a long drink of it and sat back with a great smile followed by a long baritone burp. Holmes curiously watched Cassidy's behavior. He soon dismissed the man's eccentric behavior and turned his attention to his own dinner, dishing it up and returned to the couch. As he sat down, he glanced at Cassidy who had literally inhaled the plate of food and was quickly draining the beer.

"You are not from around here are you?"

"Nay, I am not. Please forgive me, permit me to introduce myself – I am Angus Cassidy, late of...Scotland." Cassidy said, hoping that Scotland was still a place recognizable for this man.

"I arrived a few days ago."

"Wow, a few days ago – my name is Seth Holmes from Michigan, but now call Key Largo my home."

Holmes responded between chewing on mouths full of fried fish.

Setting down his paper plate, Holmes took a long gulp of his own beer, and then began to survey the man whose story and appearance really didn't seem to add up. His clothes and everything about him was a bit off – thinking this guy might be involved with the murder the detective had mentioned and why the cops were still in the marina. He got up from his couch to move closer to his cell phone; somewhere he thought was on the kitchen bar.

"I am sure thou arte thinking about where I came from – my clothing and my appearance here this evening." Cassidy said, calculating his approach to Holmes.

To Cassidy, Holmes resembled many of whom he had enlisted as keepers and guardians over the centuries; the type that lived on the edges of their own society, many that could not quite fit in, many of whom looked to him as their way out of the struggle and into meaningful existences. His plan was to first confound and subjugate Holmes by way of a technique learned during his transformation at Sogdian Rock.

Holmes would have not been Cassidy's first choice, but now he was the only choice to serve Cassidy as an interface with the people of this time, a procurer of fresh blood, food, and information, as well as the precursors needed to make precious metals according to the ancient recipes of his father Angr'a Mainyu. Smelling Holmes' growing apprehension – his increased sweat flow and his sweet rich blood seemed to glow as it raced through his veins. Cassidy sensed it was the time to act.

Standing as if to stretch Cassidy moved quickly to Holmes and pinned him to the couch with one hand over his heart, the second on his mouth and throat. He whispered for him to remain still and not struggle. Holmes' wide eyes reflected his terror and grasped both Cassidy's wrists, and gave off a frightened whimper.

"Master Holmes...I will not hurt ye, if ye remain calm and do not do anything that would appear to me as an attempt to run away or to attract the attention of the authorities still outside....do you understand me?" Cassidy whispered into Holmes' ear, his face nearly touching Holmes'.

Holmes, turned his eyes in the direction of Cassidy's face and made a nod with his head. Cassidy lightened his grasp of Holmes and backed away, then released him altogether.

"What do you want?"

"Master Holmes, first – look at images of light from this box of fire and sound." Cassidy said in a low deliberate voice, all the time motioning toward the television screen.

"Watch me hands and fingers as they tell a story of understanding and peace..." Cassidy continued moving his hands rhythmically in front of the screen as he spoke slowly, then in a low chant the Enki used to confound humans.

Holmes was immediately transfixed on Cassidy's digitally backlit hand dance and the sound of his voice. In seconds his alarmed defensive posture transformed to one of focused attention; his facial expression from one of alarm, to sublime peace. Holmes was now under Cassidy's control, and only Cassidy could break the connection. Cassidy moved away from the television and sat in a chair to its right. Holmes remained focused on the television and repeating game images on the glowing screen.

"Master Holmes, look at me."

Holmes slowly turned his trance like focus to Cassidy. Cassidy then leaned forward to Holmes.

"Seth Holmes, when I wave my hand in front of your face you will come to the present, ye will talk and appear as ye always have, but ye will still do what I command of ye as your master. I am thou'st master. Only

I will have the authority to command ye. Do ye understand me?" Cassidy said slowly and calmly.

"...Yes I do." Holmes said.

Cassidy sat back and waved his open hand past Holmes' face.

Holmes' demeanor changed. He blinked and went back to his supper.

"Can I get you anything else...err, master?"

"I want ye to listen to my story, and to work for me, and for thou'st efforts will make ye a very rich man" Cassidy said as his eyes locked with Holmes.

"Now we're talkin'...being rich...now we're talkin'. Holmes said leaning back into his couch crossing his legs in anticipation of learning how that was going to come about and what he had to do for this new boss.

At this, Cassidy got up, closed and locked the cabin door to include all the windows in the room. His plan, now that Holmes was under Cassidy's control, was to appeal to Holmes' baser instincts of greed and sex, and possibly to feed on him and that could get noisy.

"To answer thou'st first concern, I did kill that man the other night...but let me tell you why; and that will involve a story from thou'st standpoint, the incredible ranting of a lunatic – but nonetheless true...be silent, listen and believe me."

Holmes shifted his hands from his lap to either side of his hips in compliance with Cassidy's command. Holmes bid Cassidy to proceed.

Cassidy wove his tale, but at the last he commanded Holmes never to speak of it, nor question him further about his past – only thing he had to remember was complying with Cassidy as his master, and he would be greatly rewarded. Following his admonishment of Holmes, Cassidy sensed it was time to transform himself into a man of the 21st century.

"Holmes, can ye help me to find clothing and a discrete barber to bring me hair, beard, and nails under control after so many years?"

"You know, I was a barber in the Navy and trained to do all those things...and pretty good too!! As for clothing, I think I have at least one outfit – pants, shirt, and tennis shoes that would fit you. We can go shopping later...but first, how about a shower? I'll bet you haven't had a good bath in hundreds of years." Holmes said smiling.

Holmes led Cassidy to his bathroom and shower stall. He handed Cassidy a towel and showed him where the soap was located.

"Throw your clothes in a pile on the floor, and I'll throw them away. While you are showering I'll bring your new duds."

"...Duds?"

"Clothes...sorry."

Holmes went into his bedroom around the corner and went through his closet for a suitable outfit for Cassidy – both were about 5'9" but Cassidy was much thinner. After several minutes, Holmes stopped to listen for water from the shower. He heard nothing coming from the bathroom. Curious, he knocked on the door.

"Master, is there anything wrong?"

"Ye have a very small bathing receptacle Holmes...I don't know why you call it a shower." Cassidy responded.

Holmes opened the door to see Cassidy dipping the towel into the toilet bowl, and washing himself with its wet end.

"I'm so sorry master!! I forgot to tell you about a shower." Holmes said as he walked over to the shower stall.

Cassidy stood up and followed Holmes looking very perplexed.

"See, Master – this is the place you can shower, and these are the water controls." Holmes said as he twisted the hot and then the cold water faucet.

"This one is for hot water, and this one is for cold. You can adjust them to suit yourself. See twisting them counter-clockwise to start the water flow, and clockwise to stop it. After you are finished, turn off all the water – it is expensive here in the Keys." Holmes said as he stepped back to permit Cassidy to step in and begin his education in the mysteries of turning on water faucets.

Holmes was not sure if Cassidy was embarrassed and angry at him, and stood silent while Cassidy practiced turning the water on and off, and balancing its temperature. After he felt the task was mastered, Cassidy stepped back and locked his eyes with Holmes...then gave out a loud laugh and slapped him on the shoulder. Holmes gave a relieved laugh as well and fetched Cassidy a dry towel.

"Your new clothes will be on the sink here when you finish. Oh yes, if you need something for your dry skin, use this..." Holmes said holding up a bottle of aloe lotion.

Holmes then disappeared through the door. Cassidy turned his attention to taking his first shower and washing off the dust of centuries from his dry skin.

After finishing his shower Cassidy was invigorated, but needed blood to top off his evening. With some difficulty mastering the zipper, he successfully put on the clothes Holmes selected for him. He returned to the living room where Holmes had reengaged in his video game.

"How do I look?

"Great, err much better at least, but first we need to tend to that bush of hair on your head. Please come over and sit down in this wooden chair and I will get my scissors." Holmes said motioning to the chair at the kitchen table he was dragging into the bathroom..

Cassidy sat down as Holmes secured a small sheet around his neck. Cassidy sat motionless as Holmes clipped and combed his master's hair. He then applied shaving cream to the beard from an aerosol can, much to the amusement of Cassidy who took it and examined the container while Holmes retrieved a straight razor.

Sensing the razor as a possible weapon, he asked as he looked deep into the little man's eyes.

"We are not going to hurt one another are we Holmes?"

"No Master, we are not." Holmes responded returning to a trance like demeanor.

By way of the kitchen mirror, Cassidy directed Holmes how to shave him, leaving a goatee and mustache combination he had worn during his former life in Scotland. When finished, Holmes added some after shave and hair dressing finalizing Cassidy's new look with a comb.

"Now, you definitely look like a different man!!" Holmes said smiling over Cassidy's shoulder as both peered into the mirror.

"Yes...I... do!" Cassidy said as he stood up and walked back into Holmes' living room.

He got to the center of the room and turned to Holmes.

"Holmes, I need ye to do something for me. First, I need ye to walk me around your little house and explain to me things I should know about, how ye make light without flames, cook and warm food without fire, keep things cool without ice, what that thing is on the table that shows moving pictures of people and sounds of their voice, and above all how people communicate and get around; specifically about that contraption out front..." Cassidy said pointing to the car parked on the gravel lot just off the dock.

"I also want ye to take me out tonight to a place where people gather in this Key Largo, I want to be around people of this time – and have a need to feed..." Cassidy said to Holmes who stood in front of Cassidy at a position of intent interest and obedience.

"Yes Master, I can do both, I aim to please you." Holmes said as he put his hand on the television to begin Cassidy's education about the 21st century.

Chapter 12 - Warm...Warmer

"...It's hard to believe this city started as a trading post...Home to the Seminole, pirate and pioneer..."

Jimmy Buffet, *Everyone's Got a Cousin in Miami,*

1994

Looking out her cabin window, Coleen Jones stared transfixed at the runway landing lights shooting past in the final landing approach. Feeling a drop, then the landing gear touched and chirped on the runway at Miami International Airport. It had been a very long day. She stretched out her nearly six foot frame in her seat, leaning back into the cushion – grasping a lock of her dark hair, she felt sticky and imaged just how good a warm shower would feel – and needed a good long run. Seeing her reflection in the screen of her tablet, her nose looked like it was about to break out in acne. At nearly 30 she thought it a battle she was never going to win, but she had no life anyway – for now.

It had been nearly 23 hours since she has bathed or had any decent sleep. The chartered Lear 55 jet was the only way her employer would travel, but sadly did not have the range for a direct flight and required several legs that brought them from Ankora to Barcelona, then Rejkjavik, Halifax, Nova Scotia, in Canada, then finally the United States, to Key Largo via Miami in steamy south Florida.

She looked over her shoulder to Dr. Galen, her employer seated in the rear of the cabin. He was oblivious to their landing, deeply concentrating on completing his notes on what they had learned in Derinkuyu. Galen was a renowned haematologist specializing in genetics. He was also a vampire, and nearly 1900 years old, but she often lampooned an age related saying in thinking yesterday's 1900 is today's 50. Galen's life has been devoted to means of combatting his own genetic mutation and to seek out and kill the vampire who infected and made him: Tacitus Cassius, onetime commander of the Roman Legions in Syria and pretender to the throne of Marcus Aurelius; and who knows who else before him. Such was her lot now.

The revelation that vampires really exist, but not quite the same as in books or in movies, was a concept she found somewhat easier than most. She was a formally trained classical scholar, with a PhD in Classics from the University of Glasgow, specialized in deciphering ancient code and writing – her work also made her one of the leading authorities in Scotland on palimpsests, ink, and etymology. Palimpsest is a word derivative from the Latin, further derived from the Greek which means "scratched or scraped again." It was a technique used on parchment or vellum after a shortage of Egyptian papyrus occurred, and ancient writers broadened their use of parchment made from various animal hides as the common medium for books, decrees, letters, etc. The downside was that parchment was expensive; the upside was that was a very hardy medium and could be reused by washing or scraping off previously written text from the parchment with a pumice stone or something similar. It was a form of ancient recycling.

In her work, Coleen had deciphered secret writing intentionally scrapped off and overwritten to conceal the text from anyone but those initiated into the mysteries of the technique. The existence of vampires like Dr. Galen or Tacitus Cassius and their roles in world history was startling, but they were just parts of a larger body of revelation she had read in ancient text, and had to accept in her life.

As the plane taxied to the international terminal and U.S. Customs she opened her tablet and to read from the *Miami Herald* online edition on the latest reporting on the murder that brought her and Galen nearly 7000 miles. Nothing much new, just a continuing summary of what she already knew; the murder took place in a place south of Miami in the northern most tip of the Florida Keys called Carysfort Reef Marina. The victim was a man who had been savagely murdered, ripped open from his navel to throat and curiously had less than a millilitre of blood left in the body. He with his partner had been secretly and illegally excavating an undocumented 17th century wreck strung out over a reef in the waters of Pennekamp State Park. They had recovered a coffin-like box located two days prior on the wreck, and from what the police had pieced together were in the process of transferring it to the dock in the marina when the murder occurred. The man's partner was still missing, and there we no other suspects. The Monroe County Sheriff's Department was in charge of the investigation.

This was the second trip away from home in Scotland since becoming Galen's keeper/guardian and co-worker in his search for Galen's maker. The first was to examine some used and unused Latin language palimpsests discovered in a sealed jar under debris in the abandoned 1st century Panagia monastery's library, or scriptorium near Derinkuyu, Turkey. The second was to here in Florida and what Dr. Galen thought was evidence of the reemergence of the subject of his search over nearly two millennia.

After clearing U.S. Customs, Coleen found the limousine driver and arranged for their luggage be loaded into his vehicle. When all was ready, she collected Dr.

Galen in the executive waiting room and escorted him through the crowd and to the car waiting at the international arrival pick=up area. In exiting the terminal to the street she noticed the cool dry aircraft cabin and terminal building was replaced with the humid sub-tropical heat of south Florida. She quickly took her seat in the car and leaned back into the back rest and closed her eyes. After negotiating around heavy traffic they were heading south on the Palmetto Expressway and the Florida Turnpike for the Bayside Resort in Key Largo. As they pulled into the hotel entrance way, her first task after several drinks, a warm bath, a meal and a good night's sleep, would be to contact with the lead investigator in the murder. She was about to meet Detective Rusty Nash.

Chapter 13 - My Esteemed Colleagues

"...With chains upon my feet...you know that ghost is me.
And I will never be set free as long as I'm a ghost that you can't
see..."

Gordon Lightfoot, *If You Could Read My Mind*, 1969

After checking in for both Galen and herself, Coleen returned to the Bayside Resort lobby where Dr. Galen was sitting. He was on his cell phone with the pathologist who conducted the autopsy on Robert Hopkins. He was also a former student of Galen's, Dr. Sanjay Bhatnagar.

"Yes, Sanjay...I look forward to our meeting as well and thank you for an opportunity to examine the body...and for vouching for my assistant and I with the authorities. You say the findings from the lab are also available? Excellent...see you then" Galen said as he hung up and fixed his attention on Coleen who had been patiently waiting for him to conclude his conversation.

"Coleen, I know both of us are very tired, but let's get together in about 45 minutes to discuss our plan of action and your meeting with the detective tomorrow. There are a few things I need to know about this man if we are going to maximize our work with him on this important project...is that satisfactory?" Galen asked.

"Of course, and you are right about being tired, and I really could use a bath and a drink. How about I have room service send us up some supper to your suite in about an hour for both of us?" Coleen asked as she handed over his room card and envelope.

"Perfect, that would be perfect...see you then..." Galen said, getting up and motioning the bellman to follow him to the elevator with his luggage.

Coleen then asked a second bellman to take her luggage to her room; that she would be up shortly and handed him a tip, hoping that was enough. He smiled and headed toward the elevator with her luggage. She looked around the lobby for the entrance to the hotel bar. Following the rock band music, she found it. As she approached, she paused at the doorway. She thought a drink sounded good, but considering how tired she was – maybe that should wait. Besides she was not in the mood for the crowd and noise. Instead she turned and walked across the lobby to the outside pool comfortably oriented toward Florida Bay to the northwest. Away from the crowd in the bar, the evening was quite, and no one was in the pool. This was a perfect time for a swim she thought; no one around, and quite private. Moments like this evoked fond memories when she and Michael playfully piled their clothes on the beach and slipped into the warm Mediterranean while vacationing or on his business trips...nights like this became the foundations for memorable adventures routinely ending in tender love making embraced by the warm silky waters.

Behind her the automatic door slid open and a young couple walking hand in hand passed behind her to the pool, stopping to admire the moonlit bay. The interruption helped Coleen shake off her slipping deeper into the nostalgia of the moment, blinking it away, she returned to the hotel lobby. Checking her watch, she now had about 40 minutes to get a good soaking bath and change into some comfortable clothes befitting the sub-tropics. She headed directly to her room.

***

With a bath and a change of clothes Coleen felt a bit more like discussing business than before. Once inside Galen's suite, Coleen plunked herself down in an overstuffed chair in his small living room and pulled out a mini-bar sized bottle of single-malt Scottish whiskey from her pocket.

"You didn't bring any for me?" Galen asked smiling as he sat down opposite her, opening his laptop.

"...err, no, err yes – the whisky is in the mini-bar. I'll get you one; ice or no ice? She asked getting up and heading to his mini-bar and ice bucket.

"No ice, nice and neat as usual. I just gave myself a treatment and am good to go for another several days." Galen said referring to the serum he had developed to satisfy the need for human blood and decrease the effects of the rays of the sun on his skin, the former something very important in pleasant society and the latter for south Florida even in November.

After pouring each mini-bottle of the whiskey into their glasses, Coleen handed Galen his, paused and tapped it with hers, then returned to her chair. Each took a long pull on the glasses. Coleen paused to feel the journey of the wonderful liquid to its destination, and then set the glass down.

"Shall we?" Galen asked.

"I have two items for this evening. The first is how we shall proceed as consultants in this case; for any need of a cover story regarding the findings of Dr. Bhatnagar's examination of the body and the pathology reports of the foreign material found in the body cavity itself.   The second subject is the person of detective Russell Nash. I'll proceed in that order...I suspect that the pathology of the glutinous material found in the body cavity came from a vampire, most notably and likely the resurrected pretender emperor, Gaius Tacitus Cassius. The circumstances associated with the victim and his partner finding a coffin-like box from an unknown wrecked ship of the mid to late 17th century in roughly the same location the *Edith Louise* may have been lost is maybe coincidental, but what happened when the container was opened leads me to believe we are on the right track. Imagine being imprisoned on Carysfort Reef for the last 400 hundreds years in a deep catatonic-like sleep, easy at first, then as time passes into centuries the body slowing consuming itself, as it begins to smother in the vacuum of the chamber...this was the man who was on the brink of controlling the Roman Empire reduced in his imprisonment to be only the emperor of fish, of coral rock, of an insignificant crag in the ocean – from the Emperor of Rome to the Emperor of Carysfort Reef. There is one more thing, more immediate confirmation - when we got out of the car at the hotel entrance tonight I sensed his presence, one that I have not tasted in almost 500 years. It is one I remember well. It was weak, but it was there....Regarding Detective Nash...”

Just then the phone rang to announce that room service was waiting in the hallway with their dinners.

Coleen got up and invited them in to serve their dinners and wine.

"Very nice selection on the pinot noir Coleen..." Galen said swirling the wine in his glass, then tasting it.

After the service staff left, they resumed over their dinners.

"As you remember, during my last pursuit of Cassidy I went as far as the British colony of Bermuda. I learned the ship carrying Cassidy had passed through there over a month before, and put off four crewmen and the captain who were suffering from a strange illness much like the plague I had encountered in the city of Aquileia before meeting Cassius...err Cassidy...let's call him Cassidy for now...Bottom line Coleen this was not a plague of the normal variety – it was one caused by being fed on by a vampire – compounded by topical infections introduced into the body through the wound made for feeding on the host's blood. The evidence I collected from talking to these men led me to conclude they had been fed upon by a vampire, in this case Cassidy; probably on more than one occasion. Coupled with the unhygienic conditions on board ship plying the Atlantic in the 17th century – sailors didn't bath regularly or at all, rats infested their living and eating spaces – it was predictable that any untreated wound would facilitate infection of this sort to penetrate the body, in this case bodies weakened by loss of blood and the effects of the saliva of a vampire...When a vampire feeds upon a human and chooses not to take too much, killing them, or infect them to become a vampire; a very small part of the altered vampire DNA is transferred to the host via interaction between the saliva and host's blood. If the wound is cleaned and treated properly; even according to crude 17th century medicine, the host survives. There however are some side-effects: After recovery, probably in a month or so, the host experiences increased intuition, and sensory capabilities – of smell, touch, taste, etc. From a small sample of known hosts I have studied, their lifespan was also lengthened...What is interesting, is that they pass on to their male descendants; male descendants only, these same qualities. That brings me to my interviews with the crew left behind in Bermuda..." Galen said as he directed his attention to his laptop computer,

"I had all my field notes scanned over the years to a digital form just in case I needed them away from my lab...Ah, here are my notes for the period...forgive me for reading them to you...

"...Thursday, 27 October 1695 – Arrived St. George's on the morning tide. Met with the harbor master to learn the ship, "Edith Louise" had made a port call at that city on 29 August of this year, and departed on the following day's tide after taking on fresh food & water, and beer.

The ship's company beyond the crew included passengers Laird Angus Cassidy of Logie, Perthshire, Scotland and his servants, William and Gillian Brodie. Five of the crew was put ashore because they were unfit for duty. Among those sent to a makeshift seaman's dispensary run by a Mrs. Butterfield, Cut Road, St. George's Island, included –

- ∞ Captain Jonathan Bobb, Master of the Scottish privateer ship, Edith Louise.
- ∞ Michael Lea, Able Seaman, Glasgow, of the Scottish privateer ship, Edith Louise.
- ∞ Will Nash, Ordinary Seaman, Glasgow, of the Scottish privateer ship, Edith Louise.
- ∞ Philip Stone, Ordinary Seaman, Glasgow, of the Scottish privateer ship, Edith Louise.
- ∞ Wade Tynes, Able Seaman, Glasgow, of the Scottish privateer ship, Edith Louise.

I visited Mrs. Butterfield's dispensary on Friday evening, 28 October. She was an agreeable woman with much too much to do. I explained I was a physician and offered to see her patients, *with a particular interest in the men she took in from the Edith Louise. Since I also offered the medications I brought with me, she permitted me in...*

...Parenthetically Coleen, your great grandfather, let me see...about 9 times removed, Benjamin Jones, accompanied me with a small security detachment to Bermuda. Historically to that time, small private armies or security contingents were common in the entourage of the well to do. However, eventually engaging these types of men, openly armed, often caused me to stick out and eventually chose only to have a single keeper/guardian who could hire security help when needed. Back then, not knowing what I was to find there – possibly Cassidy himself, I thought it best to come in force...I did not learn until my visit to the island that Cassidy and his party sailed with the ship...

"...I first was taken to Jonathan Bobb. He was sitting up in a rope & straw bed he shared with ship's officer from another vessel. According to Mrs. Butterworth, the fever had left Bobb but he was still weak and often had violent nightmares, which was not appreciated by his bed mate..."

....Coleen, this goes on for a while with some extended diagnoses of Bobb and the crewman. The crewmen, as low ranking sailors were given hammocks in the second and third floor of her home. I will cut to the chase. All these men had been fed upon by a vampire on that ship not long after leaving Glasgow and throughout the voyage to Bermuda. Each of them shared a similar experience of something visiting them in their sleep, feeling a slight needle like prick by the base of their neck, and an unexplainable sense of stimulation, almost like being sexually aroused; then deep sleep. The more times these men experienced this, the sicker they became. Robb recalls having this experience 7 times after leaving Glasgow – and he was the sickest...Before leaving the island a ship docked from Jamaica. The master of the ship had been in Port Royal for 3 months before being commissioned to his current position. He had seen ships come and go from the harbor. The *Edith Louise* never reached Jamaica...About our cover stories - In offering substantive help to the Monroe County authorities I aim to focus on the pathology of the wound, the foreign material in it, and things technical. Tomorrow while you are visiting with Nash, I will be meeting with Sanjay Bhatnagar. He is permitting me to examine the body as well as see the laboratory results from the specimens and artifacts he collected from it. Hopefully, if he has not already conducted one, Sanjay will permit me to request a DNA analysis of the foreign material to compare against my own for evidence of a similar type of missense mutation in any of the DNA we can identify. Let's plan to have supper together tomorrow evening around 7 – I'll arrange to have them bring something in like this evening so we can work and discuss our day's findings...About your meeting with Detective Nash. He will no doubt feel a bit put out by having the two of us piggy-backing on his investigation, so, be as helpful as possible. He will no doubt be asking you what you can do for him and why are you and I so interested in this case. As my cover story is de-mystifying the pathology of the remains of the victim, yours should focus on de-mystifying the coffin and why it was found encrusted in the coral of Carysfort Reef. Remember Nash is a policeman, who is trying to solve a murder, he does not know he is on the trail of a mass murder and a vampire. He would not likely resonate with theories outside of his box, or anything close to it. Typically murders have motives attached to them. I suspect he and his colleagues have labored to establish a motive for this one as well; particularly something likely to have been taken from inside a box that looks like a bulky coffin, and underwater for over 400 years. You will have to clear your mind of what we know and suspect in this case. If Cassidy was smart, he traveled with enough resources – probably in gold species to cover everything he required until he could manufacture more. From the beginning try to link the coffin with treasure; always a good plot for murder. Ask to see the coffin and thoroughly examine it noticeably looking for inscriptions and secret compartments; ask to dive on the site where the two men found it; that should keep him occupied while I try locating Cassidy. With luck you will find some of Cassidy's traveling money and learn more than we are divulging from our new and old colleagues alike...Now, regarding the detective himself, I have asked a colleague to consult with the genealogists at the National Archives in Washington to research his family. To get them started they need his hometown, birthdate, father's name..." Interrupting Galen, Coleen asked:

"Why do we need to have this sort of information on the detective Dr. Galen, I don't understand.

"...I am interested in the connection, if any, between Ordinary Seaman Will Nash of the *Edith Louise* and Detective Russell Nash. I do know Will Nash lived a long life but did not return to Scotland. Perhaps he or one of his descendants eventually found a home in the colonies or later after independence, the United States. I know it is a long shot, but if we can make that connection, Detective Nash unknown to him, carries a bit of Cassidy's vampire DNA, enough to have a well-developed sense of intuition, and likely now, a dark presence he can't explain. We can work with that. If there is a connection, it just might aid us in quickly locating Cassidy...Finally and most importantly – The threat that Cassidy poses to unsuspecting populations cannot be overstated. Cassidy must never be arrested – he must disappear without a trace. Imagine the interrogation after his arrest and taken alive? Imagine what goodies Sanjay would find in Cassidy's corpse if his body was found? With few exceptions; I have kept the existence of creatures such as myself off the cultural radar a very long time. As we speak Cassidy is seeking or may have already recruited a new keeper/guardian and is likely planning his next feeding. We must not waste time. If we don't locate and stop him, people will soon go missing and bodies with uncommon wounds and pathology will begin to pile up here in quaint Key Largo. We need to locate and stop him, here, in the next 24 to 36 hours. If we don't, he will likely escape from me one more time. If he is able to obtain resources through a surrogate, he will be gone. Remember, this is the first in modern times a vampire is on the loose to my knowledge, a very clever one that will soon learn the ways of the 21st century and the deadly powers he can command...this is a phenomenon straight out of popular fiction come to life. If he begins feeding and killing, we will be the ones the authorities will come to for answers...If he succeeds in escaping me, he will be harder to stop than ever – Remember he is a direct descendent of a living Enki, a race that explored space when we were still entertained with the variety of things we could do by having thumbs. Think of what today's technologies can offer a man of that lineage, a man with his history of cruelty and lust for power. So, as they say - time is of the essence!" Galen said as he closed his laptop with a very grim look on his face.

"Well, those are cheery thoughts. You are right Doctor; I have got to avoid giving more information than I get from Nash. You didn't say it, but hinted that my role in all this is to distract Nash, to keep him off the trail while you track down Cassidy. Isn't that dangerous...I mean doing this solo?" Coleen asked sitting up in the chair.

"Dangerous, yes: In the past, I didn't do it all on my own. My keeper/guardians routinely engaged a several hundred men at arms or mercenaries to travel with me when hunting vampires. I recall following reports of some unusual behavior by a petty royal in the Carpathian Mountains in present day Romania. It was Cassius...err Cassidy. He was then known to the locals as Prince Vlad Dracul; he loves his royal titles I might add. He had a long reputation for occasionally having hundreds of his enemies impaled on stakes along the roadway leading to his lair; the same as he did in Syria when I first met him as Gaius Tacitus Cassius...

....He was as expected, quite openly acting an ass, and would make a show of riding up and down each row of the impaled on his horse drinking the blood gushing from their wounds. This was done for effect in full view of the local villagers – the original source of the legend.

After concluding the guy was Cassidy, my little army and I attacked and over ran his fortress. As my men fought his off, I succeeded in trapping him in the great hall of his fortress. After hacking at each other with swords and clubs for about half an hour, we found ourselves nearly spent and equally blood stained. Separated, we both took a knee on the floor opposite one another to rest. Before I could react, he escaped by crashing through a door. I tried to get up but my own wound had weakened me so I was unable to follow him and his blood trail. I was forced to give up the pursuit...

...That is the last time he was openly on the loose as a vampire in Continental Europe. And as I mentioned earlier, the spectacles he perpetrated, myth and legend took over leading to the legend of Dracul or Dracula the vampire" Galen said as he drained his whiskey glass sporting a sarcastic smile.

"Dracula, wow...wait, you mean he is the only one beside you and this Enki guy?" Coleen asked.

"No...that is not quite true. Between the time he was Demetrius Keraunos at the beginning of his bloody journey, by the time our paths crossed, he likely spawned vampires by the dozen – both male and female. I do not know if he had any with him in Syria – I did not sense any beyond myself. Many, many years later when I cornered him in Romania, he had about a half dozen with him. His flight and activities in Scotland was a different story. By September, 1305, less than a month after William Wallace was captured and executed by the English King Edward Longshanks, northern Scotland was awash with Scottish national or English loyalist raiding parties. At the time I led about a thousand men hunting Cassidy and his band under the ensign of Robert the Bruce as our cover. Cassidy's similar cover was leading a band of loyalists with promises from the English he would be granted titles and lands for his service. He was always a sucker for titles and power...

...Late in the month, near the old Roman village of Banadia, now Inverness, we located him and his band of blood drinkers. This time we watched their comings and goings in and out of the village for three days. They drank, sang, and wenched for most of each night and were slow risers. Late on the third night we struck. We killed them all, to the last man and woman in the camp. Cassidy was not there, by some way he and a personal guard of keeper/guardians had left before we struck, and we totally missed his escape...

...After the action we counted 675 dead, of which 175 were vampires likely sprung from Cassidy's innards, maybe 2 or 3 older ones that could have been with him from the beginning. I have been killing his off-spring for nearly two millennia. When not exactly on his trail it has been in one's and two's; when say at engagements such as the battle at Banadia, we did it en mass in open combat. As an interesting footnote, second generation vampires, if you consider Cassidy first generation, do not have the capacity to make others of their kind. The vampires we killed over the years were "sterile" so to speak, meaning they were second generation spawned from Cassidy. Now in a long way round to your question – No; I don't think there are vast numbers still living beyond him, me and the Enki." Galen concluded.

"That means you cannot create more of your kind?" Coleen asked.

"No, I cannot – clarity to my situation came before I tried coughing up my own mutated DNA in a glob of goo and forcing it down someone's throat."

"Yuck..." Coleen said collecting the empty mini-bottles and putting them on their used dinner trays.

"I'll call room service and have them come and get this...goodnight Doctor Galen." Coleen said covering a yawn.

"Good night, good luck with your appointment with Detective Nash..." Galen said reopening his laptop computer.

***

Coleen was jarred out of a deep sleep by heavy banging on her hotel room door. She scrambled to get out of bed and ran to the door, not only in an effort to see what was so urgent, but also to stop the annoying banging noise. Opening the door, she found Galen highly agitated and breathing heavily from his race to her door.

"Coleen, he's here, he's in this building!!" Galen said with eyes reflecting both focus and fright.

"Who's here?" Coleen asked as Galen shot past her and spun around, then back in the hallway.

"Cassidy, he's here – I feel him like he was standing between us! We must go down to the lobby and look for him!"

"Come on in while I change. Sit down and we will go down together," Coleen said as she passed into her bedroom and closed the door. She quickly put on jeans, a T shirt and sandals. As she opened her door she remembered she forgot to put on a bra...but decided it was a big T shirt anyway.

"What are we going to do if we do find him?" Coleen asked as they raced down the steps instead of taking the elevator that would open directly into the lobby.

"We are going to back off and watch. He likely will be in the company of a newly recruited keeper/guardian. We can see what Cassidy looks like now and the same for his guardian. If the hotel has a security system with video cameras on the lobby and other public spaces we will have something we can study if we can get access to the video," Galen said taking the lead as they approached the door leading to the ground floor lobby.

Galen paused and looked at Coleen, and back to the door as he slowly eased it open revealing the lobby and guests coming and going from the hotel bar and restaurant. Galen scanned the room as best he could without stepping out. Not seeing anyone that might be Cassidy he motioned to Coleen to follow him. They slowly entered the room, following the wall and taking advantage of the potted palms and other exotic plantings to screen them from open view. With each step Galen paused and narrowed his focus to the entrance door, elevators, or the passage to the bar and restaurant, asking Coleen to focus on them since no one present looked remotely like Cassidy; he could only enter through those three ways.

Arriving at the bar Galen told Coleen: "Circle the bar from the right, I will go left. Keep your eye on me as I will you. We are looking for a man looking to be in his fifties, about 5 feet 9 or 10 inches tall and rather thin. He should be with another who looks a bit nervous," Galen said over top of the thumping band.

"Do you sense him in here?"

"I sense him, but cannot pin point the source – I'm not that good." Galen said smiling to break the tension.

As they parted to walk their sides of the room Coleen's heart was racing. Never having done something like this before was frightening, but on another level felt exhilarated. With each step her eyes scoured the faces and features of each person. She felt it almost surreal as the music was in rhythm with the lighting and everyone there seemed to jump around as she walked. She also noticed Galen weaving through the crowd. He was on the hunt of his life once more. He obviously felt so close, she thought, but this time he had no sword or private army, just a classical scholar to help him. Finally, each reached the center of the bar and dance area and met.

"He's not here." Galen said. He turned and walked out of the bar and stopped in the center of the lobby, then walked over to the reception desk and asked them about Cassidy. His story was that he was looking for a friend of his that may have passed by. They were no help claiming to have been occupied with checking in a tourist group. He moved to just inside the hotel entryway, and looked out into the darkness of the parking lot.

Joining him, Coleen reached out and gently grasped his right wrist.

"Sorry Doctor – you didn't think it was going to be that easy did you?"

"No...after such a long time, and suspecting it would come after a long complicated search, then this...quite unexpectedly he shows up at my hotel. You also know what this means don't you Coleen?"

"What...?"

"It means he knows I am here, at least in Key Largo and looking for him. He was likely coming to the bar to entice a blood source away to the shadows and feed on them – its time. When he approached the bar, probably in the lobby he sensed my presence somewhere in the building. He knows about me, but not necessarily you. On the same token, he doesn't know why he sensed me here; I could also be passing through as well. This is a bit dangerous but we will continue to have rooms here. Perhaps we can use it to our advantage in drawing him in with hopes of killing me – I'll have to think about it. However, be very careful when you are alone here; be cognizant of who is around you and where you are, okay?"

"Yes, I will watch out for myself as you should," Coleen replied.

"Oh yes, do not tell what happened here tonight to Detective Nash. I still want him to struggle with motive and whatever fiction we can throw his way for the time being." Galen said as he motioned her to the elevators.

***

In the deep darkness of the hotel parking lot sat two figures in a banged up Ford. Cassidy and Holmes studied Galen and Coleen while they were in conversation. After they disappeared out of view Holmes turned to his passenger...

"Wow, that was close; who did you say that guy was?"

"That's the man who will kill me Mr. Holmes, unless I kill him first...and, he has an attractive assistant...Ummm... quite the change from when I remember him in Scotland. Things are getting very interesting," Cassidy said as he leaned toward the open window; deeply breathing in the humid tropical air to register the scent of the old vampire standing not 50 feet away.

"Let's go to the next best bar in Key Largo," Cassidy said looking straight ahead, all the while processing the appearance of his archenemy Galenicus.

Chapter 14 - A Vampire in Key Largo

"...When you said goodbye...You were on the run...Tryin' to get away from the things you'd done...Now you're back again...And you're feeling strange...So much has happened...but nothing has changed..."

Glen Frey, *You Belong to the City*, 1984

It was past 7:30 Friday morning when Rusty Nash had collected himself enough after a short night to pour a cup of coffee and slowly move to his living room. Switching on his television, Nash turned the remote to the morning news from Channel 71 in Miami. It was reporting on the developments of Robert Hopkins' murder from Key Largo. The scene was inside the Sheriff's press room at headquarters on Stock Island, the last island in the keys before Key West. The Sheriff had just taken the podium and was briefing the press on developments regarding the case to date. He began by introducing those behind him on the dais: From left to right, the Undersheriff, Colonel Janet Dixon; Captain

Phillip Evans, Nash's supervisor; Director Anne Harris, Community Relations; Special Agent in Charge of the Florida Department of Law Enforcement, Key West Field Office, Frank Alaniz; and his partner in the case Sheila Brown. He and Brown flipped a coin for the opportunity to be at the news conference and Nash won.

The Sheriff was explaining the murder in very general terms regarding what had been observed to date with some vague references to the information Brown collected earlier. When pressed on motive and specific details, the Sheriff evoked "...continuing investigation" for reasons for not providing specifics. At the end he assured the press, the residents and visitors to the Florida Keys that the department was working diligently on solving the case, sharing information with FDLE, and bringing the murderer or murderers to justice as soon as possible.

So far, FDLE had not claimed jurisdiction in the investigation, but did send an agent to help Brown when she met with Hopkins' next of kin in Kendall and were on tap to send their K-9 tracking team. She said she was grateful for that as they helped her during the interview and photographing the artifacts in Hopkins' private museum. Nash made a note to call Alaniz and keep him in the loop so to speak regarding anything he needed to know, especially if we suspected the murderer or murderers had left the county – which he thought was likely at this point. He also made a note to have Brown get a search warrant for the rest of the artifacts that were taken off the wreck.

His mind then turned to his meeting with Dr. Coleen Jones. With so much needing to be done, he hated the distractions of being wallpaper at press conferences or meeting with outside civilians forced upon him. He was not happy with the prospect of working with an egg-head university nerd, probably in her 50's, probably with the personality of a pound of human hair.

Remembering Captain Evans' warning about not wearing his usual guayabera shirt, slacks, and ankle holster – he put on a sports jacket and shoulder holster. Since his first guayabera shirt, he was hooked on their looks and for design for keeping cool in the heat of the tropics. North American guayaberas are shirt-jacs were thought to have come from Cuba in the 1970's, they immediately became synonymous with the growing Cuban American community in Miami. Today it is worn by a growing number of men for casual office wear in south Florida and most of Latin America. This morning Nash felt bold and wore his black one with a colorful flower design, linen slacks and his white linen sports jacket.

Arriving at the Bayside Resort Nash parked and exited his vehicle in the small lot near the main entrance. He had often visited the bar when live bands played and females gathered. He and his ex-wife Viktoriya had often come here to dance and drink, drink and dance.. It had a reputation for one of the best rum punches in the upper Keys...and he could attest to that and they made for many fuzzy Sunday mornings.

As he approached the entrance, he again walked into something that gave him a sense of someone being near or watching him. He paused and then turned, feeling something he could not explain. Drawn to his right Nash slowly walked in a direction opposite where he had parked. Scanning the lot and parked cars for a person or person inside, he walked up and down each row. As he reached the end, the feeling left as inextricably as it had come upon him. Shaking it off, Nash searched his mind for an explanation for this strange reaction – he decided maybe it was time to clean his coffee pot and lay off the cheap rum.

The lobby was busy with tourists and staff members scurrying about as guests checked in and out, or came and went from the restaurant. Noticing the 2 video surveillance cameras in the lobby attested to the work of the new security manager that Nash met after the Hotel's last theft of guest luggage from the lobby. Entering the restaurant Nash scanned the room for a single frumpy academic type female. The dining room was indoors except for a few tables by the pool. Most of the tables were occupied, but no one his mind told him was Dr. Jones. Checking his watch, Nash noticed it was about five minutes to nine – and he was early. She was probably having a problem putting on her shoes he thought. Nash sat down at an empty table near the door to the pool with his back to a Norfolk Pine sitting in a planter in the corner of the room. From here he could see the room and everyone in it – a habit he had learned in the military and carried over to his days as a policeman. He checked his phone for any messages cancelling the meeting – hoping to find one, but he did not.

Unknown to Nash, Coleen was at a table by the pool screened off by the same Norfolk Pine he was using to protect his back. She noticed who she believed to be Nash when he came into the dining room. She thought it amusing to watch him discreetly search each face of the women in the dining room he thought might be her. Her only impression of American police came from American television shows. *Miami Vice* was extraordinarily popular in Europe and was her only window into police and crime in south Florida. This guy dressed somewhat like the character Crockett, but certainly did not have the same hair stylist or Crockett's out of place California swagger. She thought he must be looking for someone quite different than her – probably someone older and more "booky" looking. When he made an attempt to secret himself in the corner of the room she smiled to herself that he was so cool he neglected to notice the corner was plate glass with only a potted plant between him and everyone on the pool deck. Sensing he may be annoyed by having to wait on her, she spoke.

"Detective Nash, is that you?" Coleen asked leaning into the open door form her seat on the deck behind him.

Nash turned in surprise and caught the sight of Coleen. Embarrassed for missing her just on the other side of the doorway, he got up so quickly his leg caught and dragged some of the tablecloth with him as he stepped away from the table. Not looking down, Nash pulled it away as if it didn't happen and approached Coleen hoping she did not notice. She did and thought this somewhat endearing of a man who until now only was a fictional character on the television. And he was cute.

"Good morning Dr. Jones, I'm Detective Russell Nash of the Monroe County Sheriff's Department," he said while showing Coleen his law enforcement credentials.

This was not what Nash had expected in the meeting. Dr. Jones was not the frumpy nerd he had expected. She had an uncanny resemblance to his perfect woman – She was a well-dressed tall woman who looked athletic under her dark blue suit. His eyes were conflicted as they were drawn to the white blouse with the deep open collar and then his eyes moved up her beautiful long neck to her thick auburn hair that was tied back, showing off her pale skin and blue eyes. He was smitten and momentarily at a loss for words. His anticipated dislike to working with her on the case began to evaporate all the while the perspiration on his upper lip continued to do just the opposite.

"May I sit down Dr. Jones? Nash asked running his hand over his wet lip and discreetly wiping it on his trousers.

"Please do. Would you like a cup of coffee or orange juice? Coleen asked trying hard to be charming enough to distract him long enough to get his family information and determine how far he had gone in his investigation. She also thought this man in front of her was refreshingly different and she enjoyed watching him since she had spent the last several weeks almost exclusively in the company of a 2,000 year old vampire.

Nash also noticed his mouth had gone desert dry in the last few seconds and accepted her offer. After the waiter served Nash, Coleen quickly moved to the business at hand.

"So Detective, I am sure you are wondering how a classics scholar such as me, and a physician and scientist from Scotland can help you in this case. Dr. Galen and I have spoken about this at length and are prepared to assist you with both the mystery of why the coffin was found at the bottom of the ocean, and perhaps what and who killed Mr. Hopkins and why..."

"Umm, that would help, as there are a lot of unanswered questions. We have a few theories of our own as well, however they seem go nowhere with each new bit of information. Tell me Dr. Jones just why are you and Dr. Galen so interested in this case that you traveled from Turkey to the Florida Keys at the drop of a hat?"

"Detective, Dr. Galen has been working on a mystery of his own for many years that involves the source of the Eagle standard reported just this morning at the Sheriff's news conference, the circumstances of its recovery, and the ship wreck which he believes originated in Scotland. He believes perhaps, if this murder can be solved, his mystery will also. I would prefer not to discuss specific details outside of Dr. Galen's presence or as you also would agree, at a public breakfast table." Coleen responded with Nash nodding in agreement.

"Detective, your patronymic – I believe Nash has both English and Scottish roots. Forgive me; it is the etymologist in me..." Coleen said, being interrupted by Nash.

"Patronymic...ctymolo...what? Nash asked.

"Sorry Detective, etymology is a field of study devoted to the history of words, their origin, and how they have changed through time. In this case my work has often involved the history of last names such as your own. As I recall Nash likely originates from early medieval

England. Other 12th or 13th century renditions of your name probably were spelled N-a-y-s-h-e or N-a-i-s-h. **Are you first generation American?"** Coleen asked, remembering Galen's need for further genealogical information on Nash.

Nash's mind raced to compose a learned-sounding response to Jones' obvious intelligence and mastery of a field he shared with her, almost. He also did not wish to sound like an idiot or a teenage boy trying to impress an attractive new girl in school. Giving up saying something impressive sounding or sage, he settled for a simple observation.

"Names are also a large part of my work as a criminal investigator. To answer your question, no...my family has been American for many generations, and all of us have been sailors from Boston; My grandfather Calvin Nash told me that one of my grandfathers, way back when, was in the British Navy. His father came from Bermuda where his father settled sometime in the late 1600's. My late brother Douglas was very much into genealogy and did the whole chart – personally I found it interesting - like solving mysteries, but never have taken the time to get into it as did Doug." Nash answered.

"Tell me Doctor, how long have you been working for Dr. Galen?"

"Please call me Coleen...not long at all. My brother Andrew was originally Dr. Galen's assistant, but was killed in an auto crash a few months ago while doing some field work for the Doctor," Coleen said looking past him, as the sun danced off the wake of a boat cutting through the water just off the Resort's beach.

"Oh, I am very sorry..." Nash responded, also glancing over his shoulder to the boat. As he turned back Coleen had redirected herself to the business at hand.

"Please understand Detective Nash, we don't want to weigh you down or apt to divulge state secrets while working with you. Dr. Galen is financially independent and can afford to pay me well for my services – this is his way of giving back, and at the same time advance his own research."

"And what is the subject of his research?

"That will be something Dr. Galen will have to answer completely. His work among other things has to do with forensic haematology and cures for specific blood disorders. I can tell you this; we think it involves the person that killed Hopkins and the disappearance of Mr. Walsh, Hopkins' partner."

"Then you don't think Walsh had anything to do with Hopkins' murder?"

Coleen took a long sip of her coffee before answering Nash. She felt the information gathered from Nash was enough to begin research into his lineage. It appeared he was the grandson of Will Nash, and likely carried at least a portion of the vampire's DNA. And since the vampire was likely in this same building about 10 hours earlier, as Nash moved through the lobby this morning or wherever Cassidy stood, Nash should have sensed a peculiar sensation of presence he could not explain.

"...No..." Coleen said, but before she could add anything, Nash's cell phone vibrated from an incoming call. Taking it from his pocket...

"This is Nash," he said answering the call.

"Detective, this is Deputy Stacy Wooten. I'm calling from the Tavernier Hospital ER. We have Alex Walsh here. A motorist picked him up about an hour ago. He was lying alongside Monroe Road south of old state route 905. I did not speak with him before he went in for treatment...he has been pretty much unconscious since they brought him in...You had better get down here," said the caller.

"Great, just the man I want to talk to...you say he is not conscious, what is he being treated for?" Nash asked.

"According to the ER register, Walsh is suffering from exposure, dehydration, cuts and bruises, and a concussion," Wooten replied.

"Thanks, Stacy, I'll be right there." Nash said ending the call, tucking his cell phone back into his shirt pocket.

"I've got to go. Alex Walsh resurfaced about two miles from Carysfort Reef Marina, and is now being treated at a hospital about 10 minutes from here." Nash said as he took a long gulp of his coffee, then his juice.

"Detective, I can be of help with this man. I think I know what his story is going to be. May I accompany you?" Coleen asked.

"You can call me Rusty…I would normally say not no, but hell no since this involves an ongoing police investigation – but…the Sheriff has approved you two as consultants to the Sheriff's Department. Meet me in front of the hotel in 5 minutes," Nash said as he headed toward the lobby.

After his departure Coleen took a cell phone out of her purse and texted Galen:

"….*meeting with Nash went well – convinced he is Will Nash's grandson – from Boston, grandfather is Calvin Nash; other ancestor in British Navy*

whose father from Bermuda in 17ᵗʰ C....we were
interrupted by a report that Alex Walsh has been
found and is in Tavernier hospital for treatment –
he is likely to out Cassidy – are you still at
hospital?"

Coleen tapped "send" and went to the restroom
before stepping out of the front door of the hotel waiting
for Nash to pick her up. While waiting Galen texted her
back:

"...good news about both - I am still at hospital
with Sanjay - about finished here. What I
suspected is correct – Cassidy killed Hopkins.
Sending Nash's information to DC. Call me when
you get here. G."

Nash pulled his vehicle to the front and Coleen
opened the door and sat in the front passenger seat. She
secured her seat belt and looked over to Nash and nodded
she was ready to go. Nash turned and checked for traffic,
and exited the Resort entrance and onto the Overseas
Highway, US Route 1 heading south. As they drove, Nash
was beginning to feel a bit awkward when Coleen spoke
first.

"How far away did you say the hospital was?"
Coleen asked.

"About 10 to 15 minutes south, that is, if there is no heavy traffic. A little farther south is Islamorada where there is great flats fishing and lobster diving – and of course some of the best casual, laid back Florida Keys tiki bars...have you ever been to Florida or the Keys before?

"No Detective, err...Rusty, I have not. Being from Scotland, this type of climate is a bit different than I am used to, especially the heat and humidity – yet I do love the clear warm water. When on holiday, my ex and I would go to the south of Spain or France where the weather along the Mediterranean is similar to this but not as humid...you said you were from Boston?"

Nash heard nothing she said after the reference to an "...ex." He was used to being smitten at first sight; it always triggered fantasies with the sophistication of a box of hammer handles – and an "ex" meant she was unattached, and maybe as vulnerable as Nash. When the distraction left him he replied...

"Yep – born at Boston General...the weather here took some time getting used to for me as well, especially the summers. My previous experience in hot climates was minus the humidity – Iraq and Kuwait during the first Gulf War."

"Were you there during the fighting?

"...From beginning to end; from August, 1990 in Operation Desert Shield to February, 1991 with the marines in support of the Army's 1ˢᵗ Armored Division. My last time in action was at the Battle of Medina Ridge, until the cease fire. I got back to the states in March and got out in April. To rest and forget, I came down here, dated someone who got pregnant, and we married, I got a job with the Sheriff's Department, she had a miscarriage, she left me, we got divorced – and here I am. Not a very exciting life right now," Nash said, realizing he had rambled much too long to a woman he had known less than 2 hours.

"What do you plan to do with this Mr. Walsh?"

"Well, he is still a person of interest in the death of Robert Hopkins. If the facts point to another person, it can't be overlooked he has likely committed several felonies by repeatedly and illegally disturbing an historic sunken vessel inside the boundaries of a state park, and he repeatedly stole artifacts from that vessel over a period of several years...he will have to be referred to the State's Attorney for prosecution... As I have said before, if he did not kill Hopkins, he likely knows who did and may have been a witness. That I hope to find out in a few minutes."

"Dr. Galen is also at the hospital rapping up his examination of Hopkins' body along with his colleague,

Dr. Bhatnagar – the pathologist that performed the original autopsy. He will join us there."

Nash redirected his focus to the road, thinking how this could turn into a "goat fuck" by bringing a crowd to interview Walsh. He decided one or the other, but not both would be in the room when he interviewed him. Nash also thought he should be hearing something soon from Sheila Brown who was to meet with the dog tracking team at the marina and attempt to follow what was left of the trail of the killer or killers if they did go into the mangroves from the north end of the parking lot. He pulled his cell phone from his pocket and speed dialed her number. After 3 rings she answered.

"Brown here..." she answered a little out of breath.

"Sheila this is Rusty. Saw you on TV today. Very impressive...did they call you about Walsh showing back up? Nash asked.

"Are you shitting me? Hell no – that's great..." Brown replied.

"How are you all doing?

"Well, you would call this a "Carpathian goat fuck." We are still at the marina in the north end of the parking lot. Two dog teams showed up, one from Metro and the other ours, err FDLE's. Everybody's running around smelling each other's asses. Oh, the dogs are too. I guess when we were calling everyone the other day, we never called back to tell them to disregard."

"Okay...Sheila we will get back with you as soon as we get a statement from Walsh..." Nash said with Brown interrupting.

"...We? Who's we? Do you have a mouse in your pocket? Brown asked.

"Dr. Coleen Jones, the consultant from Scotland and I are almost to Tavernier Hospital to get a statement from him," Nash said glancing over to his passenger who was focused on passing scenery. The clean sweet scent of a woman was something he hadn't had an opportunity to experience in some time.   Although his glance was momentary; then quickly refocusing back on the road – he was left with an image in his mind of her head turned slightly away, the shape of her ear, of her red hair moving rhythmically as the outside air blew in the top of the window, and her lashes and blue eyes moving at each glimpse of something catching her attention...Yes, he decided...he was smitten...again.

"...Coleen...must be a looker."

"Sheila...get ahold of the commander of the Metro team, thank him and send them home.   If he needs someone with some gold on their collar call your good buddy Captain Evans, okay?" Nash said, knowing Evans was not on Brown's favorite list.

"Screw you Rusty Nash," Brown said smiling and hung up.

Nash retuned his cell phone to his shirt pocket, slowed down and turned onto the entrance to the hospital.

"Here we are...I look forward to meeting Dr. Galen, but when interviewing Walsh, I only can have one of you to be in the room when I take his statement." Nash said as he parked the vehicle and turned off its engine.

"I understand, the fact you might still consider him to be a suspect is enough to keep both Dr. Galen and me out of the room. It is much appreciated that you will permit one of us to be there," Coleen said as she collected her purse and tablet and exited the car.

Stopping in the Emergency Room (ER) lobby Coleen phoned Galen and told him they were at the hospital waiting for him where Walsh had been moved to a room on the second floor, north wing.

Coleen and Nash took the elevator to the second floor and went directly to Walsh's room. Nash stepped inside to confirm Walsh was in the room and was able to be interviewed. A nurse in the room had just finished positioning the IV stand and ensuring the peripheral line and catheter were properly installed in Walsh's arm.

"Hello, I'm Detective Nash, is Mr. Walsh able to be interviewed?" Nash asked the nurse.

"Yes, he seems to be responding well, but not too long. He has been given medication to reduce the agitation he was exhibiting, and will likely be dropping off if your interview goes too long," the nurse responded.

Nash glanced at Walsh who appeared to have awakened. At that he turned and walked back toward the hallway. Again, before he got a foot away from Walsh's bed, Nash felt that same feeling of presence but stronger. He looked around the room. The bed next to Walsh was empty as was the bathroom. The sensation strengthened even further when he stepped into the hallway.

Walking to the waiting area near the nurse's station, he noticed Coleen had been joined by a distinguished looking man in a lab coat. He thought this had to be Coleen's employer, Dr. Mark Galen.

"Sir, are you Dr. Galen?" Nash asked as he approached the two, extending his hand.

"Yes I am detective," Galen responded, taking his hand in a firm hand shake.

As Nash gripped Galen's hand he sensed a jolt of something pass into and hold him...it was not like anything he had ever experienced. After letting go of his grip Nash, felt a release...and the feeling passed.

"I am delighted to meet you and look forward to our working together. Coleen speaks highly of you. She also told me only one of us will be permitted to join you inside...may I?" Galen asked.

"...Of course, let's go in, I am told he has been medicated and will likely drift off to sleep shortly," Nash said as he tried to rationalize the experience he had just had.

"Yes, we have no time to waste," Galen said as he followed Nash into the room, looking over his shoulder to Coleen.

Before disappearing into the room Galen and Coleen shared a moment of silent eye contact that signified each grasped the importance of this meeting and that Galen would likely have to conduct an intervention here and now should Walsh remember and communicate what Galen had been keeping from the world for so long; that his captor was indeed a man that had been underwater bolted into a coffin for over 400 years, and a vampire – a creature only thought to exist on the pages of a book or in dramatic theater.

After Galen entered the room, she returned to her chair, and began to enter her notes of what had transpired earlier and what was likely happening inside that room. Not knowing what Galen was going to do, she surveyed the number of staff assigned to this unit. She then scanned back to the door to Walsh's room wishing she was on the inside.

***

Once the nurse left, Galen took one side of the bed, and Nash the other. Nash spoke...

"Mr. Walsh...Mr. Walsh I am Detective Russell Nash of the Monroe County Sheriff's Department, can you hear me?" Nash asked Walsh who appeared to have dozed off.

Walsh, stirred, opening his eyes. He focused on both men and sat up slightly.

"I can hear you...you are a policeman right? Walsh asked.

"Yes I am. This is Dr. Galen who is assisting our department in this investigation," Nash said, introducing Galen.

"Tell...tell me, all this is a dream. Tell me Rob is okay, and none of this ever happened." Walsh said looking directly at Nash, then at Galen.

"Well, no...your friend Robert Hopkins is dead. He was murdered last Sunday at Carysfort Reef Marina. Mr. Walsh, were you there?" Nash asked.

"Oh...Fuck me. It is all true, just like the asshole that knocked me out and tied me up in that deserted military base said...yes, I was there," Walsh answered.

"Mr. Walsh it is very important if you can recall and tell us everything that happened... beginning with the last time you saw Hopkins alive. I first need to advise you of your Miranda Rights regarding your right to an attorney and that you are clear about giving me a statement you are likely to incriminate yourself." Nash said.

After Nash read Walsh his Miranda rights, Walsh paused to process the jackpot he was in, the confirmation that his longtime friend was actually dead, and the harrowing experience he had endured from the time he awoke on the damp concrete floor, his escape, being picked up by a motorist and delivered to the hospital. After sipping on some ice water he began his story.

"I know my rights, and yes am aware that we broke the law in salvaging that wreck, but I had nothing to do with Rob's death. The rest of what I have to say....well, it's really weird shit, and you probably won't believe me, but I swear to God this is what happened," Walsh replied.

"...Rob and I discovered a wreck that had been uncovered when Hurricane Andrew came through in '92. Well, diving on it we found sticking out of the sand near its ballast pile a small statue of a gold eagle Rob believed to have been a standard, the kind that fit on the end of a wooden pole and carried ahead of Roman Army Legion when it marched and went into battle. That was in 1992." Walsh said.

"Mr. Walsh, is this the eagle standard you and Mr. Hopkins found?" Nash asked showing him a digital photograph Brown had taken.

"Yes, that's the one. For the next 10 years we dived the site and picked up the normal shit found on an old wreck – cannon balls, pottery, coins and stuff like that. Rob kept it all at his home. A week or so ago we found something else. It first looked like a brass or bronze object sticking out from under a line of grass and sand where the tide and current carves a hollow depression under the grass. Do you know what I mean? He and I dug around it and discovered it was big, and very heavy. Visions of treasure danced in our heads. We developed a plan to recover it using a couple Carter 2000 pound lift bags...We finally got it off the bottom to the surface and slowly towed it back to Carysfort Reef Marina with Rob's boat. Once we tied up the boat we hooked a makeshift double sling around it and pulled it out of the water. When it was over the dock, and about 6 feet in the air when the front sling slipped and the box fell onto the deck and the top popped off. The back of the box was to me, and I could not immediately tell what had spilled out. I saw what looked like sand shot out like a wave, then there was movement. What looked like a man had also popped out, first crouching on one knee shaking his head as if he couldn't see. I couldn't believe my eyes, I moved forward to him when he turned and backhanded me on the forehead with a metal object, which later I found out was a big knife," Walsh said pausing for another sip of ice water.

While listening to this part of Walsh's story Nash also paused from writing in his notebook and glanced over to Galen. Galen returned the glance, but not in disbelief, rather fearing the secret of vampires was now going into an official account and therefore be exposed to the world. Walsh continued...

"...That explains the gash on my head and my concussion. Well...there was a flash of light and stars; and I woke up several hours later apparently after being carried by this guy a couple of miles through the mangrove and thick brush to the old missile base north of the marina. What comes next is really creepy. I woke up lying on my stomach with my hands tied behind me with telephone cable. I tried to stand but he me pulled backward, landing on my right side...Sensing where he was behind me on the floor, I screamed at him, demanding to know who the fuck he was...He asked me back who I was and where he was. He had a thick Scottish accent that, I swear to God sounded like Sean Connery. I wondered what the fuck was going on. Standing over me he put his cold grey hand on my face to impress upon me that he was in charge. It was then I recognized his face and scraggly beard and hair – he was the guy that popped out of the box. His long fingernails looked like curly fries, he smelled like something between skunk piss and moth balls...and his clothes, they looked rotten and like he was celebrating dress-like-pirate day. He told me Rob was dead. I told him we were in the United States and the date. He didn't seem to know anything about this country, about cars or the current date. Oh yes, he told me his name was Angus Cassidy, of Logie, whatever the fuck that means. Since this guy was in the box, a box that was likely on the ship that Rob and I found after it sank 400 years ago and got encrusted on the coral reef amongst the rotted timbers of the old wreck we were working. This fucking guy is someone that ain't human guys," Walsh said.

"You said he told you his name was Angus Cassidy? How did you escape?"

"Yep, he was quite clear about his name. I was with this guy a couple of days, and it seemed he slept days and moved around at night. The first day I ran my fingers along the line he had tied around my wrists. He had used some old telephone line and after slowly tracing it, I found a disconnect about 12 inches from where I was tied. He apparently doesn't know anything about telephone line and disconnects or he just missed it in the dark. Well, after he went into a deep sleep 2 days ago I managed to uncouple it and up the stairs I went. After reaching the ground level I ran far enough away that he could not see me even if he was looking from the building. I screwed up and hiked in the opposite direction and wound up on the ocean side near dynamite docks. I waded over to the island just off the shore and hid. I laid there trying to figure out how to get back without running into him. I slept that night on the rocks and took off early this morning – and here I am."

"Let me summarize what you just told me. First, you and Hopkins found the box that is now on the dock at Carysfort Reef Marina that came from the same the reef the sunken wreck you two have been working for over 10 years."

"Correct."

Secondly, in hoisting the box from the water and onto the dock, that same box slipped and crashed onto the dock and its top broken open spilling its contents. Among the contents of the box you identified a man amongst the debris – alive and kneeling on the dock...As you moved forward he struck you and knocked you unconscious," Nash confirmed.

"Correct again."

Lastly, this same man apparently carried you while you were unconscious to the closed Nike Hercules base in north Key Largo where you regained consciousness. You identified this Angus Cassidy as the same man that was in the box and struck you. This same man also appeared to be...I'm guessing here...from another time, perhaps of the time when the ship sunk...and likely one of its passengers when it sunk." Nash concluded closing his field note case.

"Yep, those are my thoughts exactly."

Galen listened stoically to Walsh's story and Nash's summary. What he envisioned as the beginning of a worst case scenario was beginning to play out. He considered what the press would do with Walsh's story; the questions he would be asked about the possibility of it being true, and the likelihood of him being exposed as well. Galen pondered the best means of mitigating or obfuscating Walsh's story and how Nash was going to respond should or when he intervene. Galen's cellphone vibrated signaling an incoming text message. It was from his colleague in the National Archives. He read the lengthy message and returned the phone to his pocket.

"Mr. Walsh, you said you suffered a concussion. I am a physician. May I have a look?" Galen asked as he pulled what looked like a physician's penlight from his lab coat pocket.

"Sure..." Walsh said looking ahead to allow Galen access to his eyes.

Galen's instrument was not a penlight but was Galen's invention. The focused almost laser like light consisted of rotating micro lenses. They focused light of varying wavelengths on the eye. The effect resulted in scrambling a portion of the subject's neural network enabling a suggestion to become reality, where real memories are erased, or false ones created.

Galen leaned forward pointing his "penlight" into Walsh's eyes. Before activating the device, he asked...

"Mr. Walsh, have you told anyone else about your experiences with this Mr. Cassidy other than Detective Nash and me?" Galen asked.

"Ah...no, I passed out before I could talk about anything with the woman that found and brought me to the hospital...and have been sleeping until you all got here." Walsh said with a yawn.

"Splendid..." Galen said as he flicked his thumb to activate the light.

Leaning close to Walsh as he focused the rotating light beam into each eye..." Alex, you don't remember anything that happened after the box fell and broke on the dock until you regained consciousness twenty minutes ago...your mind is blank. You are suffering from amnesia," Galen whispered to Walsh.

Galen turned off his device, and stood back from Walsh, focusing his attention on his almost immediate change of expression from certainty to confusion relative to where he was and what had happened to him.

"Do you have any more to add?" Galen asked.

"You know, I really can't remember. Like I told you, I can't remember anything after the box broke open – it's all a blank." Walsh said looking at both men.

Nash noticeably backed away in confused amazement.

"What the hell just happened?" Nash asked Galen in wide eyed disbelief.

Chapter 15 - The Secret

"... Friend deceives friend, and no one speaks the truth..."

Jeremiah 9:5

Coleen waited anxiously in the small cluster of chairs and wheelchairs next to the nursing unit while Nash and Galen interviewed Alex Walsh. Most certainly Walsh would be spinning a tale that Galen did not want Nash, or anyone for that matter, to hear. Nash walked into a mystery that no detective in modern times had ever run across. Police, since there have been organized law enforcement agencies have investigated crimes of all descriptions, crimes perpetrated by people who were motivated by greed, passion, or madness. Nash likely entered into this case with a bias that the murder was a product of greed, for the fruits of some treasure the box carried. Someone likely wanted it all for themselves, badly enough to kill for it. He did not expect to find himself in the middle of a centuries old pursuit – a game of deceit and manipulation whose trail was littered with the bones of the dead over the mists of time. This interview, one handed to Nash this day in the blink of an eye – one that would produce information he was not prepared as a man of the 21st century, one man of reason and logic to accept unemotionally, and would be the tipping point in his career.

The smell and setting of the hospital and nursing station, and waiting outside in the hallway conjured memories for Coleen of a recent experience involving the death of her brother Andrew. She remembered the shock of her father's message and how she frantically drove along Castle Street to the emergency department at the Glasgow Royal Infirmary where Andrew had been transported by helicopter. She remembered the blur of talking to a person at the Emergency Department who said that Andrew had been admitted in critical condition and transferred to the adjoining Intensive Care Unit. She remembered meeting her father Robert who was waiting for her. He asked her to set down, and told her Andrew had died. These were not good memories, ones still fresh in her mind.

Just then, the door to Walsh's room burst open with Nash in the lead. He had a grim look on his face, eyes fixed angrily forward. Galen followed, as they passed he motioned to Coleen to join them as the three walked briskly down the hallway. Halfway down the wing Nash looked to his right and paused in front of a small chapel room the hospital offered for families to speak privately or pray. He opened the door, found the room empty and walked in looking over his shoulder to Galen and Coleen to assure they also followed. After each entered, Nash circled back to the door, closed and locked it. Turning he addressed both Coleen and Galen.

"Please, both of you have a seat. Now, tell me Dr. Galen...what the hell did you do in there just now, and please tell me why I shouldn't arrest and load you right now for obstruction of justice and interfering with an official investigation?" Nash demanded.

Galen and Coleen sat down like two school children being scolded by their teacher. After a pause, while Nash composed himself, and got past the mysterious transformation of Walsh's recollection of the events evolving from a detailed account to total amnesia. Galen glanced at Coleen and her at him. She was so glad she was not the one obligated to tell Nash about what he had just seen and why, what and who murdered Robert Hopkins.

"Detective, I will explain...but you also should sit down," Galen said as he gestured at the chair opposite them.

"Okay, I'm setting down, and all ears," Nash replied as he pulled the chair closer, spinning it around and straddling it, folding his arms on the top of the backrest.

"The bottom line for your investigation is we know who killed Mr. Hopkins. We think we know why and we also expect him to kill again soon if he is not stopped," Galen said, being interrupted by Nash.

"...That is wonderful Doctor, I am gratified you know who the murderer is after less than two days in the Keys. Other than that tidbit of information, what I want to know now is, what the hell was all that about with your penlight with Walsh?" Nash asked waving his open hand spasmodically in the direction of Walsh's hospital room.

"...You are obviously upset about what I did detective. I used my penlight to facilitate a hypnotic-like induction to take place, thus, enabling Mr. Walsh's conscious mind to be vulnerable to a process known as dissociation, enabling me through a suggestion, to replace one memory with another..." Galen said, however interrupted by Nash.

"English Doctor, English!" Nash asked in a sarcastic tone.

"...I hypnotized him detective. Judging from your reaction in his room, you also doubted Mr. Walsh's account. I mean his account of the circumstances of the coffin falling and bursting open...and a live person tumbling out and knocking him unconscious. Shall I go on...am I correct?" Galen asked in a stressed voice.

"Well yes, that sounded like pretty much bullshit..." he quickly glanced to Coleen with an apologetic look, "...that story however won't keep him from remaining my top suspect in Hopkins' murder" ...Nobody could have been alive in that box for 400 years, pop out and have physically been able to knock out Walsh, murder Hopkins, and then carry Walsh for a mile or so into the mangrove, in the dark," Nash said.

"Detective, what Mr. Walsh told you just now was true. In repeating it anywhere would reveal the existence of a class of creatures I have worked most of my life to be kept a secret."

"True...true...!! Class of creatures...!! Holy shit, you are serious aren't you? What exactly is the secret you are protecting if I may ask? Nash asked sarcastically.

"Interestingly enough detective, part of the secret is in you..."

"Me? What are you talking about? Nash asked, leaning forward over top of the backrest.

"Coleen, please give me your tablet. I had my colleagues at the National Archives copy you when they sent their findings about Detective Nash's genealogy," Galen said as Coleen handed him the tablet.

"Part of the secret is me, my geni-what?" Nash asked, unseating himself to look over Galen's shoulder at the screen.

The screen showed a list of oldest male generations beginning with Will Nash, born circa 1640 through Detective Will Nash, born in 1972.

b.1640	Will Nash	great great great great great great great great great great	
b.1680	Rob Nash	great great great great great great great great great	
b.1706	Thomas Nash	great great great great great great great great	British Navy
b.1732	Philip Nash	great great great great great great great	
b.1758	George Nash	great great great great great great	
b.1784	George Jr.	great great great great great	
b.1810	James Nash	great great great great	
b.1836	Benjamin Nash	great great great	Union Navy
b.1870	Jonathan Nash	great great	
b.1896	Robert Nash	great	US Navy WWI
b.1922	Calvin Nash	grandfather	US Navy WWII

| b.1947 | Joseph Nash | father | | US Navy Vietnam |
| b.1972 | Russell Nash | Base Subject | | US Navy Iraq |

After Nash had a few minutes to scan the list, he continued.

"What in the hell is this? Have you people been keeping book on me, who are you guys? Nash asked with renewed indignity.

"Please detective, we have not been "keeping or writing a book" on you. This is all very necessary for us to answer your questions. If you allow me to continue...by the way, as far as you know, is this an accurate representation of the male lineage of your family," Galen asked gesturing at the tablet screen.

Nash refocused on the screen...

"As far as I can tell, this is correct. I did not know the names of any of my grandfather's past my great granddad Robert...but what the hell has this to do with this case, and me?"

"Look at the top of the list detective...Will Nash, born 1640. Will Nash had been on the ship that Walsh and Hopkins found on Carysfort Reef, the same one carrying Angus Cassidy and his guardians, the Brodie's.

This is the same Angus Cassidy Alex Walsh spoke about just now. He and several of his shipmates and the Captain of the Scottish privateer ship, the *Edith Louise,* became ill during its maiden trans-Atlantic voyage between Glasgow, Scotland and Port Royal, Jamaica. They were all put off in St. George's, Bermuda and treated at a seaman's dispensary. The ship continued its voyage the next day. That was the 29th of August, 1659. The *Edith Louise* never made it to Port Royal. It was likely lost off the Florida Coast sometime in mid to late September of that year. All were listed as lost. Now we learn where it came to rest, and only Cassidy survived...sealed in his box." Galen paused.

"Okay, okay...so you are telling me the guy that killed Hopkins is the same guy who was a shipmate of my great grandfather 400 years ago? Nash asked gesturing in amazement.

"They were on the same ship, but not ship mates. Yes, Walsh's account pretty much confirms that Detective, you can't make this stuff up. Will Nash became ill by the time they were near Bermuda because of what Cassidy did to him and the others who were put off the *Edith Louise.* Cassidy survived 400 years in the sealed coffin because he is what you call today a vampire. This is the other part of the secret I am protecting – that they as creatures really exist, they live. Cassidy fed on each of the men put ashore in Bermuda, which means he fed on your Great

Grandfather Will Nash. Cassidy is here on Key Largo, or at least was...the autopsy of Hopkins revealed he had less than ½ a liter of blood in his body. A normal person has 5 liters of blood. The reason he was 4 ½ liters short is perhaps because a lot spilled onto the ground from the massive frontal wound, but the other reason is that Cassidy drank it, feeding on Hopkins as he died on marina's dock last Sunday. ” Galen said expecting an emotional reply from Nash.

“Oh, Jesus, Joseph, and Mary...you are serious aren't you?” Nash responded.

“Yes we are serious, and this is where you need to hear from me.” Coleen interjected.

“I can attest to all this. My family has worked with Dr. Galen for generations to track down these creatures, offering them alternative nourishment to human blood or killing them to protect the secret and the rest of us from them,” Coleen said, looking Nash directly in the eye.

“Generations...your family has been working with one man for generations; how can that be?” Nash asked.

“Because I am nearly as old as Cassidy, he planted an infection in me that resulted in the same genetic scrambling that Cassidy experienced 400 years before he and I first met. Detective, I too am a vampire; the same as Cassidy, but not the same. Unlike the popular mythology vampires are not the animated dead, they are alive and can be killed the same as anyone else, they just live very long, are great manipulators, and have super sensitivity to smell, sound, taste, and have highly developed intuitions...the rest I will leave for another day. After I became infected, clarity intervened. As a physician and scientist, I eventually perfected a synthesized replacement for human blood all the while pursuing Cassidy across most of Europe. My life's work has been to hunt down Cassidy and all those he infected as vampires, my cover on the whole has always been as a physician and scientist, who I was in the second century and continued to enhance my knowledge in science and medicine as they advanced over the centuries, I became a well-known and respected teacher, writer, and lecturer. Now about you in all this...we will start with something you have been likely been trying to figure out all your life. And be honest with me...have your senses been, shall we say, extra keen...meaning you can smell things, taste things, and hear things before the people around you do...have you during your work in the Navy and here as a policeman; especially since you began investigating this murder have been able to sense something or someone's presence but can't explain it...a presence you can almost taste...especially when meeting me and shaking my hand an hour ago?"

Nash paused in his aggressive approach to questioning Galen; this was an epiphany that answered so many questions for him...reasons for which he had suppressed throughout his life.

"...Jesus....err, Yes...I have ... At times it creeped me out, and when I shook your hand in the hallway it was like grabbing onto a live electrical wire...but I ask again what does this list of my family have to do with this case, are you telling me I am a vampire too?" Nash asked with a sarcastic smile.

"No, you are not a vampire detective, but you carry a vampire's DNA, you carry Cassidy's DNA, the DNA of a mass murderer that we both seek to locate. I will be truthful, for the secret to be kept, Cassidy has to disappear – he cannot be publically arrested, interrogated, and put on trial. He would move things to the light that need be kept in the dark. He cannot be killed and body subject to an autopsy. There would be things and DNA found that the world is not ready to learn about. Frankly, the press would feed on this story for weeks – and questions would be asked of Coleen and I, as well as your connection to Angus Cassidy through Will Nash – the issue of vampire-like physical capabilities that you exhibit," Galen said as he stood up for a stretch.

Nash also stood up and walked to the door and back, then sat back down on the chair, this time spinning it back, facing forward. Leaning toward Galen and glancing regularly at Coleen, he asked:

"Doctor, this is information is pretty wild...your story does sound logical, but is one that if I would write this in my report...I would likely be off the case and assigned to the rubber gun squad tomorrow. What am I supposed to do with it?"

"Rusty..." Coleen said, "I know this is a lot to believe from two strangers and all coming to you without warning. It is a lot to process without much preparation – I know, when I was told about the actual existence of vampires, and Dr. Galen being one; well I thought of only one thing – to get up and get the hell out of there. What convinced me to stay was my father's long association with Dr. Galen, the work he had been doing, and Dr. Galen himself."

After Coleen finished, Nash turned his attention to the floor, staring silently for several minutes. Galen and Coleen watched him and as they glanced at each other, Nash finally stood up.

"Well, okay we are looking for a guy named Angus Cassidy. Do we know what he looks like? Where he might be? Will he need more blood soon....?" Nash said as his cell phone buzzed in his shirt pocket. He answered and was silent for a few minutes; both Coleen and Galen heard a male voice speaking about a double murder that had just been discovered in a nearby motel and the forensic team was just arriving. Nash told the caller he would respond.

"Okay Doctors, it looks like our Mr. Cassidy may have been busy last evening. Two female students from Pennsylvania were found murdered by a maid in an old mom and pop motel not far from your Hotel on the Overseas Highway. You are invited to tag along...and let's ride together for this conversation is not over." Nash said as he unlocked the door and headed toward the elevator with Galen and Coleen right behind.

All three walked together to Nash's car without conversation. Nash was deep in thought regarding the revelation of the actual existence of what he and the rest of the world thought previously only to be fictional creatures; that he had fragments of vampire DNA in his body – and that resulted in the heightened sensory capabilities and intuition he had served him well, especially to solve difficult mysteries; and finally the totally unethical and illegal solution Galen proposed – that Cassidy had to disappear, never be subject to a public arrest or interrogation, never to be reportedly killed and autopsied; just disappear. Upon arriving at Nash's vehicle he made seating assignments...

"Dr. Galen, sit up front, and Coleen in the back..." Nash said as an order to both. After each positioned themselves in the car, Nash started the engine, exited the hospital parking lot and pulled the car south onto the Overseas Highway.

"The motel's name is the "Come-on Inn"; I know, not one of the luxury chains...it is somewhere on the left about a quarter of a mile south of your hotel." Nash said.

"Detective, if Cassidy killed them, and if I am correct, the victims will likely be displayed in some fashion as a message to me..." Galen said.

"Why do you believe they will be displayed rather than just left for dead?" Nash asked.

Galen hesitated answering, glancing back to Coleen.

"Because Cassidy knows I am here...I know this because I sensed him last evening at the hotel. I was sitting in my room after we both had retired for the evening. About 12:30 am this morning I felt his presence, very close; it was so strong I literally jumped from my chair. I rushed to Coleen's room and got her. We searched the lobby and lounge for him. He had gone. It is my feeling he entered the hotel bar last night to lure a victim or victims to him when he sensed me inside the building and fled," Galen said.

"Why the f..." Nash caught himself. "Why did you not tell me this before for God's sake?" Nash asked making a frustrated gesture with his hand.

"I told Coleen not to tell you because I did not want to confide in you. I thought maybe we could glean information from you cleanly and track Cassidy ourselves before he could kill again; quietly dispose of him before you or other civil authorities could complicate the matter with your rules and criminal procedure for dealing with murderers. I still am hopeful we can work with one another to that end." Galen said.

"Dr. Galen, you may not know what you are asking me to do. You are asking a police officer to help you track down a person we think is a murderer and kill them; not just kill them but to dispose of them – all foreign to everything I am sworn to defend against. This reminds me of what was going on with a group of Miami cops in the mid 1980's that would kill drug dealers and dispose of them in the Miami River...I am not that sort of cop Doctor, at least I don't think so..."

"Then how would you deal with Cassidy detective? Galen asked.

"I don't know Doctor..." Nash said as he turned into the motel entrance way and past the marked cars blocking the back parking lot. As Nash exited the car, he remembered the surveillance cameras in the lobby of

Galen's hotel. He paused, pulled his cell phone from his shirt pocket and dialed the central dispatcher on duty, Jake Murray.

"Murray, this is Nash, I need you to call the Bayside Hotel in Key Largo, ask for the security manager, Ms. Elaine Mann. Ask her to pull the surveillance tapes or digital records for her lobby cameras for last evening...ah, from about 1800 to 0200. Tell her I'll be by to see them in about an hour..." Nash said.

"Sure Rusty, I live to serve you...I'll handle it but will cost you a beer next choir practice." Murray responded. Choir practice was a code for an end of evening shift get together of police and dispatchers before two days off and rotating to next shift cycle. It involved alcohol and bitching.

Turning to Galen and Coleen, Nash remarked "If you had told me earlier, we would have known what Cassidy looks like long before now – if what you say is correct, the video surveillance cameras posted in your hotel's lobby will provide pictures worth a thousand words."

Approaching the door of the end unit Nash was met with the responding officer. The crime scene team was inside under the supervision of Lieutenant Robert Hernandez, who processed the crime scene at Carysfort Reef Marina earlier in the week.

"Hey Rusty..." said the officer, looking behind Nash at Coleen and Galen, standing a few feet behind.

"Inside there are two deceased white females, both approximately 19 - 21 years old. They were reported missing this morning by their roommates just before the maid found them. Both are lying nude on the bed facing one another, and appear to have been strangled. Both also seem to have identical cuts near the carotid artery on the right side of their necks." The officer reported. Nash turned to Galen...

"Doctor, please join me inside...Coleen we'll spare you this if you don't need to be part of this." Nash said. Coleen nodded and smiled backing away and walked toward the shade of a nearby palm tree overlooking Florida Bay. Nash paused, watching her walk away, then collected himself and walked into the motel room, with Galen following.

Addressing the lead crime forensic investigator..."Hello Bob, we have to stop meeting this way..." Nash said as he leaned forward to look under the sheet covering the bodies.

"Nash, what the hell are you doing..." Hernandez said as he pulled the corner of the sheet away from Nash. "...You are contaminating the crime scene, not that the maid, the desk clerk, the gardener, the manager, half a dozen fucking tourists staying in the motel or the responding officer hadn't already."

"Can you tell me more about how long they have been dead, what is the cause of death, and anything else that might help me tie this case to my marina murder? Nash asked.

"They have been dead no more than 6 hours. It is unclear whether we can tie this to the other case except for what appears to be loss of blood in both victims. Both exhibit the classic symptoms of hypovolemic shock; largely cold clammy skin and facial pallor. However, neither one died from it, it appears strangulation was cause of death for both, but whoever took their lives, took their blood as well – damnedist thing. The pathology report from their autopsies should confirm that. Who knows, maybe we got someone who thinks he is a vampire." Hernandez said with a smirk. Before Nash or Galen could react, he continued..."There is one thing, both just had intercourse before they were killed...there are traces of semen found in "you know where" of both victims.

"Thanks Bob...keep in touch."

Nash exited first, breezing past Galen. He did not notice Galen picking up a motel business envelope with "Γαληνῷ" handwritten in Greek on the front, propped against the telephone on the small desk next to the television. He quickly slipped the envelope into his jacket pocket. Outside the room, Nash turned right toward the motel office.

"I'll be right back, I'm going to the desk clerk and find out who rented this room, then back to your hotel for pictures of your Mr. Cassidy." Nash said walking up the gavel walkway toward the motel office.

Galen walked over to Coleen sitting in a wooden bench overlooking the Bay.

"Beautiful isn't it?" Galen asked. "...it reminds me of the Mediterranean shore line in North Africa, but much more green and humid."

Sitting down on the bench next to Coleen, he pulled the envelope from his pocket.

"What's that Doctor?"

"What the police call evidence Coleen. This envelope likely contains a letter for me from Cassidy..." Galen said undoing the seal and pulling the note out.

"Hum..."Γαληνῷ", or in English "...to Galen;" the name he knew you by when you and he first met..." Coleen said examining the envelope while Galen opened and read its contents in handwritten Greek. After reading it slowly...

"The years have not diluted his capability to express a special type of hubris in writing as well as in his deeds. He writes about killing Hopkins and the two young women, and how much he enjoyed their bodies before drugging them, feeding on them, and most of all, he enjoyed killing them to insult my impotence to stop him. He welcomes me back to the chase and warned me I would lose everything important to me this time, signing it "Demetrius"." Galen said with a sigh, folding the note over, sitting silent, gazing forward as he processed his old enemy's challenge and warning.

"We will save this for Detective Nash – if it is anything, it is a confession – and confirms our story – but a confession only he will see," Galen said as he returned the letter to the envelope and back into his pocket.

Chapter 16 - The Plan

"...Graceless lady you know who I am...You know I can't let you slide through my hands. Wild horses couldn't drag me away...Wild, wild horses, couldn't drag me away...."

Rolling Stones, *Wild Horses*, 1969

Holmes had just picked up Cassidy from the Come-on Inn and they were driving north on the Overseas Highway toward Holmes' houseboat when two Monroe County Sheriff's patrol cars passed them from the opposite direction with their overhead lights flashing. Cassidy was in the back seat; his head still covered with a *chafiye*, or white cotton Persian type head cover to protect him from the sun.

"Wow, there must be something going on back there. Master, did you hear anything back there before I picked you up? Holmes asked Cassidy.

"No lad, nothin'..." Cassidy said, leaning back into the dark tinted area of Holmes' vehicle looking straight ahead. He smiled about the discovery that had likely just been made, and the taunt he left for his enemy Galen. Cassidy's thoughts returned to his plans to get out of Key Largo, the annoyance of Galen's close pursuit, and his efforts to return to where he might have the safety of home – a place to regroup, heal, and launch his next project.

"Master...! I forgot to tell you!!...Remember that guy's name you asked me to do an Internet search for the day before yesterday ...ah..."Main.." err..."ooh..." Anyway, as it turns out he is listed as president of a company in northern Afghanistan called Bactrus-Keraunos Mining Group. I did as you asked and sent them an email and attached your letter that I scanned. Well, a response came in this morning from someone from the same email address; well sort of...I could not read the note, it was in something that looked like Russian or maybe Greek."

"Excellent Holmes, we must get back so I can read it and partake of some breakfast, I'm starving." Cassidy said checking his shirt for any blood stains from his recent undertaking at the motel.

Cassidy was intrigued with the find Holmes made. Could this be that his father vampire was still alive and had come out of isolation and is dealing in precious metals? Could his longtime companion there who took his name but refused to leave Mainyu be there, and part of the enterprise? He was not only seeking refuge, but he was going back to his family, and the loving arms of the woman who nursed him through his journey to vampire.

This was fortuitous for more than one reason. He had given up any thoughts of beginning to build a new life in the Florida Keys – To confirm returning home, even with his tail between his legs was the best choice, he listed the negatives to remaining where he was. First, there were no real base metal sources or chemicals from which to manufacture precious metals to finance his enterprises; they all would have to be brought in from the outside. In the past he could challenge their power with his own. Now his power came from remaining hidden. The key reason for getting away was his activities had drawn much more attention from the authorities more quickly than they had in the past. In his experience from the beginning to the mid-17th century, communication was by word of mouth, or by ink on paper carried by courier. News spread much slower – the population was relatively in the dark about the ruling class or news beyond their own village. Gossip and rumor prevailed, and he could subvert that. He had no way to subvert the news in this age of man, anywhere, yet.

After a breakfast of eggs, ham, bread and beer Cassidy and Holmes gathered around Holmes' computer screen. He opened his email screen and found a message from gkeraunos@bkmg.af.com.

"Tis from Gulnar, m'mate...the lass and I have been separated for many years...frankly thought she was dead...Can you do something with the message I can hold – on paper?" Cassidy asked smiling, as he read.

"Yep...very easy; after do you want me to erase it?"

"Nay, I plan on answering it again. I will write down my message and thee put in that machine and send it, alright?" Cassidy questioned to ensure Holmes understood.

"Holmes, I am leaving here shortly and want thee to join me when I do. Can thee leave with me?" Cassidy asked Holmes as he knelt down next to him at the computer.

"Yes, oh yes Master – I am with you!! When do we leave?" asked Holmes.

"Soon, tomorrow; tell me the places where we can get on airplanes and fly away from here?

"You mean airports?

"Aye, airports..."

"Okay...discounting the small ones – there is the **Marathon Airport just south of here; off the Keys there is**

Homestead Airport, Tamiami Airport, Opa-Locka Airport, Miami International Airport, and Fort Lauderdale International Airport," Holmes responded.

"Tell me about which are the best; the ones that are best suited for a private aircraft capable of long distance voyage?"

"Well...the best is probably Miami International, but it is huge and lots of things could go wrong if you want to get through fast without much notice...the other is Fort Lauderdale. It is very good, but smaller and presents fewer problems if you know what I mean?"

"Which one is farthest away?"

"Fort Lauderdale is the farthest...about 20 miles north of Miami Airport."

"Good, now which ones are the next best, smaller but will still accommodate me needs?"

"Wow...well Marathon is very close, but may be too small to land a long distance jet...Tamiami and Opa-Locka are both probably okay, but my choice would be Tamiami."

"Excellent, do ye know how to get to these airports?" Cassidy asked and received an affirming nod from Holmes.

After receiving what he needed to know, Cassidy composed his note to Gulnar in Greek. Handing it to Holmes, he scanned the message, attached it to the email and sent it. With a satisfied look he looked up at Cassidy who returned his smile. With that, he reached over, lifted up the cover of the scanning screen and Cassidy took the letter, folded it, and put into his pocket. Their triumphal pause was soon to end when both heard dogs barking and sounding as if they were getting closer.

"What be that Holmes?" Cassidy asked as he looked out the window in the direction of the barking sounds.

"They are dogs Master; early this morning I noticed a bunch of police gathering in the parking lot next to where you were freed from your imprisonment. After a while standing and talking they took out some dogs from their truck and headed across the lot toward the north, I think and into the mangroves. Is that where you came from? If so, they may be tracking your scent to here...maybe we ought to leave, what do you think? Holmes said as he got up and joined Cassidy at the window.

"Yes, we should be leavin'...now." Cassidy said as he picked up and draped the long rain coat over him, topped off with the hastily fashioned *chafiye* and walked out into the light. Holmes ran to his bedroom closet. On the top self, covered in folded T shirts was the dark blue Smith and Wesson manufacturer's pistol box. He grabbed it and the paper bag containing a box of .40 caliber ammunition. He stuffed both into a backpack and rushed out. Slamming the front door; then turned to lock it. As he did, Holmes noticed through the glass he left his computer on...shrugging his shoulders, he remembered the monitor would time out and he would attend to that after he came back. Holmes got into his vehicle and drove it out the gravel track that was the back way in and out to avoid the front entrance and the approaching police dog team.

"Holmes, take me to that place where we saw Galen last night. We need to pick someone up..."

After giving Cassidy a puzzled look Holmes complied with his order, He negotiated his vehicle around the small coral boulders on the narrow track past an unfinished house on the adjoining property and onto Monroe Road south to where it merged with the Overseas Highway.

***

Sheila Brown stumbled back onto the Carysfort Reef Marina coral rock gravel parking lot from the mangroves behind the FDLE's K-9 tracking team. She was dripping with perspiration, dirty from falling down on two occasions, and thirsty. The single bottle of water she brought with her was gone the first half hour, and before the dogs led them to the abandoned Nike Hercules base about 3 miles from where they started. The trail to the base and the headquarters building got muddled as they got closer. The dogs seemed to want to go west, then east, and then finally north. After arriving at the building the SWAT team leader ordered it surrounded and a dog was sent in. It came out without locating anyone. Once they entered the structure and its basement, the dogs found a spot that had been occupied by someone recently. The vegetation and debris in the basement also had been disturbed, and according to the dog handlers appeared to have been flattened by someone or something lying on it. The only thing found out of the ordinary was a plastic wrapper from a six pack of cheese crackers found in a corner of the room. Finding the building empty, the team reassembled outside. To the amazement of their handlers, the dogs set off on a second trail, this one heading south back toward the marina.

Back at the parking lot, Brown followed the dogs and tactical team south across its western edge, passing the entrance toward the houseboat dockage.

The tracking dogs were stopped by their handlers when it became clear the trail lead to last houseboat on the dock. Brown recalled from Nash's notes this was Seth Holmes' place, and he drove a beaten up surplus Metro Police Crown Victoria; which was not anywhere in sight.

The SWAT Team Leader again positioned his officers behind cover sending 2 officers to board the vacant houseboat next to Holmes' and the another to take up a position where the water side of the houseboat was in clear view. From a loudspeaker he identified himself and instructed those inside to come out with their hands in plain view. After three requests, he, under a stretched definition of the "hot pursuit" policy, sent three officers to enter the houseboat. After they forced open the front door and searched the craft. After it was declared safe and clear, Brown moved inside to protect the scene so it could be searched by the forensic unit. She noticed the computer was still on, but the screen had timed out, and found nothing in the printer/scanner. Next to the printer under a newspaper was a handwritten letter that appeared to be in a foreign language using letters she did not recognize. She made note of what she found and called Communications on Marathon Key for the forensic team and that she would be executing and sending an affidavit for a search warrant from here vehicle's computer. She did that, and then called Nash.

"...Hcy, how are you doing, enjoying the walk in the mangroves?" Nash asked.

"Oh, more wonderful than you described...if there is a next time you walk the dogs..." Brown said.

"Did you get the Metro team squared away, and if you did, did you find anything?

"Yes and yes...the guys from Metro went home and Evans sent us half dozen guys from SWAT to help. Anyway, we followed the trail to an old building at the old Nike Hercules base about 3 miles north of the marina...it was empty, whoever was there, left...but there is a zinger..."

"Zinger...what did you find?" asked Nash excitedly.

"It's not what we found exactly, but certainly there might be something after being translated from whatever language it is....it's actually where we were lead. They dogs followed a trail back to the marina and to Seth Holmes' houseboat...it is the last one on the dock, right?"

"Yep, that's the one...was he there...was anyone else there?" Nash asked in anticipation of another body piling up.

"Nope, no one was there...Holmes' car was gone, but the computer was still on and there was a letter handwritten in some fucked up language next to the printer scanner."

"Ok, get an affidavit for a search warrant started for the houseboat and the computer, and make sure you tell Hernandez to have the hard drive imaged for any communications that might tell us if Cassidy was there, Holmes' role, any information about him, credit card accounts, money withdrawn from a bank, and if they have planned an escape."

"Believe it or not your majesty, I already started that process...but. is there anything else...would you like me to bring you lunch Rusty?" Brown said sarcastically.

"Nope, but you are sooo kind...we are getting some here at the Bayside Hotel – supposedly our suspect in all this: Angus Cassidy made an appearance last night here, and if he walked through the lobby we have got him on the hotel's surveillance system!" Nash shot back.

"What do you want me to do here...Stick around here until Hernandez brings the search warrant"

"Yes...send the dog team home and back your vehicle somewhere that is out of the way in case Holmes or whoever comes back...you said the computer was still on...maybe they were only going to be away for a short time...if that happens call for a backup; keep your little ass in the car until angry guys with guns show up, okay?"

"Gotcha...what about SWAT couldn't they wait with me?"

"Sure, who's in charge there, is it Bill Peterson?"

"Yes, I think so."

"Okay, ask him to leave some of his guys with you, but they should stay out of sight like you. If they can't stay, do what I asked you to do in the first place, okay? Nash responded with concern in his voice.

"Will do boss." Brown said.

***

In less than a half an hour Cassidy and Holmes reached the Bayside Hotel and Resort. Cassidy directed Holmes to drive him to the entrance; then park in the farthest corner of the parking lot, preferably in the shade.

Cassidy entered the hotel lobby, pausing at the edge of the room, surveying everyone who was coming and going. Although he did not sense Galen nearby, there was no reason to take chances. The tracking dogs he just avoided made it clear the authorities were almost as interested in him as was Galen. Seeing the speeding police car heading toward the motel after Holmes picked him up also likely signaled to them his handiwork. Luckily he was still ahead of them he thought. Crossing the lobby, he approached the desk clerk...

"Good afternoon, I am looking for a couple of me friends who are your guests. They are from Scotland." Cassidy said.

"Sir, what are your friend's names?" asked the desk clerk.

Cassidy, hoping his nemesis was still using a version of his name, or the name he knew him by when the parted company in Syria. He replied...

"Galen, me friend's name is Galen."

"Oh yes...Dr. Galen and his assistant Dr. Jones...they are not here right now; would you like to leave a message for Dr. Galen?" the desk clerk said.

"Ah...no; I left one for him somewhere else....I would like to leave a message for Dr. Jones..." Cassidy said with a sarcastic grin.

The desk clerk slid several sheets of paper to Cassidy, as well as a pen and an envelope. Taking the pen he tried to write without first engaging the ratchet to expose the ballpoint...the clerk apologized and helped Cassidy. Straightening the paper, Cassidy began the note...

> *...Dr. Jones, I hope thou art well. I must quickly get to the point. Thou no doubt believe'st ye are working with the man claim'n to be Claudius Galenicus – now using the name Galen. The man is not Galen – I am Galen. The man thou work'st for is really the vile villain Gaius*

Tacitus Cassius. Cassius captured me as I pursued him to Scotland. After, he put me on a sailing vessel destined for the far off wilds of ye Caribbean Sea... He sent his two most trusted guardians with orders to kill me while at sea and dispose of me body there. Fortune smiled on me when a tempest sunk the ship and I alone lived to tell the tale. Do thou'st know where he was last night after ye left him? Thou are in danger – as he pursues me to keep his secret, he will destroy ye as well. Let us escape together – there is no time to waste, once ye get this come to the front door of the inn with your baggage, I am here, I am waiting.

Galenicus...

After giving the envelope to the desk clerk Cassidy smiled and walked to the edge of the lobby, covered his head and exposed skin with his head covering and coat. Stepping out into the light, he looked to where Holmes should have parked the car – locating it; he walked across the parking lot and got in.

"...Now we wait..." Cassidy said settling into the darkness of the backseat.

In less than three quarters of an hour, a car appeared at the front of the hotel and dropped off two people who remained at the front entrance as if waiting for the driver to park and join them. Cassidy stirred in the backseat and focused on both.

"It's Galenicus and the delicious Dr. Jones... I can almost taste his presence, and lookin' forward to hers. This should not take long to find out if the lass takes the bait..." Cassidy said, smiling as he leaned back into the seat after the trio disappeared inside the hotel.

***

Once inside the hotel with Nash in the lead, they went directly to the administrative offices down the hallway left of the check in desk. Nash knocked on the glass door and opened it where **Elaine Mann** the security director was reviewing the video of the time period Nash had requested earlier.

"Hello Detective Nash, who are your friends?" Mann asked.

"Oh...this is Dr. Mark Galen and his assistant Dr. Coleen Jones.   They   are   assisting   me   in   this investigation." Nash said moving from the front in the cramped office, allowing both to come forward and exchange handshakes and greetings.

"Well...I went over the times your office gave me...So, I have them queued up. Do you want to review them in real time or in fast forward?" She asked.

Nash turned to Galen...

"...Fast forward the video to around 12:15 am this morning, then play it in regular time." Galen asked as he sat down to her left focusing on the screen.

When the video chronometer reached 00:25 Galen stiffened in his chair.

"Please slow the video down...please," Galen requested.

"Hey, the weird looking guy on the left of that guy with the mustache and goatee looks like Seth Holmes, the guy's houseboat is being watched by Deputy Brown. It looks like Holmes is up to his ass in this!" Nash said.

"The man on the right with the mustache and goatee is Angus Cassidy..." Galen said looking first at Coleen, then at Nash. "... That's our man detective. Please rewind the video once more please Ms. Mann, Detective and Coleen, pay close attention to Cassidy's facial expression."

Mann re-wound the video and played it at ½ speed. At 00:25 Cassidy and Holmes enter the hotel lobby...

"See, they enter the lobby...watch Cassidy looking around; then here...at 00:32 his facial expression changes...see, like he is hearing an announcement; then he looks around and behind him, then up toward the upper floors. He then says something to...Holmes is it...? Then both turn and are out the door at 00:37." Galen said ending his commentary.

"What was he hearing? We only use the public address system for fires or emergencies...There have been no announcements made for weeks." Mann commented.

"He didn't hear anything Elaine, but we think we know what was going on. Can you copy the video to a cassette or a computer disk or something we can have for evidence...and can you also freeze frame and print out a couple of hard copies of both these guys for us now?

"Sure can, copying the video portion will take someone smarter than me, but I do know how to make hardcopies..." Mann said smiling.

"Thanks a lot Elaine. One more thing, can you also fax a copy to my supervisor Captain Evans of the picture you print out so he can send it to all our road deputies? Nash asked.

"Sure can, any message you want me to attach to the fax?" Mann asked.

"Yes...here it is: *Suspects wanted for questioning in murder investigation; approach with caution. Contact Detective Russell Nash through the Communications Division and notify Captain Philip Evans immediately*...We are going to grab an early supper at the hotel restaurant; can you have the pictures and maybe the video ready for us in about an hour?" Nash asked.

"I think I can do that." Mann responded.

The three then walked out and across the lobby toward the restaurant. Nash motioned them to a corner of the lobby and pulled out his cell phone and dialed Brown who was waiting in the parking lot for either Hernandez and the search warrant or Holmes. He put the phone on speaker mode in case what she found was germane to Galen's link to this case so he would not have to retell the story and finally to give Galen or Coleen a direct opportunity to question Brown.

"...Brown here; hey Rusty the search warrant got here in record time – I guess Evans or someone is greasing the skids of our fabulous Keys criminal justice system."

"Very good, I have you on speaker, Dr. Galen and Dr. Jones are here – we have surveillance pictures of the suspect Angus Cassidy and Seth Holmes; who we can now consider to be a conspirator in this case. Where are you now?"

"We are in the houseboat…Hey Doctors!! We discovered that whoever Holmes was entertaining, likely Cassidy, they had just finished breakfast – the egg yolks have hardly had time to dry on the dishes in the sink. We also found a handwritten letter in Greek next to Holmes' scanner/printer; and are you ready for this? The computer was still on and Holmes' email was still on the screen – the guy apparently didn't put anything behind passwords…anyway, there are a couple of emails here from a gkeraunos@bkmg.af.com.

The computer tech imaging the hard drive told me it originated in Afghanistan. Galen then addressed Nash…

"Detective, can we get an image of the letter so I can read it, or do we have to go over there…?"

"…Rusty I can answer that, I can take a picture of it with my phone and send it to Rusty's – how's that?" Brown asked.

"That would be splendid, thank you!" Galen said

Nash then returned the phone to standard talk mode and thanked Brown and asked her to keep Captain Evans informed about the houseboat and the evidence they are collecting. He also asked her to request the officer be taken off the front entrance to the marina, replaced by a couple of plainclothes task force officers to conduct a surveillance on the houseboat in case Holmes and Cassidy returned. Nash told everyone to get a shower, change clothes and get some dinner because they all are in for a long night.

Sitting down in the dining room each ordered their suppers from the "Early Bird" menus – Nash looked around and observed that the "Early Bird was a Florida restaurant phenomenon to attract elderly visitors and residents looking for a reasonably priced meal before the traditional evening dining hour. These folks are catered to as they are literally a backbone of the state's economy. Galen and Coleen looked around to find many in the dining room fitting that demographic and snickered.

"It seems I am in the right place that caters to people of my age...almost." Galen said smiling.

"Detective, we also have another handwritten note in Greek to share with you..." Galen said as he reached into his sports jacket and produced the envelope he picked up at the motel before it was noticed by Hernandez. Nash's body language reflected that of a house cat about to hiss and swipe its claws.

"I know detective, bear with me – this is addressed to me...me. It was written by Cassidy in that room likely with 2 dead women lying just behind him in the bed where they were killed! Suppose your associates would have collected it? Remember our earlier conversation?"

Galen asked as if he was repeating the same instructions to a child with a short attention span.

"Alright, what does it say Doctor?" Nash asked leaning back and taking a long drink of his iced tea.

Opening the letter and flattening it on the table, Galen translated it word for word. He paused each time as Cassidy described in graphic terms how he picked up the women, drugged them, had sex with both before he fed on their blood; and then in the coldest terms..."...after I took what I wanted...after I enjoyed everything their bodies had to offer; I then crushed each of their larynxes and they suffocated...holding their throats and gagging for air to the last..." Galen then silently looked up from the letter, folded it, put it back in the envelope, and handed it to Nash. Nash gave Galen a hard look and tucked it into the inside pocket of his jacket.

Their silent gazes were interrupted with the arrival of their suppers. They ate in silence except for a few good comments about the fish or the mango salsa each lathered on top of their blackened fillets. Near the end of their meal Nash's phone buzzed in his shirt pocket, it was from Brown.

"Ah, here is likely the picture of the letter Deputy Brown found at Holmes' houseboat." Nash said as he opened the text message.

Embedded in the text page was a small photograph of the letter. Nash attempted to enlarge it but was only partially successful.

"Can you make any of this out?" Nash asked Galen as he handed him the device.

Galen took the phone and squinted at the image for an extended time.

"No, I am sorry; can we go and see the original? Galen asked.

"We will have to." Nash said, dialing Brown's cell phone. Brown answered and confirmed she was still there, but Hernandez was packing up and he had planned to take the letter in as evidence, with him.

"Ask Hernandez to wait, we are coming right over. Dr. Galen can translate the letter and it is very important we see it before being sealed away as evidence." Nash said. There was a bit of silence from Brown, and then came back on.

"Okay, he says they will have everything wrapped up in 20 minutes if you can get over here by then." Brown said.

"Tell him we will be there before then. See you in a few..." Nash said putting his phone into is jacket pocket next to the envelope Galen had given him.

Nash turned to Coleen and Galen and asked them to accompany him to the marina to read over the letter Brown had found. Galen agreed; with that, all three got up and began walking toward the lobby.

"If it's alright with you Dr. Galen, I'll stay here and rest while you and Detective Nash go to the marina to see the letter. You don't need me to help read Greek, and I'm a bit tired and could use a change of shoes and time off my feet." Coleen said.

"Of course Coleen, once we look at the letter, we will be back for what it looks like a long night. It's good that you take a few minutes to refresh and rest." Galen said as he followed Nash through the lobby toward the security office. Mann had left for a few minutes and the uniformed officer handed Nash the photo print outs and computer disk in an envelope. At the door Coleen hugged both men before they left the hotel. Nash, who was pleasantly surprised thought how events had been distracting him from his infatuation with Coleen, he concluded he would have to pay more attention to her as well as working the case.

Opening his vehicle, Nash was met with a rush of heated air from inside the closed car; a well-known gift of the Florida sun. He slipped off his sports jacket, the one he really didn't like wearing, and tossed it in the back seat.

He set the air conditioner on high cold, and with Galen, set off to the marina and the mysterious letter.

After walking the two to the entrance door, Coleen felt relieved she did not have to go back to the marina. It had been a long and exhausting day with no doubt more to come. She took the elevator to the second floor and once inside her room, placed her purse and her briefcase on the small office desk on the way to the bathroom sink. Once there she stopped and assessed how her makeup and hair had survived the day...and...she decided they hadn't. She gave up, washed her face and brushed her teeth; and kicking off her shoes lay back on the bed and closed her eyes for a short nap.

***

"Master, what are we waiting for, I have to pee." Holmes announced in what Cassidy thought was a whine.

"We are waiting for a wee young woman, the same one we saw enter the inn an hour ago. We are waitin' for her to come to the front with her baggage to wait for me to come and save her...get out and piss in the bushes." Cassidy said.

Cassidy had noted that Galen and another man, likely an official of the local police had just left the hotel without the woman. He theorized she may not have been given his message straight away, and it would be a short time before it is delivered, read and a decision made regarding his proposal. A positive reaction would be as he told Holmes, she would appear at the entrance as he instructed; a negative one would be a hasty return of Galen and the policeman. In the latter case, they would make a hasty exit and head to the rendezvous with Gulnar's people and return home and safety.

***

Coleen rolled over on her left side and opened her eyes. She noticed her room telephone blinking which indicated a message was waiting. Strange she thought, the only people that would be trying to contact her either had just left and certainly she did not sleep through a ringing phone. Picking up the phone and dialing the front desk she was told a gentleman had left a message for her earlier in the day. Perplexed, her mind raced as to who it could have been. The only other person could have been...Cassidy! Cassidy had been in the hotel and they had evidence of that, he knew Galen was on this case because he wrote a letter to him... practically in the blood of those two poor women found in the motel down the road. But...did he know anything about her? Had he been watching her? Did he know her name? And...why would he write her a message?

Deciding the only way to end the suspense was to retrieve the message and see what was in it; maybe it wasn't from Cassidy at all. Maybe it was from a fan of Galen's work saw him at the hospital that thought it best not to address him directly, but through his executive assistant...she hoped. Exiting the elevator she scanned the room for Cassidy or that weird looking man who was with him in the video. It was clear. With a decidedly lessened sense of concern she approached the desk and retrieved the envelope. On it was handwritten cursive, *"To Dr. Jones...."* Coleen did not open it until she returned to her room. Sitting in the desk chair she kicked off her shoes and put her feet on the bed to get comfortable.

Opening the note she read the message from Cassidy, then read it again. Cassidy was a good liar and this deception would have made her think twice. However, a good deception needed facts and things known to the target to resonate in order the lie seem to be true. This simply was not the case. Cassidy did not know the relationship she had developed with Galen, and trusted him emphatically; her family had served him and helped him in his quest to return Cassidy's progeny to the world of light for centuries, or to put them in the ground. Galen was respected and had served science and medicine – and whatever name he was using, whatever identity he assumed – it was of a good man, a philanthropist, even though the wealth was from an out world recipe. This note was from a person who was an evil thing; it was from

Cassidy not Galen who had been shut up in a box by some vile villain.

She decided to act independently, if Cassidy was waiting, he was also watching. It is likely she theorized that he is watching from the outside and say Galen and Rusty Nash leave and would see them upon return. She suspected Cassidy wanted something from her, perhaps secrets of Galen's money or his property, or to use her to harm him. Whatever his plan, she decided to thwart it and position Cassidy where Galen could capture and try to reason with him. Galen had brought ample supplies of the serum he developed for himself to give to Cassidy to enable him to live a reasonably normal life if he so chose. She thought that unlikely however, largely based on the content of this note alone. Cassidy could never become a man of the light, especially from what Galen told her of Cassidy's origins, he had never been such a man – he had always been a liar, a creature of the dark and always will be and had to be exterminated. To get everyone on the same page she needed to call Nash and let him in on her plan and for her eventual rescue when she lead Cassidy into a trap, now she just had to come up with a plan.

Dialing Nash's cell, she ran over in her mind how she could accomplish her mission. Nash's cell rang until it transferred to his voice mail...she tried again, same results...his voice mail! On the third time she decided to leave a message and trust he would get it in time.

"...Rusty, this is Coleen Jones. It is 7:05 pm. While you and Galen were gone I was notified I had received a message left by a man earlier in the day. I retrieved it and it was from Cassidy pretending to be the real victim and claiming he was really Galen – and that Galen is really Cassius, aka Cassidy. I am meeting him at the front of the hotel with all my bags as he instructed,. I left my tablet and laptop with the concierge. I hope to let you know later where he is, so you can come and capture him. I hope you get this soon...very soon!" Coleen said as she tapped end on her cell.

She hastily gathered her clothing and packed her bags. She would stop at the concierge and leave her tablet and laptop. They contained detailed information on Galen to include the bank account numbers she had been instructed to protect. She could not let Cassidy have access to this vast amount of information on his adversary – homes, and money – with it he would likely disappear until he was ready to re-emerge in a new, more dangerous and independent persona.

After checking out she slowly walked across to the concierge desk. She handed the case containing her computers to the young man on duty. She then, garnering all her courage, turned and walked through the front door of the hotel, sat down her bags on the curb and waited.

Chapter 17 - Now We Begin Again

"...Deep in my soul, I've been so lonely...All of my hopes, fading away, I've longed for love, like everyone else does, I know I'll keep searching, even after today..."

Bob Seger, *We've Got Tonight*, 1995

Stepping onto the coral rock parking lot in front of where Seth Holmes' houseboat was docked, Nash felt a rush of the presence he now knew heralded evil. It was much stronger than he had felt before. Being with Galen was distracting enough, but this added sensual cloud was almost overwhelming; likened in his thoughts to sitting on a bar stool all afternoon drinking 151 floaters and then trying to walk...it took some effort. As he and Galen approached the houseboat entry way Brown came out to meet them.

"Rusty, good to see you...in a few minutes I'm taking your advice about going home and cleaning up a bit – that walk with the dogs kicked my butt..." Brown said.

"Deputy Brown, this is Dr. Mark Galen, he and his assistant are helping us on this case...Dr. Galen..." Nash said motioning toward Galen who was patiently waiting beside him.

"I am delighted to meet you Deputy Brown. Detective Nash has been very complimentary of your work." Galen said extending his hand and took hers in a quick handshake.

"Brown, where's the message, and did the IT guy found anything on the computer email that is of any interest to us?" Nash asked.

"It's inside on the desk in a evidence bag...you know how Lt. Hernandez is about keeping the chain of evidence to a minimum...and to answer your question about the email, it timed out before the warrant showed up, and got locked behind a password; he said he would take the CPU and image the hard drive to get the emails – whatever that means." Brown said leading the two inside the houseboat.

"Lt. Hernandez, don't you ever go home?" Nash asked jokingly.

"Nash, can it. Your cases are occupying more of my time than I really need. Can't you catch the bastard that is at the bottom of this so I can sit on my ass in the office like I am supposed to...oh, Dr. Galen you're traveling in bad company?" Hernandez answered pointing at Nash.

"Detective Nash has been very helpful; Lieutenant was this letter the only one your team found in your search?" Galen asked.

"Yes, it was. Our computer forensic guy has pulled Holmes' CPU and took it back to his lab to image it and look into the email folders; can you read this stuff? Hernandez asked motioning to the message Galen had been focused on.

"Yes, I can, its Greek; actually written in an archaic style; I will have to look at it closer with a dictionary, perhaps after you get into the emails – I can look at them all together. Detective Nash, if there isn't anything else, may we return to the hotel for a joint meeting with Coleen?" Galen asked as he nudged Nash out the door.

"Err...yes. Bob, it looks like we will be tied up on surveillance tonight. Please have someone give me a call when the contents of Holmes' email are ready. They could give us a clue to our suspect's next move, instinctively tapping his shirt pocket for his cell and noticed it was not there. Searching his memory of where he might have put it, he remembered it was in his sports jacket lying on the back passenger seat of his vehicle.

"...send it to this email address; it's Dr. Galen's, we can access it remotely," he said, handing him the address written on the back of Nash's business card to Hernandez.

"Sheila, you haven't left yet?" Nash said turning to Brown.

"I'm outa here too...see you at the Bayside in a couple hours?" Brown replied as she headed toward her car.

"See you then. As always Lieutenant, keep in touch and keep smiling..." Nash said with a wink as he and Galen left the houseboat. Once inside his vehicle Nash reached back and retrieved his cell phone and placed it back in his shirt pocket. After Galen seated himself Nash turned to him.

"So you couldn't read the message without a special dictionary?" Nash asked.

"No, I was trying to get you out of there without having to give up the content of the message to anyone outside you and me. I read the whole thing. Cassidy has made contact with his maker. How he found him I do not know. My memory is vague on this one, but his maker retreated to a very remote area of what is now likely northern Afghanistan. It was there Cassidy and he parted company. If that is so, Cassidy plans and escape soon and expects to find sanctuary with the community of vampires likely concentrated there. My experience with these creatures tell me they likely have a front organization backed by endless financial resources; and they are coming for him – probably in a chartered or personal jet, and soon! We will find out more from the emails and even where he is likely going. We have no time to lose!" Galen said.

While listening to Galen, Nash's cell phone buzzed intermittently signaling a missed call. After Galen finished Nash opened his phone and listened to the voice mail left by Coleen a half hour earlier. The voice mail explained she was contacted directly by Cassidy and she had decided to meet Cassidy in order to lead him into a trap set by him and Galen.

"...Holy shit!...Christ, Coleen has been contacted by Cassidy, he claims to be the real Galen and wants her to escape with him. She is meeting him to help us catch him. What is she thinking!" Nash said as he flipped down his interior blue police emergency lights attached to the sun visor, engaged the transmission and headed toward the marina exit, careening out of the parking lot.

Galen said nothing. In shock he feared for Coleen's safety. Cassidy had threatened to take everything away as Galen had done to him 400 years before. He now saw Cassidy's evolving logic. Lure Coleen to him, learn what he could about his operation through deception, learn the rest through duress, and when he decided he could get no more, rape and kill her as he did to the two women found around mid-day. He sat stoic. His only movement was to push his hand onto his side of the dash board to steady himself as the car sped down route 905 and then the Overseas Highway with blue lights blinking and siren wailing.

In less than 30 minutes Nash and Galen arrived back at the front of the Bayside Hotel. Nash had turned off his lights and siren ¼ mile before the hotel entrance to avoid alerting Cassidy if he was still on the hotel property. Coming to an abrupt stop, Nash locked the transmission into "park" and jumped out without closing the car door. He ran to the hotel front desk clerk.

"Have you seen a young woman that is a guest here...Coleen Jones; tall, athletic, red hair – beautiful! She should have been in the lobby in the last hour!" Nash said nearly out of breath.

"Coleen Jones. Just one second sir, I think she checked out about an hour ago," the desk clerk said as she scrolled down her data base records. "...Yes, she checked out at 19.35, err...7:35 pm, left a package with the concierge and went out the front door carrying her own bags. I think a car pulled up and she got in and left almost immediately. "

" Is something wrong?" The clerk asked.

Checking his watch, Nash noted it was 8:15 pm. He calculated they had almost an hour's head start. In the meantime Galen joined Nash in the lobby.

"Okay, they left and likely are heading north – and likely they have made it to Homestead by now. What they plan to do next, I haven't a clue..." Nash said as he opened his field note case to find the 10-28 or registration check he printed out on Holmes' vehicle. After he found the information he ran back to his vehicle to radio central and give the information and provide a general BOLO or "Be On the Lookout For" the vehicle likely heading toward Miami or other airports or unknown points north. He added the vehicle was occupied by two murder suspects and a hostage. He further asked for a statewide FDLE broadcast with special emphasis on police departments in Metro Dade County, Florida City, Homestead, Miami, and Broward County, all up and down US Route 1, Florida Turnpike, and US I-95. While Nash was making notifications Galen went inside to claim Coleen's computer and tablet.

"Okay detective, now that you have notified all your colleagues, what do we do next?" Galen asked.

"Well, there is no sense racing up US 1 into the night unless we know we have somewhere to go. Although everything inside me wants to do that, we first need to wait for the emails on Holmes' computer, and for reports from officers up the line now looking for that beat up surplus police car," Nash said writing into his field notebook.

As they paused for a moment in Nash's car, Deputy Sheila Brown pulled up in her vehicle and parked behind Nash's. She got out and came over to Nash who was sitting in the driver's seat half in and out of the parked car.

"Rusty, I heard the BOLO on the radio and saw the statewide broadcast on my vehicle computer. What do we do?" Brown asked.

"We get a couple of sodas and go to Galen's room and wait for the email images being sent to his laptop. The emails, both sent and received versions should show us any other messages Holmes likely scanned and attached to his email message, as well as any direct messages from the people Cassidy has been in contact. This should give us an idea where Cassidy is now or heading. We just needed it an hour ago," Nash said pecking in the numbers on his phone of the forensic unit in the Roth building.

The computer forensic technician answered the phone and assured Nash the images, both received and sent for the last week will be to Galen's computer inbox in ten minutes. He then had planned to look for credit card and banking information that could help to establish intent and items purchased during flight.

"Let's get our cars away from the front of the hotel and get inside. The images should be here in the next several minutes. Dr. Galen, go on up and we will join you shortly...oh, what room number?" Nash asked.

"...314" Galen said.

While parking his vehicle he heard officers on the police radio checking the marina parking lot. Holmes had not returned to the marina. Returning to the hotel Brown and Nash took the elevator to the third floor. Passing the ice machine and soda machine Nash bought 3 cold drinks. Handing Brown a soda they arrived at Galen's room. Nash knocked and Galen opened it. Nash handed him a can of soda and walked to the laptop which was in the process of booting up. They sat down popped open their sodas and each took a long drink. Putting his can down, Galen entered the password and sat down waiting for his email icon to appear and access his inbox. In a moment the computer icon appeared and Galen selected his email and waited for it to load. The email from the forensic unit had just arrived. He double clicked on the message from a

@keysso.net address with 3 attachments. Nash and Brown stood behind Galen as he clicked on the first.

"Well, this looks like the first email message Holmes sent out...obviously it is in English.

> "...*Dear Sir:*
>
> *My name is Seth Holmes; I am in the service of an old friend of yours who left your company long ago. The name you knew him by is Demetrius Keraunos. He was The First of Lord Mainyu. He wishes to return home to his father and his family. Attached is a note written by him.*"

The attachment was from Cassidy in archaic Greek. Galen read is word for word...

> "...*Lord Mainyu – I am Keraunos. I am greatly gratified thou art well and have built a great fortune and enterprise. My fortunes are now much less, and need help from you, my father. Please father, send thou'st ship for me!! I am frightened. One of my progeny has pursued me for nearly all my life as your son, and is close by even now. I am in a land called Florida in the United States. I have recruited a servant*

and he has told me I am in Key Largo. Please grace my eyes with your words soon. Keraunos..."

"...That pretty well confirms this is Cassidy, aka *Demetrius Keraunos*. And he is our killer, and Holmes is his accomplice." Nash said.

"Yes, but there has been no doubt since I examined Robert Hopkins' remains; let's see what message is next," Galen said clicking on the second attachment. The second attachment was an email from Gulnar in Greek...

"...My Lord Keraunos, I cannot tell you how overjoyed I was when Lord Mainyu spoke to me about you; that you were still alive and will be coming home soon...I pleaded with him to permit me to come on the air ship to retrieve you from the land of Florida. He was so overjoyed to hear from you he permitted me to come, and is preparing a feast upon your return. We are preparing for the journey and can leave at any time. We can be in Florida in 30 hours. Tell us where to land our air ship and where you have taken sanctuary. I am coming. Gulnar..."

Remembering Deputy Brown's knowledge of Galen, Cassidy, or the world of vampires, and missing each other over the centuries, Galen so far had successfully omitted any reference to that part of the story, especially present in Cassidy's initial letter when he wrote

> "...*For centuries my body was imprisoned in a transport chamber meant for days or weeks – but thanks to my loyal guardians I survived there at the bottom on the sea for centuries. I was discovered and brought ashore. I escaped from my imprisonment and find myself to be as a child in the new age I have found myself...*"

Galen would share this later with Nash but Brown had to remain uninformed.

"Well, now we know they are coming for him. If the message in the last attachment is Cassidy's response about which airport and where he might be hiding in the meantime then we will have a place to go tonight and wait. Judging from the date/time stamp on the email that carried the next message – and they left as soon as possible after getting it. I estimate they will land somewhere in the Miami area around 20:00, or 8 pm tomorrow evening." Nash speculated.

"Here is the last message..." Galen said, carefully reading the contents...

> *"...Lord Mainyu and Gulnar, I am so happy you are coming for me. The airports that my servant has suggested are Miami International airport, Fort Lauderdale airport, Tamiami airport and Opa-Locka airport. All of these I am told will accommodate you – your air ship captain should know the best one to go and get out fast. I will make communications with you after we reach our sanctuary from the telephone numbers in your message. All these things are so new and magical; I cannot wait to be in the arms of Gulnar and being taught the mysteries of this new age -Keraunos..."*

Nash asked Galen to step over to the corner of the room.

"Given what we know or think we know, where do you think they are coming from?"

"...Either Afghanistan or, if borders shifted, Tajikistan or maybe India." Galen responded.

Nash returned to the hotel desk and lifted Galen's room telephone receiver and dialed central dispatch identified himself and the case number to the operator.

"We are expecting an incoming private international flight coming from somewhere in Europe to pick up a murder suspect who has taken a female hostage...I need Air Route Traffic Control Center Miami to provide a list of all known private incoming flights in the following airports: Miami International, Fort Lauderdale International, Tamiami, and Opa-Locka; or any aircraft radar transponder interrogations assigned to private transport aircraft from Afghanistan or Tajikistan. Send the list to my department internal messaging email," Nash said, nodding to a comment made by the operator and hung up the telephone.

The Air Route Traffic Control Center (ARTCC) Miami is located approximately 2 miles north of Miami International Airport. It is responsible for airspace management over south Florida from Tampa International (KTPA) south to Key West International (KEYW) as well as the Miami Oceanic Airspace over the Bahamas. Any inbound aircraft would be visible at some point at the ARTCC Miami. Nash, with the help of the Florida Department of Law Enforcement Fusion Center liaison with ARTCC Miami was to be informed of any aircraft coming to their attention.

"How did you know that stuff about transponders?" Brown asked.

"When in the Navy, I did some counter-drug work at the US Southern Command in Panama before the war. I worked with guys who used these codes to track smugglers; or as long as they had them turned on. When they turned them off, they didn't disappear from the screen, but became unknown blips – smugglers usually flew with no transponders. The guys at Miami Central should be able to see any aircraft coming in and let us know as long as they are at an altitude where radar can see them, "Nash said.

"What do you mean see them?" asked Brown.

"The aircraft has to be at a certain altitude...jet transport aircraft of the size we are expecting usually fly at about 450 knots below 200 feet off the deck and it is not unusual to see aircraft flying 50 feet over the open ocean to avoid detection by radar. If these guys know they are picking up someone being chased by the police, how do you think they will arrive? My guess is no transponder, travelling about 500 knots, between 50 and 75 feet off the deck until they are in sight of Florida. Once they reach the Florida land mass, they will likely ascend to about 3000 feet, circle into the wind; execute a quick approach and then a landing. Wherever they land, we will never see them coming until they are here,." Nash said.

After being picked up by Holmes and Cassidy, Coleen briefly shook hands with the creature claiming to be Galen. She immediately understood how a woman would be confused by his presence. Despite his recent resurrection from centuries in the vacuum of the coffin without any nourishment, Cassidy appeared to be none the worse. He could almost be considered attractive had she not knew who and what he was. After exchanging pleasantries he told the long story. This was a practiced deception regarding who he was, his life of the victim and how wonderful he thought of her decision was to join him.

"...Where exactly are we escaping to Galen?" Coleen asked.

"Lass, we are going far from here, to a place that we can rest and plan for our work to rid the world of Keraunos and his progeny. In less than a day from now we should be in the arms of a protector. Tell me, as this fiend's guardian, do you have control of his wealth. Can you access it? " Cassidy asked.

Coleen knew exactly where this was going with this question. He was getting to at least one purpose of luring her to his side. That was precisely why she thought it was important to leave her computers at the hotel, hopefully in the safe hands of Galen. Also suspecting Cassidy remained ignorant of modern day banking and means of tracking purchases, she chose to only bring Galen's credit card used for travel and small purchases while on the road. Large expenses such as air charters, vehicles, or equipment were purchased by online banking assets and transfers. Access to these accounts could likely be devastating; this credit card had a very high limit, to include cash withdrawal – and can be tracked.

"No sir, the man I knew as Galen never confided in me regarding the extent of his wealth or bank holdings. He gave me a credit card I used to make all his arrangements for travel and expenses up to the financial limit of the card," Coleen said looking Cassidy straight in the eye trying to seem as certain as possible.

"...and what is the limit, lass?" Cassidy asked.

"The credit card is limited to £ 100,000 and cash withdrawals to £ 5,000."

"That should be enough..." Cassidy said.

"Master, forgive me for speaking, but credit cards can be cancelled at any time; if you have plans for using her card, you had better do it soon. As soon as they learned Dr. Jones has switched sides, her privileges will end, and the card will be cancelled." Holmes said looking over his should to Cassidy in the back seat.

"Thank you Holmes. Let us get some spendable currency, how do we do that?" Cassidy asked.

"The banks are now closed and that means the limit cannot be drawn, but we can go to any automatic teller. They are available," Holmes replied.

Coleen had hoped they could use the card at a location where they would be for a while. It could be tracked and Nash could come to the rescue. Using an ATM Nash will know where money was taken, but no location to match it to after leaving the bank. She decided she needed to eventually contact Galen or Nash by cell phone once their plans are clearer.

"Let us go to one of those automatic tellers; sounds fascinating. We can also stop for some food, correct Master Holmes?" Cassidy asked smiling.

"Now you're talkin" Holmes said.

Krome Avenue is one of the most western of the north-south highways in Miami-Dade County. It runs almost 37 miles from Florida City in far south to Opa-Locka airport just south of the Broward County line. Cassidy had planned to use Krome Avenue as back way access to both Tamiami and Opa-Locka, or if need be, Miami or Fort Lauderdale Airports. His plan however was first to find sanctuary at a remote motel off Krome Avenue and await the impending arrival of Gulnar and transportation back to the fabulous underground caverns of Balkh, in mythical Eucratideia.

"Holmes, when we reach a midpoint between Tamiami and Opa-Locka airports, choose a place to get currency, food, and find an inn to await our friends," Cassidy said looking at the passing landscape thinking of his second purpose for bringing Galen's assistant, one he likely cares a lot for – and the pleasure he will have achieving that end.

""Dr. Galen, you mentioned the computers contained the accounts and passcodes necessary to access the money, is there any other access money that Coleen may have like a credit card?" Nash asked Galen.

"Yes detective. She carries a credit card that has substantial but not limitless purchasing authority. Should I call to cancel it?" Galen asked as he searched for the account number on his laptop.

"No, no, let's keep it open, we can track where she is told to use it – maybe a motel, restaurant, or whatever. Our liaison with bank security people will provide us almost real time notification of it being used. We just need the account number, bank and the type of card," Nash responded.

"What do we do now? Brown asked.

"Given they are likely waiting for the arrival of their getaway aircraft, and that won't be here until tomorrow evening – unless we find out something in between regarding their location – we wait here." Nash said.

***

"Are you ready for a road trip Sheila? Until we get more information about credit card use, I suspect being somewhere close to the Miami area airports mentioned in the messages between Cassidy and his overseas friends. We can head up to Metro's Northwest Sub-station in Miami Lakes. That would be 2 miles north of Miami International, close to Tamiami airport a bit more to the south, Opa-Locka airport a couple blocks east, and a quick ride to Fort Lauderdale to the north east. Get our stuff. Sheila, take your own vehicle. Dr. Galen and I will go in mine. We may have to split up should we get information about their location that is not really clear. Got it?" Nash asked.

"Got-ya!" Brown said.

An hour later with Nash in the lead heading Route 826 North, both cars passed the first of many exits for Miami International Airport. Nash's cell buzzed. He answered and put it on speaker.

"Go ahead, this is Nash..."

"Detective, we got access to Seth Holmes' credit card account on the hard disk of his computer. The latest transaction on the card was at a Key Largo car rental agency. He rented a dark blue Ford Explorer yesterday morning for a round trip rental for a week. That's good, since the DNR (Department of Natural Resources) marine patrol located and identified a Ford Crown Victoria registered to him in about 10 feet of water on the bayside of Largo Cut just before dark today. It was empty," The operator reported.

"Thanks, we are in Miami-Dade County heading north to stand by at the Metro sub-station in Miami Springs. Have you cancelled the BOLO for the Crown Vic and replaced it with the Explorer?" Nash asked.

"We are changing that now and should be on the network in a few minutes." The operator replied.

Nash thanked the operator and turned to Galen.

"What type of danger is Coleen in once Cassidy figures out she can't access the large accounts and that she knows who he really is?" Nash asked.

"Coleen is in grave danger detective. Once she does not serve any other purpose to him – he will become what he always has been, a calculating narcissistic killer. This means he will want to send me a message. He will likely do much the same as he did with those two young women in the motel," Galen said with a pained look.

Chapter 18 - Road Trip

*"...Tell me why you're smiling my son...Is there a secret you
can tell everyone?
Do you know more than men that are wise?... Can you see
what we all must disguise..."*

Peter Yarrow, *Day is Done*, 1969

After withdrawing cash from an automatic teller
the trio bought grilled chicken and French fries and
brought it to a motel north of Tamiami Executive Airport
on Sunset Drive. Cassidy directed Holmes to check in for
the group and get 2 rooms. Coleen volunteered to help
Holmes check in and pay for the room with her card.
Holmes informed Cassidy on the drive up that his card
was nearing its limit after paying for the car rental costs.
Inside the office, Coleen looked for a surveillance camera
hoping that it was attached to a video recording system to
document their visit and a restroom where she could go
and make a cell phone call to Nash. There was a camera
but no restroom. It was not a tourist motel, not one she

would normally choose. It was selected by Cassidy after being advised by Holmes that it was out of the way and not place that police looking for them would find before Cassidy's transportation arrived and they had departed. Coleen did hope that Galen had not cancelled the card and was using it to track her. The card worked and they were given keys. Coleen speculated about but could not understand the purpose of the second room.

Once back at the vehicle, Cassidy emerged and took both keys.

"Let us go inside and have our suppers. I will call and notify Gulnar where we are waiting and learn how long we have to wait before they come for us." Cassidy said motioning to one of the room doors, handing the keys to Coleen to unlock and open it. Inside Holmes tossed the SUV keys and bags of food on the table, and turned on the television. Turning to Cassidy...

"Master, what can I get you to eat? Holmes asked.

"Thank you Holmes, but please serve the lady first." Cassidy said smiling, turning his attention to Coleen.

Holmes' facial expression changed to one of annoyance, and turned to Coleen.

"It doesn't matter Mr. Holmes anything would be fine." Coleen said as she took her purse off her shoulder, placed it on one of the beds and sat down at the small table.

After Holmes separated the chicken and French fries, all three ate their dinner in silence except for Holmes who questioned Cassidy about where they were heading and what they would be doing there. Cassidy was non-committal. He did reveal his plan for their escape once transportation arrived.

"Holmes, we will separate and travel in 2 cars. I will travel with whoever is sent for us. Ye and Dr. Jones will travel in the other vehicle. This arrangement should make it harder for the police to track us to the airport," Cassidy said.

"That's good thinking Master. When did you say we were leaving for the airport?" Holmes asked.

"I will call home soon and confirm the plan. You and Dr. Jones remain here, whilst I go next door and make the call on this magical device. Dr. Jones, please relax. I want to speak with you more after my call. I will come and get you," Cassidy said as he closed the door and went next door to the second room.

Coleen sat back in the chair, folded her arms in front of her and processed the signs of what she expected

Cassidy to do next; and where Galen and Nash were at this time. She thought about trying to use her cell phone but that would tip off even Holmes about her motive for using it. She sat still waiting for Holmes' attentiveness toward her to wane as he became involved with the television program. Since Cassidy would return soon she decided it was now or never, and Holmes was now glued to the television.

"I am going to in the restroom to freshen up," Coleen said as she got up and headed in that direction.

Holmes glanced over his shoulder at Coleen and made a slight grunt of acknowledgement. Inside she located her cell phone and opened it. The was an alert to an unread text message from a "305" area code. After thinking a moment, she concluded it was Nash! Accessing the text message, she confirmed it was from him. It read...

"...Coleen, you are in a great deal of danger!! Keep your cell phone on, we will attempt to locate you if we can. We are tracking Holmes' and your credit cards – Be very careful. We are coming for you - Nash."

Just then Cassidy burst through the door catching Coleen attempting to type a message into her cell phone. Surprised, Coleen backed up abruptly into the bathtub and fell backwards striking her head on its back edge, knocking her unconscious. The cell phone flew out of her hand landing in the tub next to her.

"Holmes, come here. Help me pick her up and put her on the bed," Cassidy shouted to Holmes.

After placing her on the bed, Cassidy directed Holmes to retrieve Coleen's cell phone and discover what she was doing with it when he surprised her.

"Master, she received a message from a guy named Nash," Holmes said, then reading the full text of Nash's message to Coleen.

"It was sent about an hour ago...I guess this means the police are getting close...huh?" Holmes asked.

"Turn off her cell phone. We will stop using any more of those cards to purchase anything. If Dr. Jones paid for the rooms with her credit card this means they will know soon where we are. Throw her in the back of the car and we'll go to another place and pay with the currency you got from that automatic teller machine."

Once they relocated Cassidy called the phone number a second time and reported their new pickup address. Like before Holmes had secured two rooms. Coleen had been placed in the second room, hands and feet tied and mouth gagged. For Cassidy this was the time of reckoning; to begin taking things from his enemy Galenicus.

Ordering Holmes to remain in the first room, Cassidy entered and closed the door behind him. He paused and looked down at Coleen who was lying on her side on the bed. She was regaining consciousness and slowly began to tug at her bindings.

"Dr. Jones, I am so sorry ye came to me under false, circumstances...ye should not have done that. Ye should not have tried to deceive the old man...for I have been deceiving men and women even before your ancestors knew how to find their arses with both hands. I am the great deceiver, you and your kind are not...now the piper must be paid for offers rejected," Cassidy said sitting down next to her.

Reaching over, he ran his hand up her legs until he reached her buttocks. Sliding his right hand under her panties he fondled her, chanting the same mesmerizing incantation he had used on Holmes. But this time it was for much more nefarious purposes. Continuing to chant and stroke her thighs, and between her legs, Coleen responded by ceasing to struggle. Then breathing deeply, almost as in a fever of passion, her body pulsated as if lying next to her lover. Cassidy took his lancet and cut the tape on her ankles and wrists, whereupon she pulled him to her slowly all the while groaning passionately for the lover he had conjured up into her subconscious. Cassidy quickly removed her panties and entered her – she opened wide for him, pushing back again and again against him until she climaxed in a muffled scream.

He was not finished. At the moment of his climax he made a deep opening in her skin at the base of her neck with his lancet. The warm sweet liquid he needed flowed out like a mountain spring. He covered the opening and fed on Coleen, drinking the living nectar until he felt her body grow limp and cool. He would not have stopped but was interrupted by a shuffle of feet and noise coming from the room occupied by Holmes.

***

Dialing Central Dispatch, Nash identified himself as a police officer and gave the case number. He asked if they had learned anything new about use of credit cards.

"Negative detective, there is an issue with the system that tracks the Jones card – the system is down and I can't get an estimated time it will be back on line. We did get a broad read out reported for her cell phone, It was tracking north until got to about 25°40'13.10"N" by 80°28'16.48"W, somewhere just south of SW 88th Street, then it disappeared...that was about 18:47 hours," reported the operator.

"Is that close to any airport?" Nash asked.

"Let me, see....yep that was about 3 miles northwest of Kendall-Tamiami Executive Airport," the operator said.

Nash thanked the dispatcher and asked her to keep him advised. The Tamiami airport was definitely one of the locations listed in the emails on Holmes' computer – but not a likely spot since it was small and any aircraft coming in would be noticed. The good news is the Miami-Dade Police Incident Containment Team (ICT) could be there in less than a half hour if they had to come from Miami International.

Challenging this theory he speculated that whoever was coming was not likely want to challenge the armed reception team...then too it all could be a deception. A small plane jumping from another location landing on a non-commercial runway...or perhaps driving straight through to the west coast of Florida, or even someplace around Boca Raton. After thinking about it, he dismissed any likelihood of the pick-up attempt would be made at Tamiami, just too risky for a couple of guys flying an airplane.

Arriving at the Metro-Dade Miami Lakes sub-station, Nash pulled up to the front with Brown pulling into the space beside him.

"We will wait in the squad room until we are notified by ARTCC Miami of the approach and landing of the getaway aircraft. It is now 19:47. If I am right, we should be hearing something in an hour or less." Nash told Galen.

***

After an intermediate fuel stop at Lydan Pinding International Airport in Nassau, Bahamas, and once again airborne, the pilot resumed the flight plan filed earlier on course to Santo Domingo, Dominican Republic. The cover for the flight was a cargo run of mining machinery to a client on the island. At 00:36 hours Zulu (7:36 pm East Standard Time) the pick-up location was received a second call via cell phone link with the target, adjusting the pickup point. Heading south, after passing over a channel called the Tongue of the Ocean and onto The Great Bahamas Bank, the pilot brought the aircraft to a slow descent. At 200 feet above the clear waters best known in legend as the Bermuda Triangle, he switched off his identifying transponder and banked the aircraft northeast at a heading of 311.2 degrees, programming the target location to 25°38.87"N 80°25.97"W. Readouts from his onboard radar showed a blip of a second identical aircraft. It had been flying without a transponder and 200 feet off the water for the last 6 hours in a bumpy parallel course to avoid detection from Bahamian and US air traffic control radar. The second was a sister aircraft that now took its place on the

Dominican cargo flight plan. The decoy headed on to Santo Domingo with the load of mining equipment.

The cargo of the first aircraft was very much different than on its original manifest. In less than a half hour it and its passengers would be near the Florida coast and implemented of a bold plan to recover Cassidy and return him home to Angr'a Mainyu, now the controlling partner of a mining and pharmaceutical empire. It was defined largely through networks of shell companies with no real business functions other than to hide his identity as their owner.

The plan involved a quick unannounced and under the radar approach to the target airport, then ascending to an altitude of 2800 feet, circle the airport, put its nose into the wind and land. Given the unauthorized nature of the landing to pick up what they suspected was a fugitive from the police, the owner of the aircraft, Angr'a Mainyu sent a reinforced team of his best personal security to assure things would be handled professionally and without a hitch. The aircraft was an American made C-130J Super Hercules tactical lifter. It was equipped with auxiliary fuel pods to feed its 4 powerful turboprop engines and some special electronics. In addition to the assault team an armored sport utility vehicle was secured near the aircraft's ramp. The SUV was equipped with a GPS land navigation system preprogrammed with the coordinates of the pick-up location.

In the noisy open cargo hold team members discussed preparations with the precision of a military operation. Each member of the team strained to see the leader's laptop screen depicting the 1 meter imagery obtained of the airport layout, as well as the known location the pickup team would deploy once on the ground.

When the aircraft was within range, the co-pilot would activate onboard electronic active countermeasures designed to jam all radio and cell phone communication for a mile until the tower and airfield was secure. Once they were on the ground, the mission commander knew that speed was the key to getting access, and interrupt any land line requests by the tower or security personnel for additional police support.

The assault team consisted of three elements: aircraft security, the main element to secure the tower and neutralize airport security, and the last the SUV pick up element that deployed off the airport grounds to where the target was waiting, retrieve and return him to the aircraft for an on time departure.

The team leader was a comrade of Cassidy's during the Roman age of his many lives, the Centurion, Antonius Maecianus. Fleeing Syria, and after they reached Greece, he and Cassius decided to equally divide the force to avoid undo attention by Roman patrols in the region.

Maecianus took a contingent of troops to the east and, with benefit of a letter from Cassidy, then Cassius, joined Angr'a Mainyu in his fortress. During the first year with Mainyu, Maecianus also became his vampire "son". As a vampire, he too had morphed into many persons over the centuries, the latest as the head of Mainyu's corporate security, known as Anthony Lucas, an Englishman. Lucas fit this role well, first working with the British during their long unsuccessful imperial quest of Afghanistan in the 19th and early 20th centuries, then with British NATO forces after the 2001 invasion. Lucas took personal lead of the pickup element.

Over the years, many invasions by foreigners had changed the man Cassidy left to pursue his dream of power with the Romans. Mainyu was drawn out in the 9th century as the great tide of Islam swept over the country and challenged his supremacy in the far north. The British came 900 years later. Only after they left in 1919 did Mainyu regain control over his realm. The Soviets invaded roughly 60 years later and sent their tanks through his territory. This was the last straw for him. He could no longer seek to remain untouched by foreigners or men. This time Mainyu organized his own militia and joined the Islamists in their war against the invaders. During this time Maecianus remained loyal to Mainyu and rose to a position Cassidy had reached before he departed from their father several millennia before.

Maecianus, now Lucas, looked forward to reuniting with his former commander, but learned also to fear what his return to Mainyu's protection would mean to him both in his relationship with Mainyu, and also with Gulnar who had shared his life far longer than did Cassidy. He was conflicted, happy yet suspicious and angry about the return of the man he knew as Cassius.

The plan was finalized and to be executed after the aircraft taxied and stopped adjacent to the airport tower facility. Teams 2 and 3 would immediately deplane and separate to achieve their own missions. Team 1 would establish a security perimeter around the aircraft. Once the first boots were on the ground - the plan allowed for 25 minutes until wheels up and over the darkness of the Caribbean Sea and into the southern Atlantic.

Each member was dressed in black military uniforms, equipped with ballistic vests and armed with suppressor equipped .45 caliber automatic pistols and Russian manufacture 5.45mm AKM assault rifles with four 40 round magazines. Team 2 was additionally equipped with flash bang stun grenades and one AKM fitted with a 20mm grenade launcher with smoke, CS tear gas, and fragmentation rounds should they met stiff resistance. They were authorized to kill, but only if their own lives or the target's life was in danger.

Chapter 19 - Wheels Up

*"...And I come chargin' off the jet way, the Dream is in my eyes
When I see you there at curbside babe, I'm kissin' you at
sunrise..."*

Harry Chapin, *Northwest 222*, 1981

At 01:40Z (ZULU) (8:40 pm East Standard Time)
the lights of Miami and Miami Beach were visible from
the cockpit as the aircraft skimmed stealthily 200 feet off
dark Biscayne Bay. Gulnar switched from white to the red
interior cockpit and cargo bay lights signaling they were
approximately 10 minutes from touchdown. The overall
mission commander, Anthony Lucas, climbed up the
ladder from the bay to the cockpit. The pilot turned and
reported the flight status:

"Commander, the weather is clear, winds from the
east at approximately 10 knots, and temperature 23° C – a
very nice evening with no rain or clouds on our radar. We
will ascend in approximately 5 minutes to 850 meters, fly

over the landing zone, turn east and land. We should be on the ground in less than 10 minutes".

In the pilot's seat was the still beautifully striking Gulnar, Cassidy's long abandoned companion. She was monitoring ground communications at the airport and all Miami-Dade and southern Broward County police frequencies that had capabilities to respond to their landing and foray to the pickup location in less than 30 minutes. She also managed access to cell phone contacts on the ground. Her additional responsibility involved activating the communications jamming equipment once the aircraft reached an altitude of 500 meters, keep it active until departure, and until their disappearance from Miami ARTCC radar screens.

While the co-pilot made his report, Lucas and Gulnar momentarily made eye contact. At the conclusion, Lucas nodded and returned to the cargo bay and his 3 teams.

Lucas ordered everyone to their posts and insert ammunition magazines into their weapons and chamber a round. He reaffirmed that no ground personnel should be killed unnecessarily – that incapacitating wounding shots where the rules of engagement since these men or women were only doing their jobs. As were each of them. With that Lucas strapped himself into the passenger seat of the SUV next to the driver and in front of the third member of the pickup team. Both these men were specifically handpicked by him for this mission. Two members of the aircraft security team would release the SUV retaining straps after landing and would be the first to exit the aircraft, immediately driving to the pickup point 3 kilometers from the airport. The 25 minute ground time limit began when the SUV touched the tarmac.

The aircraft engines roared as they strained to lift the heavy aircraft 700 meters in altitude and past the airport. As it banked left and assumed a back azimuth of 49 degrees east, everyone was on their feet. Each member of the mission steadied themselves against one another, interior posts or fuselage wall, waiting in silence amid the deafening drone of the engines. Some were staring straight ahead, others conducting last minute personal equipment checks. In quick descent, the aircraft dropped onto the runway and the wheels grabbed hold. Immediately the pilot reversed pitch on the four thick propeller blades producing an additional roar. Steadying themselves as the aircraft slowed the crew chief began lowering the rear ramp to permit the SUV and other teams exit immediately once the aircraft reached full stop. As the aircraft ended its linear landing tack, it began to slowly taxi to the airport control facility. Information from the facility Internet web-site detailed where to expect the control and security staff to be located. Just prior to full stop, the SUV restraining straps were loosened, unhooked and its engine came to life.

With a jolt, the aircraft brakes engaged and brought it to full stop approximately 100 feet from the airport tower. By this time the ramp found the tarmac and the SUV dashed out and turned left past the control tower, and turned right on Miami-Dade County's SW 128th Street to the airport exit. It was 01:55Z. The pickup and return to the aircraft and departure were scheduled for 02:20Z. At the intersection with SW 137th Avenue the driver turned north for the 3 kilometer drive to the pick up location.

As the SUV and its occupants disappeared behind the tower facility, the assault team entered the ground level doors. Fanning out inside, three members of the team searched the ground level for occupants. The remaining team members scurried up the one level stairway to the control room and security offices.

The ground level team found two men in the coffee room. They were caught completely by surprise and quickly taken into custody without a word. The ground floor was declared secure by 02:00Z. On the second floor of the control tower the team encountered the 2 person FAA Air Traffic Control Team and a security officer. As the team entered the control room the security officer was picking up the phone. The officer heard the team enter the room and fan out. Before he could react, a team member rushed to the man and pointed his pistol at his head, ordering him to stop what he was doing. He slowly turned and stared down the barrel and hung up the phone. In response to their questioning, the team learned no calls were made to the Miami Dade Police or to their Incident Containment Team (ICT) at Miami International Airport located approximately 24 kilometers to the north east. With the tower and aircraft secure they waited. It was 02:05Z. The pilot and Gulnar were checking onboard computers for a 02:20Z departure, fifteen minutes from then.

Lucas and his assault team had reached their destination but did so immediately behind a single Metro Dade police cruiser. Lucas ordered the driver to slow to a stop and turn off the headlights as the cruiser entered the court yard of the motel. As the police cruiser passed behind the blue Chevrolet SUV Lucas saw its break lights flash into the darkness of the parking lot. Lucas looked at his wrist watch. It was 02:06z.

"We have 14 minutes to get our target into the aircraft. I will attend to this policeman. Listen closely. When you hear my pistol discharge twice, drive into the parking lot. General Cassius is in room 12," Lucas said as he exited the SUV with his assault rifle. He walked quickly to the police car. As he approached, the lone officer exited the car.

"Err...who are...? Get back sir..." the officer said holding his right arm out as if in a blocking gesture.

With the assault rifle in his left hand. Lucas drew his pistol and shot the officer once in each leg, causing him to fall on the pavement. Lucas was thankful the young man did not scream or raise an alarm to those who might be in earshot. He rushed to him and took the officer's pistol, portable radio and cell phone. The SUV darted into the lot and stopped in front of the police cruiser. The driver and third team member exited and entered room 12. After ensuring the wounded man was no longer a threat he moved the selector on his assault rifle to full automatic aimed it inside the driver's compartment peppering the cruiser's radios. Stepping back he shot out the driver's side front and rear tires. He was very impressed that suppressors on each weapon made less noise than the impact of the bullets. While the teams were organizing and bringing out Cassidy and those with him, Lucas redirected his attention to the police officer he had shot. The officer seemed dazed from the shock effect of his wounds. He pulled a first aid pouch from his assault vest and crouched down at the officer. Moving quickly, Lucas wrapped a compression bandage around each leg wound and injected him with a ¼ grain of morphine from a preloaded syrette. The young officer immediately responded to the pain killer, relaxed and focused on Lucas crouching over him.

"You will be alright mate. I am sorry," Lucas said.

Lucas stood, turning in time to see Cassidy emerge smiling from the motel door.

"General, it is good to see you after all these years. We are on a schedule," Lucas said. After Cassidy Holmes emerged, followed by Lucas' driver carrying Coleen who was very pale and unconscious.

"Put her in that car with Master Holmes," Cassidy said pointing to the blue rental SUV.

"Holmes, leave now for Ft. Lauderdale Airport...we will meet you at the Executive Terminal. Good luck," Cassidy said getting into the front passenger seat of Lucas' SUV. Lucas was now occupying the driver's seat next to Cassidy and gave him a puzzled look about their rendezvous destination. Cassidy returned the look that clearly meant to "stay silent".

Holmes closed the door to his SUV and gave Cassidy a thumbs up signal through the glass.

"We have 10 minutes to get to the airport, secure ourselves on the aircraft and into the air," Lucas said to Cassidy as he exited the motel courtyard turning south in the direction of the airport and waiting aircraft. Holmes, thinking they were taking a different route north, turned right with Coleen. With her wrists and ankles again bound, she was lying across the bench seat behind him.

***

"Detective Nash, please come to the telephone. We have some updates on the movement of your suspects," said the Officer in Charge (OIC) of the sub-station. Interrupting Nash's late dinner from a local chicken barbeque joint.

Nash put down his chicken, entered the dispatch room and picked up the phone.

"This is Nash," he said.

"Detective Nash, this is DHS officer Andrews. We have a few things to report regarding the inbound aircraft your office has asked us to track if they enter our airspace. First, after checking with ARTCC Miami, there are no inbound flight plans filed tonight by private aircraft. If your inbound is coming, it is without benefit of a flight plan. If they land, will be doing so illegally."

Nash thought to ask her to tell him something he didn't already know. These guys seem to be very good in stating the obvious. If someone was coming to pick up a fugitive from justice, they would not likely file a flight plan anyway. He needed this officer's cooperation and decided not to tell her she was a dick-weed and to get to the important stuff. He bit his tongue.

"Right, thanks..." Nash said.

Continuing, the officer reported "At approximately 20 minutes ago, at 20:47 hours (8:47 pm) ARTCC Miami radar momentarily picked up what looked like a bogy (unknown) aircraft appearing in the vicinity of 25°36'53" by 80°19'59" taking a west north west track in the vicinity of 25°40'53" by 80°30'23", then turning east again and disappearing from our screens at 20:55 hours (8:55 pm) in the vicinity of 25°38'52" by 80°26'51.""

"Hum..." Nash again biting his tongue..."Can you tell me by land marks where those LAT-LONG coordinates are located?"

"...Sure, we first noticed the bogy roughly over Goulds and Cutler Bay in Miami-Dade County. It appeared to turn around after passing over Krome Avenue and into the Redlands, and disappeared in the vicinity of Kendall-Tamiami Executive Airport," reported the officer.

"Christ! Is that what you might consider a landing pattern Officer Andrews?" Nash asked.

"From my experience, and unless we are getting a false hit, looks like this guy flew into our airspace at a very low altitude to avoid our radar, and ascended into radar coverage in order to safely make his approach and land. Yes, this looks like a landing pattern and as best we can see the aircraft is still on the ground. Oh one more thing we just got off the phone with the Kendall –Tamiami control facility – they claim an aircraft did a fly-by but did not land," The operator added.

"Do you think he was lying?" Nash asked.

"I don't know Detective, although these things do not happen all the time. Fly-bys do occur and tracking private aircraft are like trying to herd cats in south Florida," She said.

"Did they say what kind of aircraft flew by, and did you notify the ICT at Miami International?" Nash asked in exasperation.

"No...he did not, but I did," she replied.

Nash thanked her and hung up.

Thanking the sub-station OIC, he told him DHS already notified the ICT element at Miami International. He asked they send someone to Kendall-Miami airport regarding the aircraft and likelihood of Cassidy escaping from there in an undocumented aircraft.

"Can you guys also call ICT and confirm the request?" Nash asked. After making the request Nash returned to Galen and Brown who had finished their dinner.

"...Let's get out of here. It looks like the people we have been waiting for have already landed at Tamiami airport, and the plane is still on the ground. DHS sent the Metro ICT to Tamiami and will meet us there. It's now 20:22. Dr. Galen, you are with me. Sheila come in your own unit. When we get there, and if there is a plane on the ground, it is likely our man and his people. If we get there before Metro's ICT, wait for backup. Galen and I will head directly for the aircraft. Consider them armed...and they have Dr. Jones. That's all I'm going to say about that," Nash said being interrupted by the OIC who ran from the control room.

"...Detective, we just got a call from Pinecrest PD. One of their officers spotted the Blue Chevy SUV you're looking for on US 1 around Suitland. It appears that it is occupied by a person fitting the description of Seth Holmes. The officer also reports seeing what looks like a female in the back seat, appearing, then going out of sight, like the person struggling," he reported.

"Thanks, can you get some backup over there? Deputy Brown will head over there as well. Where are they now?" Nash asked.

"The last from the officer indicated he had just passed the University of Miami heading north. He reported being joined by University police and Coral Gables marked units."

"Okay, please request an unmarked Gables or one of your detective units drop in behind the SUV as soon as possible, and have the marked units drop back. I suspect he is either heading toward Miami or Fort Lauderdale International airports. I don't understand why he got himself jammed up in traffic on US 1. Deputy Brown will head over there if the Pinecrest patrol unit can keep us advised of his direction of travel. Let's not spook him. I think he has a hostage in the back...okay?" Nash asked.

"Right..." the OIC said turning to request what Nash had asked for regarding the vehicle operated by Holmes.

"...Oh, can you ask the sector supervisor from either Metro or the City of Miami to call me on my cell...and after they figure out the best place; a place with the least danger to everyone. Stop him. Doctor Galen and I are heading to the Tamiami Airport," Nash said handing his business card with cell phone number to the officer.

"Rusty, do you think we rather should be going after Holmes if he has Coleen with him?" Galen asked as they headed to the parking lot.

"...Err, no. Maybe you should go with Deputy Brown. Coleen will likely be interested in seeing and knowing you are safe..." Nash said.

Before Brown got in her car, Nash asked that she take Galen with her. He instructed her to report to him as soon as she joined with the units following Holmes, especially when either Metro Dade or the City of Miami Police made the stop. He instructed her to take care of herself as Holmes was likely armed. Nash looked at his watch. It was 20:30. He slid into his vehicle, activated his blue law enforcement emergency lights and headed south on Florida Route 826.

Unknown to Holmes, who was 2 miles south, Miami Police Captain Ben Cavada ordered his sector units to close the entrance to I-95 and funnel all traffic onto north bound South Dixie Highway, US 1, into Miami at the split of South Dixie Highway and US I-95 just north of the famous Coconut Grove. It is here where US 1 narrows to one lane that was the best location to identify and stop Holmes' SUV and send traffic safely back onto I-95.

It was a typical Sunday evening in Miami. The Dolphins had just defeated the Baltimore Ravens in a home game. The sports bars and watering holes in Coconut Grove and Key Biscayne were buzzing with fans. South Dixie Highway was jammed with traffic going or coming from activities on that warm late fall evening. Seth

Holmes had been watching in the rear view mirror for the black SUV his master, Angus Cassidy was in when they left the motel in different directions. At each red light on South Dixie Highway he strained to see the profile behind him or for them to pull into the next lane and take the lead. In the back was Cassidy's hostage. He thought she didn't look too good. When the men who came for them placed her in the back of his car, she looked pale and "out of it." Why did his master want her in his car and why did he go with them and not him? For some reason, he was feeling very alone on the road. He reached to his backpack on the passenger seat next to him and felt around until he found what he was looking for. It was the pistol he brought with him from his houseboat the day before. Feeling the end of the grip, he assured himself he had loaded a full magazine into the weapon. He sat it on top of the open backpack in case it was needed.

Deputy Sheila Brown came down I-95, the fastest route she knew from Miami Lakes. She ran into some traffic generated by the home football game. As she passed through Miami and I-95, the highway transitioned into South Dixie Highway. She saw the barricades Miami PD had set up on the north bound lane to her left. Switching her radio to the south Florida emergency communication channel she asked Miami Police Dispatch to pass on to the supervisor at the scene that she had arrived from the north and was turning around to join them. Describing her vehicle and herself, at the intersection of SW 16th Avenue she made a U Turn and headed back north on South Dixie Highway. Passing several cars she came upon what looked like an unmarked police Ford Crown Victoria and just ahead, the blue Chevrolet SUV occupied by Seth Holmes.

Her pulse began to race as she pulled next to who she suspected to be the detective following Holmes and Dr. Jones. She reached into her gun purse and pulled out her police credentials and badge. Flipping down the blue emergency lights attached to her sun visor, she activated them momentarily to get his attention. It worked and the officer looked over. She held out her credentials and motioned for him to allow her to take direct lead behind Holmes. He nodded and backed off permitting her to pull into line about 20 yards directly behind Holmes.

Following loosely for the next several blocks, the road block came into view. The blinking blue lights of the police check point were about a quarter mile away, and were about to slow behind a short line of cars and brake lights. Brown confirmed with the Miami Police that she was approaching the check point and was immediately behind the suspect vehicle.

Holmes began to fidget and suspect the police barricade he was approaching was set for him...no maybe not. This was Miami. After all this sort of thing happens all the time...they are always having construction or road painting...this is nothing to worry about!

As he got closer he noticed the officers were checking the driver's licenses and looking inside each vehicle that passed by. Just then Coleen who was lying tied up on the back seat groaned. *"Fuck me...."* he thought to himself. What to do? Where was Cassidy? No time to think about him. He had to look out for himself. If he actually stopped at the check point he was toast. They would pull him through the driver's window and that would be that. Looking left, he saw no escape. He could not turn around. He had to go forward until he could turn off to the right. On the right were a line of homes and offices, with no side street. His hands began to sweat. He looked in the rear view mirror and cars were beginning to back up several deep. There was no way he could get past them without crashing the car. Finally as he got to the check point an opening to the right appeared. There was a sign for the Science Museum, and possibly a way out and around the checkpoint from their parking lot...

As Holmes approached the checkpoint, the officers focused on him even though he was several vehicles back. They glanced at each other in anticipation of Holmes' next move. Suddenly Holmes made it, he turned quickly to the right and entered the parking lot. He rounded and followed the road, then noticed he was loosing control because he was probably driving too fast. He could see in the roadway dark objects like sections of cabling across his path. The car shuddered as he passed over each one. He soon realized his tires were flattened, and had run over police spikes. Flooring the accelerator, he tried to exit the lot but the rubber of his shredded tires made steering impossible. He slid sideways and impacted a large tree on the driver's side pinning his door shut.

After the crash Holmes, although stunned, grabbed his backpack and pistol and crawled over passenger seat, opened the door and fell out onto the pavement. While still on the ground, he pushed the slide back on the pistol and chambered a bullet into the weapon. Standing up, he pointed the pistol at the bright search lights of the police vehicles that were positioned to block escape from the back of the lot had he missed the spikes laid in the road.

"Put down the weapon. Put down the weapon!" an officer on a loudspeaker demanded of Holmes. Holmes looked around as if to find Cassidy. He hoped Cassidy, his master would appear and magically transport him away from his fate. Licking the perspiration from his lip, Holmes decided to run into the darkness where Cassidy had promised him he would be. For him to get away, he had to move very fast. He broke to his left and fired a single shot. The police response was immediate. Several shots from behind the lights echoed into the night. Holmes recoiled sideways as several bullets impacted him. Slamming him into the hood of the SUV, he slide off and collapsed near the shredded front passenger side tire.

Several police officers rushed to the lifeless body of Holmes and kicked away his pistol and checked him for signs of life and other weapons. Brown followed and tried to open the back passenger side door. It was still locked. Aggravated, she dived across the front seat and opened the rear door. Returning she opened the door and found Coleen on the floor between the back and front seats. Coleen groaned, opening and shutting her eyes as if trying to orient herself, and regain consciousness.

"Can we get a medevac here now?" Brown asked as she brushed Coleen's hair from her face and checked her pulse.

"She is still alive, but I can hardly feel her pulse..." Brown said to Galen who had joined her at the crash site. He remained silent, knowing it was Cassidy that had done this to her as a way to get at him. He felt helpless to bring any relief to Coleen just now, but turned his thoughts to Nash and what may be happening at the airport.

Miami officers transported Coleen in their SWAT vehicle onto still blocked northbound I-95 where they and Galen awaited for helicopter transport to the trauma unit at Jackson Memorial Hospital. The air ambulance arrived shortly and lifted off for a short flight to the hospital. Brown returned to her car, and while waiting for the medical examiner joined in to prepare Holmes' vehicle to be searched and towed; and finally to notify Nash of Coleen's recovery and Holmes' death. He would likely be angry since he ordered her to call when she arrived, not after everything was over.

Driving south and exiting the Don Shula Parkway, Nash zigged-zagged through some back streets and came to the entrance of Tamiami airport. In a few minutes he was able to make out the blinking blue lights of the Metro Police ICT unit from Miami International Airport. They were parked at various locations around the airport air traffic control facility. There was no aircraft there, they were gone... and Cassidy had escaped!

Parking his vehicle Nash walked to the front of the control building and stood on the tarmac peering east into the night sky. A slight wind blew from that direction. Except for the humming sound of the rotating lights on top of the police vehicles the night was quiet and peaceful. Turning toward the building he was again hit with a feeling of profound presence. This one he could almost taste – this wasn't Galen, this was Cassidy and many others of his kind. He turned back toward the east. They had been here. They were now gone, but he would find them and bring Cassidy to justice, maybe not the way he would like. Possibly more like Galen had described, but it would happen.

Inside he made his way to the second floor control room where everyone was gathered. Lieutenant Chip Gerlach, commander of the ICT opened the meeting. "Welcome to Miami-Dade County Rusty! I guess we just missed them. The guys here said they all came in a dark colored military transport plane, probably a souped-up C-130. They taxied that big ass thing right up to the front of the tower and were inside and had everyone in flexicuffs in less than 5 minutes after they arrived," Gerlach said. Flexicuffs are plastic hand cuff type restraints that are much like electrical wire binders. Once employed, needed to be cut off.

"Did anyone get hurt?" Nash asked.

"Nope. These guys were professional and well disciplined. What really confused the staff was their aircraft was like the type our military uses. They were all dressed in black tactical clothing, tactical vests, and armed with U.S made assault rifles. They thought they were either U.S. military or other federal agency doing an exercise. Only when they actually started pointing weapons at people did they come to realize they were not. Oh yes, one more thing. An officer a few blocks from here located the SUV you were looking for at a motel and was shot before he could get a call out." Gerlach continued.

"He ok? Nash asked.

"Yes, actually the guy who shot him put bandages on his leg wounds and gave him a shot of morphine. The perp said he was sorry before he left. Kind of fucked up if you ask me," Gerlach said scratching his head.

"...oh yes, I'm just full of news. Your Deputy Brown asked that you be notified that Miami PD stopped the SUV Holmes and Jones were in. Miami PD set up a check point where South Dixie Highway splits and I-95 forms. Holmes tried to get around it, but they channeled him into a parking lot and he ran over some "stop sticks" and crashed into a tree. He then made the mistake by shooting at a dozen Miami police officers. He is dead. Coleen Jones was found on the floor between the front and back seats. She was flown to Jackson Memorial for treatment. She and Dr. Galen are there now," Said Gerlach

"...Treatment for what?" asked Nash.

"I don't know really, but she wasn't shot."

Great. At least we did score one in this game. Tell me Chip, do you know who called you down here?

"Why yes. It was you. Remember you asked the Miami Lakes station OIC to call us. Well he did and here we are, a little late."

"You mean DHS did not call you guys first?"

"Fuck no, DHS...nahh!"

"Where is the guy in charge here?" Nash asked. He looked toward the office staff giving statements to the sector officers brought in to prepare that segment of the report.

"Here, Mr. Ackell," Gerlach said.

Identifying himself, Nash asked "Mr. Ackell did you get a call from an Officer Andrews from DHS, a female with a slight accent tonight?" Nash asked.

"Officer Andrews...from DHS, a female...No, there is no one I know at DHS in Miami by the name of Andrews. My contact is male; from New York."

Nash thanked him and walked out of ear shot.

"Those sons of bitches...they called me. They told me exactly what I wanted to hear, slowed me up by saying no one landed, and that they were sending the ICT. Son of a bitch!" Nash said pounding his fist onto a desk.

***

By the time Nash reached Jackson Memorial hospital, Coleen had been put on an IV and transferred to a room. Inside were Galen and Deputy Brown standing next to the bed. Coleen now was sleeping.

"How's she doing?" Nash asked as he entered the room.

"She had a close call – a concussion and loss of blood. Now that she has been given over a liter of blood, she now appears to be responding well; as well as one of my own injections I gave her just now. She will be fine." Galen said smiling.

Nash approached Coleen's bedside, gently placing both his hands on the safety rail used to keep patients from falling. He looked down at her for a moment and then turned.

"Deputy Brown, this has been a long day and tomorrow will be another. At least you and I won't have to write up a shooting out of your jurisdiction. Good job on that! You are relieved, go on home, I'll call Captain Evans and give him a verbal tonight with a report to follow tomorrow. Besides there is a lot for me to talk to him about. This chase is not over just because they outsmarted us this time. We...err...I totally underestimated what resources they had available and their organization. That will not happen again." Nash said.

Brown smiled, shook Galen's hand and gave Rusty a hug before leaving the room.

The two men turned and looked at each other. This was a moment of clarity for Nash. Coleen was raped and nearly murdered by this vampire and Cassidy was still on the loose. He was now likely more dangerous than ever. If the people he was now with have military aircraft, teams of people that can perform preplanned tactical operations with military precision, and deceive him directly over his own cell phone, he needs to be stopped by any means possible. Alone he was a public safety threat, With the resources of these people, who knew what was to come?

"Well detective we both learned a bit more about our adversary this past week. Before this adventure I chased Cassidy through time as single prey. At times accompanied by many of his own kind and sometimes less. He was predictable; he was masterful, yet vulnerable in a way. Now it appears that things have changed. He has learned how mankind has advanced in its ability to communicate instantly over long distances, and to rapidly travel over land and in the air – things totally unknown at any time in his long life. He has seen how technology has provided weapons so lethal even he could be impressed. Lastly he has joined an old friend – apparently the father of our kind who has exploited his knowledge and capabilities as a vampire to amass an organization that, if it wished could challenge the present world order; whatever that might be....and now, what he has done to Coleen. It was his cowardly narcissism that drove Cassidy to exhibit his power over Coleen and me when he raped her. He knew I would feel helpless, and I do...he also planned to kill her by feeding on her – leaving her body an empty sack as he often put it when we were together; but something intervened. Whatever that was, I am thankful. The bottom line...this is not over. The trail is cooling but we both know it must be followed. It must end now not just with Cassidy's death, it is likely that at the end of the trail will be a great den of vampires that will gather around him, and even now he is exploiting them to gain the power denied to him so many years ago..." Galen mused aloud as he stared out the window at the passing traffic and lights of Miami.

With that said, Galen turned and addressed Nash directly. "What will you do now?

Nash was standing at Coleen's bed side. He did not answer Galen's question immediately. He continued to hold Coleen's hand and stroke her hair. He then turned to Galen.

"Dr. Galen, it was hard for me to swallow what I thought was a bullshit story about you, vampires, and all the weird shit that comes with that. You, particularly Coleen, convinced me that it is not bullshit and the importance of what you have been doing. Cassidy is a criminal by Florida standards. He has taken lives, he has opened a can of worms from the minute Hopkins and Walsh found the box and it crashed on that dock at

Carysfort Reef Marina. The fact that his activities can be characterized as criminal provide us both with a cover story. The secret is still safe for now. Holmes would have likely been "Baker Acted" or adjudged crazy if he would have survived tonight. Except for what might be found in the pathology of Robert Hopkins, those two young women he killed a few days ago, or of Coleen. There is nothing that is not explainable, right?" Nash asked Galen.

"No, there is nothing we cannot explain. Cassidy, as far as the authorities need to believe, is nothing more than a killer; having taken something from the box of great value and was aided in his escape by persons unknown to a place long considered to be lawless and out of reach."

"I haven't answered your question. First I need to hear more from you."

Galen again turned toward the window. "We are in pursuit. After Coleen regains her strength enough to leave hospital, we will conclude some business with colleagues of mine regarding the pathology you so accurately described. We will then follow leads developed by my own organization who are now tracking where Cassidy is heading and where we may find him. Detective, we will follow him to whatever rock he crawls under and deal with anything or anyone he puts in our way. It is only a matter of time before he masters living in the 21st century.

As I have mentioned before, He can become a global threat. With what you know about him, you could be an asset to Coleen and me. As we both have noticed – this week has taught us many things. One of these is I must recognize the danger Coleen is in when accompanying me as my only close associate. I am in need of another...and can make it worth your while financially."

Nash walked to the window next to Galen. He clasped his hands together behind his back and fidgeted a bit, but finally answered.

"This certainly is the case of my lifetime. I will call my captain in a few minutes and characterize it as a criminal matter, then make an effort to request a leave of absence or be attached to Interpol to continue the investigation. Even as a criminal case, this may be considered too big for a puny Monroe County detective to handle. Likely the FBI will step in and assume jurisdiction with a few other federal agencies in support. In any case, they will not likely let me go. What kind of salary did you say you were paying?" Nash asked he reached out for Galen's hand.

Chapter 20 - Heading East

"...When you reach the part where the heartache come...The hero would be me, but heroes often fail...And you won't read that book again because the ending's just too hard to take ..."

Gordon Lightfoot, *If I could Read Your Mind*,

1970

Lucas gripped the steering wheel of the SUV as he and his passengers were pushed back into their seats when the powerful aircraft lifted off and banked to the right. Assuming a southern track until it reached the Florida Straits, the aircraft would then descend below minimum radar visibility and turn east to a refueling stop at a private location before heading home.

Once they became invisible to Miami and Bahamian radar, the pilot switched the cargo hold lighting from red to white. The crew chief motioned over the drone of the engines it was okay to undo their safety belts and move about. The teams gave a shout, and began breaking

---

out bottles of wine and vodka to celebrate a successful mission with no problems.

Cassidy remained sitting and looked over to Lucas, his old and most trusted subordinate when he walked the earth as Cassius. He extended his hand to Lucas. Lucas looked back and grasped Cassidy's right hand sealing their reunion. Suddenly, Cassidy felt dizzy and nauseous.

Less than a hundred feet off the water having long passed to the west of South Andros Island in the Bahamas, the aircraft began overflying three commercial shrimping vessels. The vessels were a bright spot on a dark sea, flooding the water with powerful spot lights to attract shrimp in the brightly lit water. Everything had gone like clockwork so far, but that was about to change.

Distracted by the vessel activity as they approached, Gulnar and her co-pilot failed to notice a dark swarm of sea gulls diving and feeding on the bait fish and shrimp from the nets. As the aircraft passed directly over the boats, the first gulls impacted the cockpit plexiglas windscreen and portside engines 1 and 2. Passing through the cloud of panicking birds, the plane rocked and fire began to shoot out of both turboprop exhausts.

"What the hell was that?" shouted Gulnar into her headset microphone, straining to assess what they had just run into.

The aircraft shuddered and cockpit alarms sounded loudly over the roar of engines. The cargo hold lights went to red followed by the intercom with the co-pilot telling everyone to sit and buckle their seat belts.

"Excuse me General, I will go forward and check our situation," Lucas said as he also handed Cassidy a bottle of water and a box containing a sandwich, apple and power bar.

Lucas raced forward and quickly climbed the ladder from the cargo deck into the cockpit. He strained to look past the co-pilot at the burning engines, then to the cracked wind screen. Holding on as the plane continued to lurch, he frantically tried to make sense at the blinking emergency lights on the instrument panel as the emergency engine alarm bleeped loudly.

For what seemed like an eternity, the aircraft cut through what they would soon learn was a cloud of sea gulls smashing into the windscreen and fuselage. Then came silence except for the engine alarms.

"We have to find a place to land, soon" Gulnar shouted over the alarm.

Lucas reached to the panel and pushed the alarm disconnect while Gulnar turned off the fuel boost pump to both engines and placed the engine bleed air switch to the "off" position. The fire in engines 1 and 2 sputtered before going out.

Although the aircraft was designed to fly on 2 engines, Gulnar struggled to keep the flight path as smooth as on 4.

"Find us a place to land and soon!" Gulnar shouted to navigator.

Engine number 1 began to shutter and vibrate with pieces of cowling breaking away.

"Oh shit!" Gulnar gasped as she strained to put maximum force on the rudders of the good engine side, simultaneously fighting the yoke to regain control of the aircraft as it yawed toward the port side lifeless engines and the dark water below...

www.ingramcontent.com/pod-product-compliance
Lightning Source LLC
Chambersburg PA
CBHW060150260626
47160CB00001B/197